Vicious Texts

CAPTIVE WRITINGS
BOOK THREE

M.L. PHILPITT

Note

Vicious Texts is the third book in the Captive Writings series, which must be read in order. There will be moments you may not like the character of Teagan, and this is okay. I encourage you to look past her actions and continue to the end of the book. Her actions are rough, her thoughts may be cold, but there is a purpose that is later revealed. I implore you to hang on for this insane ride.

Vicious Texts is a dark romance with content some readers may find triggering. You can read the content warning list on the last page.

This book uses Canadian spelling. This means words will have U's in them, "re", or double LL's. (colour vs color, centre vs center, signalling vs signaling, etc.) These are not typos.

Playlist

"Russian Roulette" by Rihanna
"Princesses Don't Cry" by CARYS
"Stockholm" by Bianca
"Like a Vampire" by Catrien
"Still Here" by Digital Daggers
"Treat You Better" by Shawn Mendes
"Battle Cry" by Beth Crowley
"Love Me Like You Do" by Ellie Goulding
"Without Him" by Christina Grime
"Ember" by Katherine McNamara
"Rise" by Katy Perry
"Tattoo" by Jordin Sparks
"Infinity" by Jaymes Young
"Denial" by Sevendust
"Here Without You" by 3 Doors Down
"the lonely" by Christina Perri
"Requiem" by Avenged Sevenfold
"Punching Bag" by Palaye Royale
"How Do You Love Someone" by Ashely Tisdale
"I'm a Mess" by Bebe Rexha
"Move Like a Solider" by Kristina Maria

For all survivors still fighting the trauma

Preface

He ensured he kept his promise to protect me. At one point in my life, his text messages were the shining light—the proof someone cared. But presently, his texts have changed, and I'm merely a tool, no different than I've been for *him*.

Brent Thorne was my best friend. No—he was more than my best friend; he was my soulmate. The guy who kept my secrets, held my hand when I needed, and gave me his shoulder to cry on. He knew everything about me, and no matter what life brought, he loved me through it.

Until the one unfortunate day during senior year when I got with *him*, and it all changed. *He* calls it love, but I label it as obsession—fixation in its unhealthiest form. *He* took me for himself, made my life toxic, and even when I thought I escaped from the pretty monster he eventually showed himself to be, *he* found me, tightening the leash around my neck as *he* dragged me home.

He changed my life, but not for the better. For their safety, I let go of everyone I cared for. The day I lost Brent was the day I lost myself too, for nothing mattered any longer. Nothing beyond surviving.

I've been living the lie for five years, until a random Sunday night becomes the catalyst for change. When Brent appears in my life again.

Only, he's no longer the white knight I left behind; he's an anti-hero who's come to slay me.

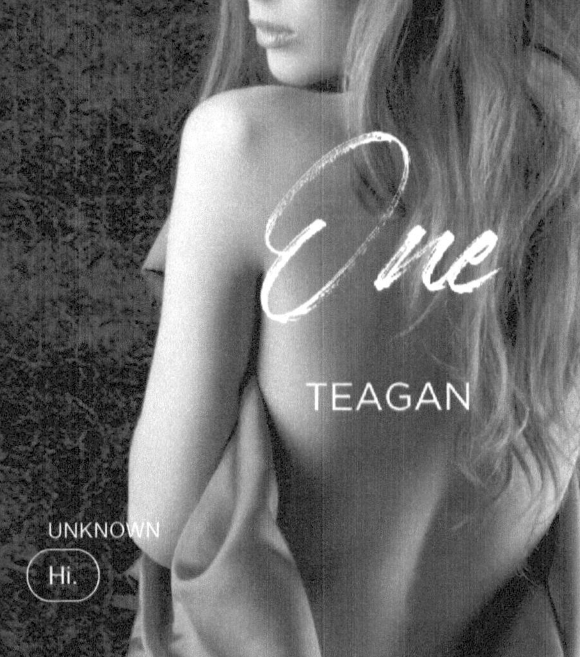

SCOWLING AT THE MESSAGE, I tuck the phone away in my purse. It's likely some overeager customer who somehow got my number, but at the moment, it's not my problem. I'll delete it later, after this night concludes, and I return home, pretending I'm a normal woman.

"Evening." Josh, the linebacker-sized security guard, opens the staff's side entrance and lets me slip in. "Have a good shift."

My lips lift in a polite smile as I flick my hair back around my face, so he can't see my actual feelings. It's not his fault I'm stuck here, so I have no reason to be a bitch.

I slip down the dark hallway, only lit by a few white pot lights in the ceiling, and enter the girls' changing room, shutting the door and muffling the erotic music from farther down the hall.

Being ten o'clock, the club's in full swing. Starting later in the night, like now, is preferred because it involves less waiting around for clients to arrive, which means I'm able to pick whatever man doesn't currently have one of my co-workers hanging off him, do my job, and move on to the next. The nights go quicker, the men a blur of faces passing by, and before I know it, it's two in the morning and Josh is telling me to have a good night's sleep as he walks me out of the club before assisting the other girls.

The changing room is empty, leaving me to prepare in much welcomed and needed silence. It's almost deafening, increasing the awareness of the music's volume past this room. When the girls are in here, they try to spark up conversation, but I'm never in the mood.

Ever.

Because they're choosing to be here, and I am not.

If I have to pick a moment to hate the most, it's this part. When I'm forced to sit on the cushioned bench in front of a lit-up mirror and primp and prime myself for strange men. Sometimes women—those that are curious, accompany their own guys, or the few open lesbians, but mostly, it's men.

Strangely enough, when I'm out on the floor, it's not the most-hated portion of this whole ordeal. Not when I'm undressing for their greedy eyes or touching my body in ways meant to tease and heighten their desire. Those moments are easy to tune out as I let my mind wander to a place outside these four sin-soaked walls.

The worst part is when I can feel my self-loathing growing as I apply heavy amounts of makeup, douse my body in glitter that'll sparkle beneath the stage lights, and slip into a bikini so revealing, I wouldn't dare wear it outside this building.

Right on schedule, there's a quick rap on the door and my boss, Mason, pops his head in, his somber expression devoid of emotion. He's not surprised to see me; it's why he's come here in the first place. It's our nightly routine in which he needs to retrieve me, aware I'll never willingly stride from here on my own.

Mason, help me. Save me from a madman. Words that are always on the tip of my tongue, but never spoken.

Like Josh, my situation has nothing to do with Mason, so I can't hate him. Secondly, for a club owner, he's damn good to us. Nothing like the girls from other clubs say about their bosses. Mason never forces us to do anything we don't want, isn't unmannered or disgusting, and seems to genuinely care about his staff. But like me, he works under a bigger boss—the same as mine, actually—and it's why he'll never speak his pitying thoughts.

"Sorry, Teagan, it's time. You're up in a minute. DJ's readying to announce you."

Not me. He won't introduce Teagan Faber to the strangers beyond this changing room because, to everyone else, that's not who I am. I transform into a different person to make it through these nights. It's yet another way my identity has been yanked away from me.

"All right," I agree, not that I have a choice in the matter.

Through the mirror in front of me, I see Mason still waiting by the partially open door, frowning expectantly. I sigh and fluff my hair —a deep red and a signature colour around here—check my matching lipstick and stand, taking one last glance at the small silver bikini. If it can even be called that. Triangles that barely cover my nipples, while the thong bottoms call attention to my ass. It has *maybe* two inches of material covering my pussy.

I lower my eyes and breathe in so deeply, it echoes through my ears, before turning my back on the reflection and not giving self-hatred a chance to intensify any more than it already has. Mason closes the door behind me, throwing a tight, understanding smile over his shoulder.

"You're beautiful. Do your usual out there, and it'll be over before you know it."

For the second time tonight, I smile politely and walk by him, heading down the hallway and toward the music. I approach the stage just in time for the DJ to announce my name.

"Please welcome... Cherry!"

Cherry. The day Mason asked me to select a stage name, it's the one that slipped out. A name I stopped hearing years prior, so I'm not sure why I allowed it to resurface in my life, but it has. It's a name to remind me of everything once good in my life. A name—

I halt my thoughts before they get anymore wayward. I know why I chose the name, but it doesn't mean I need to think about it. Like every other good past memory, it went into a little box, which I locked and stuck under my bed.

Compartmentalizing is necessary.

Between clenched teeth, I suck in and hold the breath in my lungs before bracing my foot on the bottom step leading to the stage. The mile-high heel wobbles, a sign of how my insides vibrate with hate—a frequent feeling—before I block all emotion.

Cheers rise from behind the curtain as I'm swallowed by the stage and leave the service hallway behind. Like usual, the club assaults my senses, though nothing in my view is new. It's the same scene, unchanging over the past couple years.

A rainbow spattering of lights rain down on me, blocking my vision from anything beyond the edge of the stage. I'm fine with that, since it means I won't need to meet any hungry gazes ogling me. My attention remains focused on the pole in front of me. It's a job, a task, nothing more. One song, approximately two-and-a-half to three minutes of dancing, and it'll be over.

There's a reason I'm on the stage every night, and my body's perfect curves are part and parcel to that. Because *he* always ensures I stick to my morning exercise routine, I have breasts that are large but never spill out of a man's hand, an ass that's round and eye-catching, toned legs and arms, and a perfectly flat stomach. I'm thin without being skinny—a body men flock to see. I dance to increase the desires of the observing clientele, silently encouraging them to purchase dances from myself and the other girls.

I'm the piece of meat the club offers up to encourage buyers to check out the other stock.

Stock. It's all any of us are, really.

My hands grasp the cool, metal pole, and I lean onto it, twirling around with one leg lifting high in the air. I hover it there for a beat before wrapping my ankle around it and spinning in an arc. I feel the pole all over my skin, and it becomes a symbol of what every man in here wishes they could be right now.

With my back to it, I survey the crowd, the subtle shape of them I manage to make out through the bright lights. I may not see every individual person here, but I feel them. Feel their sick eyes studying every inch of my body, wishing they could touch what they salivate over.

A particular beat of the familiar song comes, signalling my next movements. I turn, giving the crowd my ass as I shake it, fingers playing with the strings at my hip. I won't be removing it; my dance is centred around the tease of it all. It's then, I lose myself. My mind drifts elsewhere, finding blackness. My moves continue, but I'm no longer on stage with them.

Another beat comes through the nearby speakers, reminding me of the next step in my dance of seduction. My hands slide down my sides, pausing for a brief second on my bikini top. I take another spin around the pole, and when I return to the front, my fingers find the tie at my back.

I undo it and a hush travels over the gawkers. The entire room adopts a beat of silence as they wait for more. I roll my shoulders and hips against the pole, expanding the moment, before finding the tie at my neck and tugging the dangling string once.

My bikini top falls away, my breasts shining beneath the stage lights. The air, though warm, perks my nipples. Whistles pierce the dimness, entering my safe space on the stage. My eyelids fight to remain open and not block them out completely because Mason won't approve of me physically checking out too. Mental is enough. I know what they see though, and that's the point in the dance.

I roll my body around the pole again, pressing it between my breasts before grasping the bikini top and flicking it into the crowd for added effect. Almost always, someone tries to steal it—the pathetic guys they are—but I require it for after the show, when I do this again for someone else in private. Mason or one of the other servers oversees retrieving it after the dance.

The routine continues, me flipping and twirling around the pole until the song comes to an end. The lights dim and the DJ calls, "And that's Cherry!"

Without waiting another beat, I escape the stage, my mind returning to the moment. The room's air pierces me, hot and heady, knowing I've increased the men's desires and they're waiting for me to enter the main floor. Instead, my chest heaves, catching up with the exercise I've just completed on stage.

As usual, Mason is right there in the service hall, my silver bikini top pinched between two fingers. I grasp it and get to tying it on my body again, right in time for him to jerk his chin toward the other hallway.

"Room two. You know the drill."

He means the button on the far wall if someone is too overeager and not following the rules. It'll ring his cell phone and the pagers the security guards keep on them.

"Yep." Despite the familiarity of this conversation—since we have it so often—my body grows hotter, and irritation makes my neck prickle. It's harder to check out during a private dance, though I've become semi-proficient at it.

"Two guys, but only one to start. The other will be a few minutes late."

"Sure," I mumble, brushing past him and stalking toward the private rooms. I walk quickly, my five-inch heels eating up much of the floor in my rush to arrive, but also to ensure no one else stops me on the way there.

I make it to the line of four rooms, nodding to the guard stationed there. He ensures no patron who shouldn't be here makes their way to the back. The men who pay for private rooms pay well and will never be interrupted, as per Mason's rules.

I slip inside the door marked with a two, instantly swallowed up by the dark red light. It flashes against my skin, reinforcing my stage name, a theme Mason really enjoys playing on.

Seated on the couch, at the opposite end of the room, I spot my customer. He's bathed in the red light, and no part of him is hidden, for my safety. The colour washes his hair, but I can tell it's light in colour, like a blond. Dark tattoos creep up his neck from his plain white shirt and down his arms, stopping short at his wrists. Bright eyes blast through the light, pinning on me before he grins, his lip ring lifting with his movements.

He's hot, but even if I was free to fuck anyone, he's not my type.

"Hi there." My voice is low, a tone meant to be sultry and inviting to the clients.

He doesn't answer, not that I'm necessarily expecting him to. Sometimes my clients do, and sometimes they don't.

"Heard you'll have a friend joining us soon," I go on. "Do we wait for him or begin now?"

"Now." The voice isn't one I can identify, not that I recognize everyone who comes through here, but he's certainly no regular.

Private dances are worse than the stage. On the stage, I can pretend no one is watching me. Pretend that while I'm up there, I'm all alone in the room and merely dancing for my own entertainment. I'm meant to captivate eyes, but not keep a single one for myself.

But in the room with a single person, there's no way to pretend their attention isn't soaking up everything I do—every look I give, every move I make. It's as though they can see inside me, and yet, they still want to search deeper and bare all of me. People are selfish like that.

I tap a button on the far wall and a popular song blast through the speakers. With its beginning beat, my eyes slide shut, and I allow it to move me. It controls my hips and my arms with every slow step I take.

My eyes lock with his in time for my hands to find the tie behind my neck. Biting my lip, I fiddle with it, aiming for playful, but when I stop in front of him, I find him looking... well, bored.

I'm doing my job. I'm fucking sexy, and if he's not into this, it's his problem. Perhaps he'll want to end this sooner then I can move on.

My hips bounce from side to side as I turn, giving him my back and bending my knees until the bare skin of my ass brushes against his rough jeans.

Before I can move again, his hands clamp my hips and he spins me quickly, placing my tits in his face.

Okay, so no lap dance. My hands slide up my side, skirting the outline of my body until they find the edges of my top and I toy with the strings again. Clearly, he wants more of what he witnessed on stage.

Again, his hands find mine, and he pushes them away from the string. Shocked, my hands go slack and allow it—allows my hand to land by my hip, where he puts it. Usually, they're not permitted to touch, but that's to prevent over-eagerness and keep us safe. I've never had a guy push me away not only once, but *twice.*

Then the door opens and shuts as his friend likely arrives, but instead of twisting to get a glimpse of the new addition, I'm locked in a silent battle of confusion with the one in front of me.

The guy's bright eyes flash to mine, hardening as he speaks, "Don't strip. You're not my type."

Not his type? My skin flushes hotter, and it has nothing to do with the dance. Anger bubbles to the top and I jerk away, straightening my spine and stepping back a few inches.

"Then why the fuck pay for this? If I'm not your type, why not choose someone else?"

"I didn't," he says simply, shrugging and lifting one leg until he drapes his ankle over his opposite knee.

"Then who did?"

"*I* did, Cherry-Girl."

Everything comes to a screeching halt. My mind, my body, my heart, and even my fucking soul stops working, because the voice that just spoke isn't the guy in front of me. The name he called me is one I've heard countless times before, and still sometimes do, buried deeply in my dreams and memories. Of the boy who uses that name while he saves me from the darkness I'm constantly locked inside.

With my heart thumping so loud, it overtakes the music, I turn to face my past.

Two

TEAGAN

TEN YEARS AGO

I'M THE NEW KID.

Again.

You'd think after being the new kid five different times, I'd be used to it by now.

Used to the comments. Used to the anxiety as my new grade eight classmates all stare me down, pre-placing me into their already-existing social hierarchy. Used to the struggle of catching up to whatever subject the teacher is working through.

But mostly, used to the rumours that'll float around. Once classmates discover I'm not like them—that I don't have a pretty home filled with adoring parents who love, cherish, and spoil me, or have siblings who can be my honorary best friends—they'll start talking.

I'm a foster kid.

And after my last family decided they already had too many kids in their house, regardless of the income accompanying me, I was the one booted since I was the newest and they felt it fairer to the others.

"Class, please welcome Teagan. She has recently moved to town."

Thirty-some eyes narrow on me. The girls scan me, noting my

ripped jeans and baggy shirt, and already label me an outcast, deeming me different from them. My jeans are faded from use, not from the designer who made them so. My bright red hair isn't because of a dye job my parents forked money over for. It's all-natural, which somehow makes it uncool.

In the end, it doesn't matter. I give it a month before my current foster family tires of me, and I'll have to start all over again.

"There's an empty desk at the back you can take." My new teacher, Mrs. Novak, gestures toward the back of the room.

"Thanks," I mumble and haul my bag closer to me as my feet eat up much of the floor in my rush to get to my seat. Every single kid's eyes stalk me, watching me calculatingly, waiting for me to slip-up so they can use it in their attacks later.

I keep my eyes locked on my tattered shoes as I slide into the desk Mrs. Novak indicated. My back is so hot I'm shocked I don't stick to the plastic chair. My hair falls in my face, and I wait for my classmates to find something better to stare at.

Only when Mrs. Novak takes command of the class once more, commenting, "All right, everyone. Get your math books out and we'll check how you've done on the homework," do I look up.

Homework. Which means I'll sit here bored until they get to the new stuff and hope it's not a subject already covered at my last school. Worse part about switching schools partway through the year is being retaught topics I've already learned, while missing out on the subjects I haven't studied yet.

I sit back, crossing my arms across my chest, and listen to the teacher drone on as I study each one of my classmates, searching for anyone with at least a shred of kindness within their judgy looks.

Life sucks.

WHEN THE END of the day finally comes, after hours of the same thirty people sneaking looks at me constantly, the only thing I want to do is curl up in bed and forget today happened.

As I exit the school, a scuffle at the edge of the school's property catches my attention. There's two guys towering over another one. Shorter and wider than the two, he steps back, arms up in defence.

I sigh, shoulders lowering. Bullies suck worse than first days. No matter what, I don't ever allow myself to be bulled. People can speak negatively about me behind my back all they want, but they'll never say anything to my damn face and make it out unscathed.

I glance to the right, seeking out a teacher on duty, but most of them seem occupied with organizing the bus lines for the younger kids. Everyone's so worried about young kids' safety, leaving the older ones to fend for themselves.

Maybe it's dumb of me. Maybe I shouldn't make waves on the first day. Either way, it doesn't stop me from marching over there and pushing between the three bodies, even noting the two bullies are *much* larger than me and can easily squish me if they wanted to.

"Hey!" I call, shoving my hands on one's chest. "Back the hell off. What is wrong with you?"

Both guys stop what they're doing, their gazes dropping to me. One sneers, but his attention remains locked on the kid they were pushing around. "Thorne, you're pathetic. Needing a girl to friggin' protect you."

"You're pathetic," I counter, before the guy—this *Thorne*—can speak, "for picking on people. God, what is *wrong* with you? You realize there are bigger issues in the world than your pettiness, right?" Past the bully's body, I catch the eye of a teacher, who's finally turned around, noticing us. "Look, a teacher is watching. There's nothing you can do now anyway, without getting in trouble."

The one I pushed away steps farther back, his fist clenching his friend's shirtsleeve. He rolls his eyes, scanning me, his gaze stopping on my ratty shoes. "Whatever, you two are made for each other."

Grumbling, they run off, and once there's a few feet of distance between us, I do too, marching in the opposite direction.

"Hey, wait! You can't just leave after that."

I spin on my heel, arms crossed and hip cocked out, as the kid I saved jogs closer to me. His blond hair hangs over his eyes, as is the style with most guys my age right now, but his kind smile shines through.

Still, I don't fall for it. Every foster family I've ever had smiles kindly in the beginning. Then it goes downhill. "Why, because you want to insult me for 'taking care of you?' Sorry for having a heart." Guys are all the same—unable to handle being "saved" by a girl.

"No, I wanted to thank you." His hands at his sides curl, his sapphire eyes darting all around my form.

Oh. "No worries." I turn to leave again, shrugging off his apology. Being a decent human doesn't mean I need a reward.

And again, as if he's a glutton for punishment, he speaks, "It *is* a big deal. Not everyone does stuff like that."

He's not going to let this go apparently. I spin again until I face him and roll my eyes. "That's the issue. Too much bad in the world, and we're not saving each other often enough. Why were they bullying you anyway?"

"Look at me." His hands gesture to his body. "I mean, they're on the track team. Fit. Popular. And, well, I'm not."

Like he suggests, I scan him. I suppose he's on the thicker side. Some would call him fat, but I'm not some. Weight doesn't really matter. Fat or skinny, if someone is evil, they're evil. Everyone worries about looks, but it's personality and having a heart mattering more.

"Still no reason for them to make fun of you." I shrug again, wondering when he'll be satisfied enough with this conversation to allow me to leave.

Not yet, apparently, since his next words are, "You're the new girl, right?"

Of course he knows me.

"I'm in the other grade seven class, and well, you were mentioned," he adds, stuffing his hands inside the pockets of his baggy jeans. "What's your name?"

He seems harmless enough and is, so far, the only kid to look at me like I'm worth a moment of their time.

So, I say, "Teagan. Yours?"

"Brent. I like your hair," he comments, his bright eyes landing on my head. "Cherry red."

My fingers find the edges of my most noticeable feature. "Yeah." *Does he want me to say anything more to that?*

"It's too bad we're not in the same class, but tomorrow for recess..." He trails off and shuffles his feet side to side as his teeth sink into the corner of his lip. "Wanna hang out?"

Is he trying to be friends with me? I tilt my head. It happens so infrequently in all the schools I've been to, I forget what friendship looks like.

He's—Brent—is offering me a hand. Kindness. Friendship. And though I may not be in this town for long, there's no reason I shouldn't take the leap and risk it. Time will tell if he remains so, or if he'll tire of the new kid, like so many others have in the past, and ignore me.

"Sure."

LITTLE DID I know on that random Tuesday, Brent would become my everything.

My friend.

My hero.
My enemy.
My saviour.
My future.

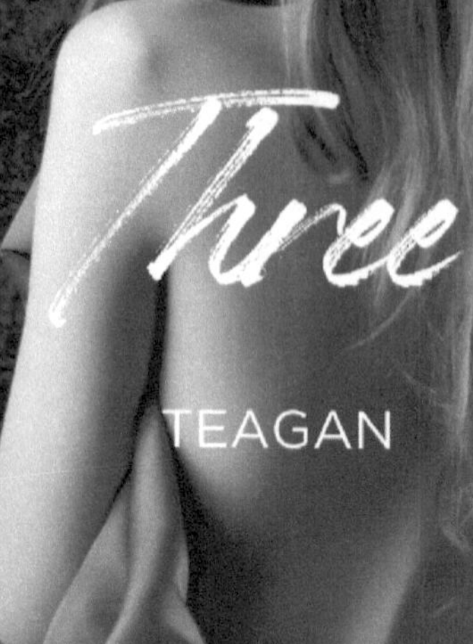

Three

TEAGAN

"BRENT," I breathe, my mind finally alert enough to speak—though with my barely-there volume, you can hardly deem what I did as talking. "H-how... What?"

My words are disjointed, as are my thoughts. Nothing makes sense. He shouldn't be here. He *can't* be here. What he's searching for—the girl he's hoping to find—she doesn't exist anymore. She withered away with every passing year.

Brent's appearance steals my breath, making the room suffocating. Because even through the red lighting and the four years that have passed since I ran away, I know it's him.

My Brent.

But he doesn't look anything like the version I left behind. The Brent I knew in high school was a chubby kid, but now, I'm not sure if there's an ounce of fat on him. Not in his muscular arms, his shirt pulled tightly against his chest. His jawline is pure bone. His blond hair lies flat, making it easier to see the hatred spewing from his eyes —bright blue ones that hold none of the sweetness I once revered. Now it's something else.

Darker.

Deeper.

He needs to go now before *he* finds out Brent is around.

The guy behind me moves, and I realize I'm boxed-in between them. My nails sink into the skin of my thighs, being my only defence mechanism against the onslaught of what the two of them can do.

"Surprised?" Brent prowls closer, his tone chilling the air around me. Brows lift and a cocky smirk hints on the corner of his mouth.

I open my mouth, waiting for something to come from my lips. Some form of a sentence that'll verbalize everything flying through my disjointed mind.

What are you doing here?

How did you find me?

Do you still hate me?

Do you still love me?

But he doesn't give me a chance to speak. "Not as big of a shock as I had when I found out you're *still* in the area, despite me previously searching for you."

His steps bring him no farther than an inch away, his dark eyes—normally such a bright colour—narrowing down at me. They're cold. Winter cold, and not at all like what I remember.

But then I recall I've changed too. Not for the better but changed, nonetheless. There are reasons I shut that door on my life and pretended there wasn't once an ounce of happiness in it, and these reasons haven't changed. *He* ensures it, and it'll be safer for Brent if he continues to avoid me.

My spine stiffens, and I lock my knees, jutting my chin and giving back every bit of hate, needing to push him back to wherever he's come from. Hopefully, my voice remains intact long enough not to waver through my next words.

"It was my choice to leave, Brent. Exactly like it is now. Excuse me." I sidestep him and his friend, who is still hovering at my back.

I manage an entire step toward the door before I'm yanked backward, a hand clamping down on my arm. In a flurry of movement, I see nothing but the blur of the red light and his snarling expression as he walks us to the far wall. I swallow, my hands flying up to his and pushing at them, but making no headway to rid the clasp on my arm.

"B-Brent." It's so obvious now that this isn't the childhood friend I abandoned. The Brent I once knew protected me, and would never lay a hand on me. "Stop."

"Not," his teeth bare, "until you answer a few fucking questions."

I shut my eyes briefly, mentally praying this isn't how I meet my end. I always assumed it'd be at the hands of a psychopath, and while that option is more painful and horrifying, it's expected. Not this. Not from someone who once loved me.

My nerves freeze beneath tingling skin. "What?"

"Who are you to Alex Miller?"

Everything in me comes to a halt again. *What does he know?* He *can't* know. I won't *let* him know. I've done so much over the past few years to save who I could, and it's with my next words, I hope he'll accept my response and leave. Leave and forget me and remain safe.

I'm not the friend he left behind, and it's with this fact, I push my ex-best friend away all over again. Self-sabotaging, perhaps, but *I* need this—need to know Brent will be safe from what Alex could do to him. From what Alex has threatened to do to him, time and time again.

"Nothing," I whisper, shaking my head. I'm nothing to Alex. Nothing and everything all rolled into one.

His grip tightens, sparking a gasp from me. I yank at my arm but, somehow, he holds firmer.

"Brent." His friend's warning tone comes from behind us.

Please listen to him.

He does, letting me go but not moving away. "I ask you again, Cherry-Girl, who are you to Alex Miller?"

Cherry-Girl. The nickname came out of nowhere, sometime after he stated my hair reminded him of cherries. It stuck though, and I never minded. In truth, I loved it. It made me special. Made me belong to someone. Little did I know then, I *would* belong to someone, but it wouldn't be Brent, the person I had wanted it to be.

"No one," I murmur, as my heart shatters all over again. "Why do you want to know?"

His mouth opens again, but instead, it's his friend who speaks. "Brent, our time is up. Her boss will come looking soon."

Brent doesn't seem to hear him. His eyes bounce around my face, and despite the darkness in his normally-bright depths, I see something else there.

Fear. Pain.

It crushes me inside, but I breathe through the feeling, forcing my mask in place. He steps away, putting space between us, but still, I don't move. I won't until he leaves my life again.

"I *will* find out, Teagan. You have information I need."

Need? Oh, Brent, what have you gotten yourself into? Nothing good comes from needing to know about Alex Miller.

Hell, if time travel is a thing, I'd go back and tell myself that in high school. That instead of panting over the popular kid, I should have been running far away from the power he wields.

"Don't," I offer a warning. "Don't go down this path, Brent. Alex Miller isn't worth your time."

He freezes, his steps coming to a quick stop. "You know something. Tell me, Teagan. Tell me what you know, so I can help you." All the ice in his tone melts away, leaving a flicker of the guy I once knew.

Help. He wants to help me. But he can't. No one can...

The door bangs, followed by a "Hey!" It's Mason coming for me. "Time's up in there."

Brent drops his gaze, scanning my body, for, I believe, the first time since entering. It's no different than when we used to go swimming during the summer months, so many years ago. Yet, as his eyes stroke my bare skin, breasts much firmer and larger than they were last time he saw them, in a bikini, leaving much more of me visible, it feels—*No. Don't go there.*

"It's a fucking shame, Cherry-Girl. After all this time, you've popped back up like a dream come true. It's as if my hopes and prayers have finally been answered... all to discover, you're on the wrong side."

He leaves then, taking his friend with him. The door opens and I see Mason peer through, noting my still-dressed appearance. Noticing I'm physically okay, he goes too, following them out.

Key point in that is that I'm *physically* fine.

Physically, yes. Emotionally, no.

When the door shuts behind them, I drop to my knees, bowing over on the ground as I allow countless memories of the past invade my mind until I hurt. Until the pain and agony of the past swells up like a huge wave and wipes me out.

Brent believes I'm on the wrong side.

Alex believes I'm on his side.

What neither of them realize is, I'm on *my* side.

And my side involves surviving.

Four

BRENT

"WHAT NOW?" Hawke asks as we make our way outside the strip club.

"Now, you leave it to me." I clap him on the back, striding toward his car parked nearby. "Thanks for helping, but I'll take it from here."

Hawke slides into the driver's seat and starts the vehicle. Once it's rumbling beneath us, he checks, "You're not going to pull a Tristan, right, and stalk the girl?"

I chuckle, laughing at our friend's antics. He's a crazy motherfucker, who truly did what he needed to do. Alex's sister, Natalie, gave the answers we required, plus more.

She gave me Teagan.

Cherry-Girl, how you've grown.

She was my best friend and first love, even if our relationship never made it to the point I once hoped it would. My childhood crush didn't take the title of girlfriend. Regardless, it never changed anything for me.

But she's not the teenager who once left me. Far from. Her body has filled in, her curves perfectly round, and her chest—*God*. I groan, recalling the way they spilled out from that tiny bikini.

"Brent?" Hawke glances over, a dip between his brows. "Dude, tell me what's in your head. If this is too far for you…"

"No." I blow out a breath and lean back against the leather headrest. I gave him the basic details of Teagan and me, but not everything. "I'll be fine. It was just a bit strange, you know? I mean, we were best friends, inseparable—or so I thought. It's been four fucking years."

His eyes cut to me again. "You sure you're okay to do this? I could get her to talk. Maybe even through legal means."

"No," I repeat, shaking my head. My hand tightens around my phone, where my text to her remains unread. "No, I'll be fine. In the end, she's on the wrong side." And I'll be reminding myself that often.

Alex Miller. She's his fucking girlfriend, according to Natalie.

"What if Natalie is correct, man? She seemed very firm in her claims that Teagan tried to warn her away from Alex. Teagan may be with him, but she knows he's bad. Just… don't treat her like the villain. Don't do that to yourself."

My eyes cut to him, annoyance swirling in my chest. "In your house, you seemed to take my side."

"Because she has information we need, and that hasn't changed, but be careful how you go about learning it. Brent, I know you're hurt she never found a way to contact you, but think about who we're dealing with. Alex Miller. Fuck knows what horrors she's seen and endured." His own gaze slides away and his hands tighten for a second around the wheel. "All I'm saying is think about what she's been dealing with before you act too rough. Be smart."

"There's no proof. I'm not sure why she said what she did to Natalie, but I struggle to believe she would have found herself on the wrong end of this situation. No," I purse my lips, "she might have warned Natalie away, but not for the reasons we're all assuming. Back then, she was too much of a fighter to be trapped by Miller."

Hawke makes a noise in his throat. "People change."

I hear him. I do. But as I stare out into the darkened streets, watching my reflection in the window's glass, my eyes appear hollow, like a broken man.

I can't be broken for the next part.

I was soft for her once. Let her have everything she wanted from me. When I wanted more but she only wanted friendship, I let her have it, even when it killed me nearly every day.

This time, I'm the one controlling the reins, and if I need to, I'll tighten the collar on her fucking neck until she submits and gives me what we need to finish Alex.

Only when my eyes harden again in the reflection and my expression is unrecognizable, do I glance at Hawke again. "I'll react how I need to, to get what we need. Our history helps me because I know her tells. I know what she likes and hates. What she fears. I'll use it all to break her. When she's broken and vulnerable, I'll get the answers we need.

Hawke frowns, skeptical, but he asks, "How do you plan on doing that?"

"By taking her on a trip down memory lane." I grin to myself, thinking of all the ways to win my round in the elaborate game Ryker, Tristan, Hawke, and I have been playing.

Cherry-Girl, this time you have nowhere to run.

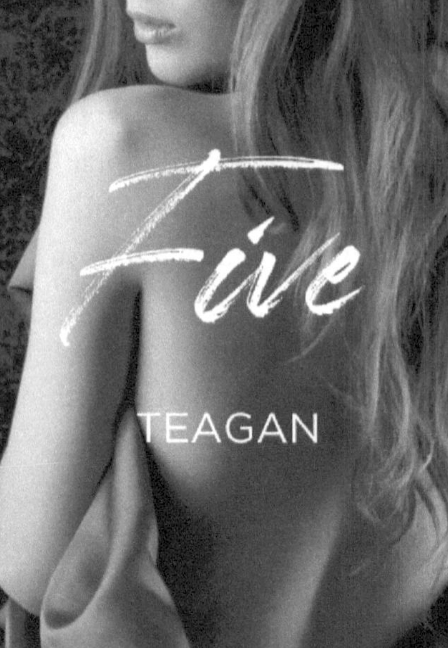

Five

TEAGAN

THE NEXT MORNING, I awake to another text message.

UNKNOWN

Morning, Cherry-Girl.

I falter, staring at my screen. *Of course it was him texting me last night.* All these years later, and he still remembers my number. After high school, and after him calling and texting it constantly, he eventually gave up trying to contact me. I assumed then, he deleted my number and moved on.

But am I surprised? Not really. This is exactly what my Brent would do.

I huff, standing from bed and bringing my phone with me, mind wondering in what other ways I can make him comprehend the importance of deleting this text thread and forgetting me.

ME

You texted me yesterday too, I assume?

Instantly his answer comes in.

UNKNOWN

Yes.

ME

You've kept my number this whole time.

UNKNOWN

The digits have been imprinted in my mind since
the moment you gave them to me.

A second later, another one comes through.

UNKNOWN

I've memorized everything about you. Including
what you've become.

Back on this, I see. Groaning, I drop down onto the couch and hoist my feet under me as I respond in a way to satisfy whyever he's returned.

After all, what I've "become" is someone he won't recognize. I've made my mistakes—over and over and over—and I'll pay my dues without getting more people wrapped up into it. What I see is bad enough, and I couldn't handle witnessing Brent in *their* place.

ME

I don't know what that means.

Tired of staring at the *unknown* moniker, I input his name into my phone's contacts, ignoring how the simple sight makes my stomach flip. Once, he was at the top of my phone's messages, but after everything went down, I deleted it, aiming to remove the temptation to contact him. It was safer for him that I left his life completely, based on Alex's ongoing threats.

So, it's what I did.

But now, re-labelling him feels right and wrong all at the same time. Wrong, because if Alex were ever to see my phone... I let the thought trail off, not willing to input the words that go along with it. Wrong, because the moment I convince him to leave me alone, I'll need to delete the number all over again. But right, because for this slice of time, it's my selfish act. My penance for surviving.

BRENT

> I know you're with Alex Miller. I also know he's into some bad things.

The phone slips out of my hand and onto the couch. Brent is claiming to know things, and for the sake of his own life, he needs to let it go *now*. Knowing about Alex will only get him killed.

So that's where I leave the phone as I prepare, wandering through my small paid-for apartment as I dress in jeans and a shirt, pulling up my hair into a ponytail. I avoid the couch at all costs until my phone dings again, but this time with an identifiable sound. One I've specifically labelled to be sure I never miss a message from *him*.

With the strength of everything inside me, I stalk to the couch again and pick up the device between two fingers, as if it's on fire. I swipe away Brent's message in favour of the only other man in my life.

ALEX

> 6 p.m. Business dinner at my house. Wear a black dress. Knee-length. I'll pick you up.

Once, I had him referred to as *asshole* in my phone, but Alex noticed and then, I couldn't sit for a week without it hurting.

I type him back a response quickly before he can find a reason it wasn't fast enough.

Alex Miller. My first boyfriend.

And my jailor.

When I believed myself to be in love with him, he used me in the worst way possible.

When he was in the hospital, healing from injuries after getting beaten, I ran, using the opportunity to get far away from him. What I didn't know at the time, is how much power his name brought with him. Of course he had people watching me.

To ensure I wouldn't escape again, he trapped me. Threatened Brent and Elena, and their families. Trained me. Showed me how lucky I am, compared to the others.

When six o'clock rolls around later this evening, I'll be dressed in what he instructed me to wear, and I'll smile when he tells me to. I'll be his happy girlfriend and ensure no one has a reason to second-guess my acting.

It's what I've been trained to do, and it's how I'll act. For my own safety and well-being, along with those I care for.

BRENT

You never answered me, Cherry-Girl. Is this your way of admitting I'm correct?

I SCOWL AT HIS PERSISTENCE, at the use of that damned nickname, and tuck my phone into my clutch in time for Alex's shiny black Mercedes to pull up.

Good. I like when the Mercedes arrives because it means Alex is driving. When it's his town car, it's his driver, Billy, chauffeuring us around, which gives Alex easier access to touch me if he so desires.

He always wants, though less in the last couple of years.

He found a new outlet, but I've learned it's not a positive thing. For me, maybe, but not for my guilt or sanity. I'd almost prefer it *only* be me. I walked into this when I young; the others unwittingly get jobs for a monster who soon turns on them.

Beneath my skin, my muscles and nerves tighten in wariness, but still, I pull open the passenger door and immediately slide in the car before he finds a reason to complain I'm stalling.

Never keep Alex waiting.

"Good evening, Teagan."

I shut my eyes briefly—*very* briefly—hoping he doesn't see my quick inhale of bravery. The simple purr of his voice used to have my thighs clenching with desire, back when I was a young, naïve girl, but now they only have me wishing I could sew my thighs shut tight forever.

"Good evening, Alex," I reply in a tone that isn't too loud or too quiet. He doesn't like when I'm quiet on nights like this one because it could raise alarms with our guests. This conversation during the drive is practice for later.

Through my peripheral vision, I spot him nodding, pleased with my response. Then he puts the car in gear and pulls away from the curb, the vehicle a rumbling hum beneath me. Thankful for the distraction, I keep my face tilted to the outdoors, watching as the city's lights pass us by until they're fading into the dark highway. It's a trip like Alex himself. He started bright and starry, but I soon learned that it masked the truth.

Unfortunately, the drive to Alex's mansion is much too short, and he swings to a stop in his curved driveway, like one of those ones you'd see in movies. While Alex gets to climbing out of the car, I suck in the largest breath possible as I look upon my jailcell.

No debate, his mansion is *gorgeous* from the outside. The type rich people who only ever host successful business parties own. It was his father's, back when Alex's family lived here, close to the city, and before his father took a break and moved to Newton.

Sky-high cement walls with many lights shining through the multiple windows. Pillars line the double doors that are easily triple what my townhouse's doors are. It's always reminded me of the castle from Beauty and the Beast, and like that story, deep inside the walls, there is a monster. Only unlike that story, this monster prefers to leave his safety of his estate and bring forth his fear onto others.

The monster in question opens my door wide, a hand reaching inside for me to grasp. Doing so means handing myself willingly over to him, like I have so many times before. His hand is representative of everything I've come to know—pain, agony, and loss.

Still, I'm aware of the outcome of not taking it, so I do, using him to stand from the vehicle. He nods, satisfied, and leads me up the grand front steps, leaving one of his multiple staff to move his car to its proper place.

We pass the front doorman, because yes, he has literal staff to hold his door open for him. The moment we're across the threshold, Alex grasps the skin of my upper arm, wrenching me to a rough halt.

I wish I could say his expression was scary. Furrowed brows and evil eyes, but it's a lie. His passive expression is worse than anything else he can send my way because it hides my horrible reality.

"You will behave tonight. I have two important guests coming and they wish to see me in my comfortable home life, which means meeting my *girlfriend*, who will smile when she's spoken to, will reply appropriately and politely, and will limit herself to one glass of wine with dinner. Understand, babe?"

Babe. I shiver, despising that word. He uses it as though he's loving, but rather, it's a meaningless endearment. More so, there's always a knot in my stomach when he does, as though even my body dislikes the term.

Still, I nod, as I've been trained to, biting the inside of my lip to not flinch from the pain up my arm. The sooner he's satisfied with my response, the sooner he'll release me.

After a final pinch to the bone, he moves his hand away before adjusting his suit jacket and taking the lead toward the dining room. I follow along and wipe my damp, sweaty hands along the edge of my dress, cursing the day Alex Miller noticed me.

A figure plops down in Elena's desk in our Math class, but I know from the bold blue jeans—clearly new and not faded—collared shirt, and blinding smile, it's sure as heck not my best friend.

I drag my gaze up from the pencil I'm fiddling with to find Alex Miller smiling at me. His hair flops over perfect eyes. Eyes that easily get him any girl he even glances toward.

"Hey, Miller," I say casually, aiming to not show him how he affects me. As long as his eyes aren't an x-ray machine, he shouldn't be able to spot my speeding heart, since nonchalance when speaking to Alex is next to impossible.

"Faber." He nods his head, shifting to position his chin on a propped-up arm. "Think we can get on a first name basis yet?"

Alex wants to use first names? *My already speedy heart quickens to an unimaginable rate. He's gorgeous and easily the most popular guy in school. His family is rich, though very secretive. His father is our principal, and I've never heard mention of his mother.*

My faded jeans are insanely pale compared to his. My shirt is a size too big and isn't even mine. My current foster family gave me one of their other child's clothing when all mine got too tight. Begrudgingly, of course, because all I'm good for is getting them a cheque. Heaven forbid they actually use some of the money on me.

Alex and I are the total opposite from one another.

Whoa, settle down, Teagan. *All he's asking for is a first name.*

My lashes flutter, like how the other girls he speaks to do. "I guess we can be."

"Teagan," he purrs.

Oh my, why does my name sound so amazing in his mouth?

I wrinkle my nose playfully, knowing full well I'm flirting. "Alex."

He readjusts his position, leaning back in the chair and appearing lazy and relaxed. Any moment the teacher should call the class to order, but I hope she never does. Doing so will end this interaction.

"How is it that we've never spoken to each other?"

Because we exist on different planets.

Instead, I shrug, leaving him to extend the conversation if he chooses to.

"Well, I think we should fix that. You want to hang out later after school?"

I never should have said yes.

It only got worse after that.

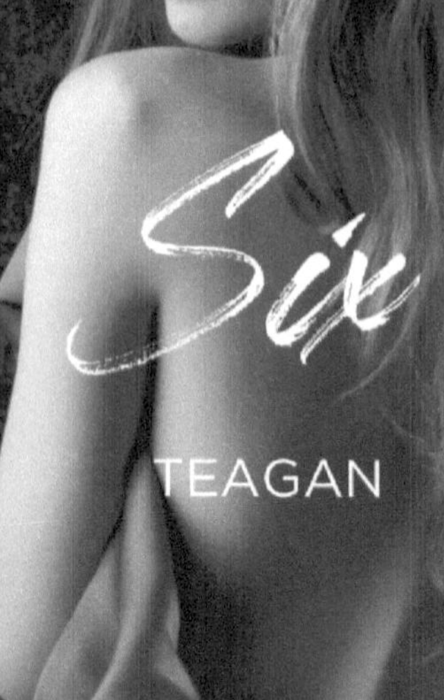

Six

TEAGAN

"TEAGAN."

I blink away the memory of a better time. A better time because that day, being a normal teenager flirting with the cute guy, was nice. It was everything that occurred *after* that was less so.

"Sorry." I hurry, quickening my feet until I catch up to Alex, where he stands a few feet ahead of me.

"Eyes up," he orders, ensuring I look the part of a happy girlfriend.

His cold hand wraps around my own, and together, we enter the lion's den, smiling at the elderly couple already waiting.

The rapes, the beatings, the abuse, the horrors—but this is the part I hate the most.

The pretending.

Pretending I don't know how Hell is only a floor down, behind the padded locks, steel doors, and misery, so thick it alone keeps people out.

Pretending Alex and I are truly in love. He tells people we've been together since high school, which isn't a lie, but it also horri-fying masks one.

Pretending I'm happy when really my smile is fake. It's chock full of pain and the knowledge if I don't smile convincingly, I'll feel it for the next while.

Pretending I'm not alone inside, when really, I'm screaming from the mountaintops, hating how unwanted I truly am. Hating how my own foster family basically sold me to Alex in exchange for a lifetime of wealth.

"Mr. and Mrs. Sully, what a pleasure it is to have you in my home." Alex spreads his arms wide and inviting, and the idiots fall for his charming persona.

"And what a lovely home it is." The male steps forward—Mr. Sully. "And it's Dave and Sherry, please." He grasps Alex's hand in a firm shake before gesturing for his wife, Sherry, to also approach.

"Thank you for having us." Her smile meets her eyes. She means what she says.

Alex sweeps his hand to the side, motioning to me. I swallow, forcing moisture down my dry throat. From the outside, they appear like a gentle elderly couple, so how much do they know about Alex's true form?

"Dave and Sherry, please meet my Teagan."

My Teagan.

Mine.

His.

I'm an object to him, to be pulled from the cupboard for when I'm useful, such as events like this one.

I tilt my head and lift the corners of my lips in a demure smile, one I've practiced many times before. "Nice to meet you both."

Beside me, I spot the telltale glow of pleasure in Alex's eyes, which allows my shoulders to unknot by the smallest fraction. I've gotten through the hardest part of the night with Alex's attitude intact. Anything past now will be easier.

"Come," he says, stepping toward the sitting room. I follow in his shadow, keeping my shoulders straight and rigid as his guests walk behind us.

A few more hours and this will be over.

THE NEXT TIME I breathe is when Alex drops me off at the club. Before I exit the car, his hand clamps down on my arm, keeping me in place. No doubt there will be an onslaught of verbal abuse, even while my mind speeds through the boring night we just had, seeking anything indicating I pissed him off.

Instead, his eyes lighten, and he smiles, but it's not pretty or nice. It's the smile a serial killer has right before they stab the knife into their victim.

I've seen this smile before.

In no way does it make me feel the slightest bit proud of myself that he's not angry. Instead, he's calculating, which is worse.

He leans across the console, lining his face up with mine, and I force myself to remain still. Flinching won't do me any favours.

"You were a good girl tonight. Run along and show every other guy what a slut you are, babe."

The nickname sends a chill down my spine. I hate it, and yet, it makes me nod—makes me obey his command.

He continues, "I have plans in my basement."

Bile shoots up my throat and I swallow the bitter taste. It's not the crude nicknames he uses on me—I'm used to those. No, it's the knowledge of what his plans will be.

That poor girl.

I've seen her once before—because he forces me to see every single one of them, permitting me to keep a tally of his sickness while lording his power over me. He knows I won't tattle. He knows I won't because no one will believe me over him. He'll pay off whoever he needs to and then take penance from my skin.

Fear is a powerful motivator.

And the exact reason I smile and nod and say, "I will. Have a good night, Alex," despite the crushing weight of guilt making it challenging to breathe.

How easy it'd be to march myself inside and demand Mason call the police, so I can report Alex. How easy it'd be for me to be free, and to free the innocent woman he has locked up.

I won't because I know how this game goes. The rich wins and the weak loses. To keep both our lives going, I won't do what I dream of all the fucking time.

Alex releases my arm and I finish opening the door, forcing my speed to remain slow and paced to not appear too overeager to escape.

"Goodnight, Teagan. I have a work function next week."

Which means more of the same. I nod again and shut the car door behind me, waiting until he peels away from the curb before turning toward Josh, waiting by the staff door.

"Have a good night?"

"Peachy," I respond with an attitude-lined snarl. Peachy, if peachy means sitting on the edge of my seat while I pretended to associate with *those* people.

As I stride past him and inside the club, I switch my phone back on, getting greeted by an onslaught of messages.

BRENT

If you continue to ignore me, I will continue to message you.

BRENT

Teagan, answer me.

BRENT

Why are you protecting him? You know
something and all I'm trying to do is help you.

And finally, the last one, sent only ten minutes ago.

BRENT

Fine, you win.

Scowling with annoyance, I toss the phone in my purse again. Ideally, he'll stick to his *I'm finished* plan because it's ridiculous for him to believe he can invade my life and make such demands. For his own safety, Brent needs to remain far away from Alex. I'm doing him a favour by not telling him anything. He can consider it a tribute to the feelings I used to hold for him.

That's *all* it is. At least that's what I tell myself.

Brent's interruption into my life has me in all sorts of disarray. So much, I don't wait for Mason to come find me, but rather, I bump into him on my way out of the dressing room.

"Oh!" His hands fly in the air with surprise, causing him to seem like a cartoon character. "Teagan, you're... ready?" His tone is a question, mixed with surprise, and if I wasn't in such a shit mood, I'd find his dumb expression hilarious.

"Yep. Stage first, like usual?" I'm already walking past him and toward the stage entrance for my usual dance.

But stop with Mason's, "No." Surprise makes me do a double take and glance behind me. As long as I've worked here, my nights begin on the stage.

Mason gestures to the side, toward the hallway leading to the private rooms. "A fan of yours requested you right away. He paid double. First room."

Without waiting for the comment about to explode from my mouth, he spins on his heel and walks away. But then I wonder, *Is it really that bad not to be starting on stage?* Perhaps this will be a welcome change.

By the time I make it to the private dance rooms, it hits me. The realization I should have had right away. It's not a coincidence someone paid double for my company right away. A someone who can't wait to get me alone.

By the time I enter the room, I'm fuming. My teeth are pressed painfully together, my jaw, a rock of irritation and frustration, has me slamming the door, uncaring how much noise my arrival makes.

Got to hand it to him. He's fucking determined.

The red light cast over the room may as well be a white spotlight, the way my gaze zeros in on Brent's cocky grin. He leaning against the far wall, his arms and ankles crossed, appearing at ease.

"Why won't you leave me alone?"

"Are there cameras in here?" he asks instead.

I gesture to one in the corner. "Yeah. For the dancers' safety. Sometimes people get handsy and rough."

His expression remains passive, and he only comments, "If you're not dancing, will that raise suspicions?"

Probably, but I don't admit that. There is someone who monitors the surveillance room, but as I said to Brent, security only really steps in to prevent abuse. I don't mention it to him though because I do not want to rub my body over his—his that has clearly hardened into a man.

Looks never mattered to me. Even when Brent thought himself unworthy of a relationship because no pretty girl would look twice at him, *I* did, because he was my brightest light. I always saw the boy who viewed me as me, and not as the poor foster kid with nothing but the clothes on her back and whatever lunch my family found it fit to send me to school with that day. He was the one I was saddened to leave behind each day after school, scared that each goodbye would be our final one. I never cared about his weight because I was the one to see his amazing soul, when his personality shone so bright.

He was the guy who went to the nurse's office to retrieve pads when I got my period at school and didn't have the necessary items in my locker, and although I was awkward as fuck about it, he didn't seem to care about anything other than helping me. He was the one who soothed my emotional wounds against the verbal abuse from my foster family. I may have been more outgoing, between the two of us, and shut the bullies up, but he was the kind one. With everyone, not just me, because that's who is is—*was.*

With time, I grew to want him as much as he wanted me. Then I got with Alex and learned his dark desires and how he doesn't share. Which is why when Brent finally asked me out, I had to break his heart.

But now, scanning how his shirt stretches tightly over his chest, and how his arms bulge from where they're crossed over his chest, I can't imagine any girl *not* giving him the time of day now. Or night. Or whatever time it is the second he wants them.

While not dancing may raise some questions from Mason, it's worth it *not* to press my body all over his and reawaken desires that have no place in the present. It'd be a silly fantasy—a momentary thrill—that'll only end up shattering my heart more.

"I'm only here to talk," he says, after waiting for me to respond.

"Y-you need to leave, Brent." Despite my stutter, my hands form fists at my side, and I straighten my spine, keeping it firm and steady for his next round of begging.

Instead of asking about Alex, which is what I expect Brent to do, he kicks off the wall and murmurs, "I've been thinking about the past."

My head tilts, my annoyance pausing in momentary interest for what he has to say. "Our past?"

"Mhm." His arms drop by his side and his shoes echo against the floor as he slowly comes toward me at an unhurried pace. "Mainly high school. Do you remember our first day?"

Like it was yesterday. It was an entirely new world after elementary school, and I wasn't handling it well at all. I'm not normally an anxious person, but that day was different. It was so much *more,* and I wanted nothing to do with it.

"Yes."

"You remember how I walked you to each of your classes and made sure we found you the best routes through the halls?"

"Yes."

"Do you remember your first crush?"

A name I haven't dwelled on in a *long* time, but I've never forgotten, for all those first-crush reasons. He was nothing special, other than being hot. Eventually, he dated some other girl and I moved on.

"Yes."

"Me too. I remember how excited you were when he greeted you one day. You swooned for the rest of the week."

Brent takes another step, this time bringing himself close enough that the warmth from his body touches my bare skin. I refuse to admit to myself how it electrocutes my nerves—how it makes my spine tingle with desire. Despite everything, some long-buried part of me wants this—wants Brent in my life again.

It can't happen though, because outside these walls, it's no longer the reality we live in. I need to return to being the bitch he met last night and chase him away.

"Do you recall when you urged me to become friends with other people so we both could expand our social circles? Or how you were so happy we shared two out of four classes together in the second semester of that first year? Or the first sports game of the season and how thrilled you were to dress up in the school's colours and cheer in the stands." His warm breath blows sweetly over my face, and I inhale the scent, locking it inside me. "I relive those years *all* the time, Teagan. All. The. Fucking. *Time.*"

A knot forms in my throat. His words do not sound as if they come from a fond place. I step back, placing distance between us again, needing the space.

Space he instantly deletes by stepping closer. His words come faster, harder, and harsher, full of agonized memories. "I relive how I fucking fell in love with my best friend. How you were the greatest thing in my life and how I humiliated myself in front of you, but still, was able to move on because I couldn't lose you."

I know what he's doing. He's saying all this shit to break me—to force me to relive our teenage lives, believing it'll what—make me talk?

Instead, I step back again, watching as he follows along. We continue our dance until my back lands on the wall and Brent stops less than an inch from me, his mouth curled in an evil grin, knowing that I can't escape. He bends slightly, tipping his head until our faces line up.

"I would have done *anything* for you, Cherry-Girl. Any-*fucking*-thing. You were the best person—thing—in my life. Your heart was larger than this damn country, I swear. But that was before you became *this.*" He steps back, removing his heat and putting distance between us once more. Every inch he replaces between us is another breath I take. His nose lifts, his chin jutting, until he's peering down at me through a sneer. "You've become this person who aligns herself with a criminal."

Words sit on my lips—denial of what he's claiming. I don't want to be aligned with a criminal. Don't want to know what I do or have witnessed what I have. Rather, I'm forced to live through these horrors, knowing there's nowhere I can run that he won't find me; no one I can tell who'll help me.

"And now," he sneers, his eyes flickering darker, but all his words do is painfully curl my insides, "I'm here, fighting with you, when I should be helping save those women."

He does know. I still, right down to my beating heart. *How does he know? He* can't *know.* This will ruin him—endanger him. I won't watch as Alex takes Brent away, in ways worse than he already has.

His responding chuckle slackens my nerves, loosening them until my tense muscles relax the slightest bit. "So, you do know what I'm speaking about then. Good. We've made progress."

A damn set-up. My arms fly toward his chest, but end up missing his body entirely. "Fuck you, Brent. You know nothing."

"I know more than you think, but would prefer if you filled in the gaps."

Not happening. I cross my arms and fuse my expression into one I hope he finally understands as needing him to drop this. Nothing he says will make me admit anything.

"Brent, I don't know why you've randomly showed up, but you need to leave. For your own safety." I swallow. *And mine.* No doubt Alex would remember Brent, even with how different he looks now. Alex is aware of who Brent was to me and made sure I knew better to ever reach out.

Brent's head tilts, and instead of seeming hurt, he appears pensive. As if something I said sparked a thought within him. "*My* safety? Teagan, *my* safety isn't the concern here. You need to tell me what you know for the safety of those women. For you. Why did you warn Natalie away?"

I falter. I want to ask how he knows Alex's sister, but I suspect it's one more thing in a line of facts he's aware of, based on what he's said so far.

The moment I met Natalie at Alex's party, I knew. Even without him saying anything, simply because I'm aware of his habits and the purpose of those fucking slave parties. His sister was next on his hit list, and while I couldn't do anything then, because Alex was glued to her side, the moment I saw her enter his office the other day, I couldn't let it go on.

He gave her some pretty speech about an arranged marriage with a "business associate" and how giving her some of the Miller fortune —money that should be hers without the strings—would accompany that marriage.

Right. There would be no marriage, but rather a bargain, made only to benefit Alex and that associate. No doubt, Alex would have received large sums of money, or stocks, or trades, or whatever the fuck he was chasing in the moment in exchange for his sister, but the little I learned of Natalie proved to me she's not like her brother.

I can't save myself, nor anyone else who finds themselves in an entanglement with Alex, but I tried for her. A gamble, sure, as she could have turned on me entirely, but I took the chance to help her because what I saw in her eyes wasn't villainy. It was fear. Discomfort.

I swallow around the lump forming in my throat. "How do you know Natalie?"

"That's not what I asked, Teagan. Why did you tell her to run away from Alex's office?"

Because Alex is the devil. But I can't admit that to him. Giving Brent a facet of the truth will do the opposite of what I want; it'll keep him around when I need him to go away.

So, I lie. "Alex is trying to give her money. The more he gives, the less I get. It's as simple as that."

A weak fable, but one I hope he believes. As I'm already horrible in his perspective, adding money-hungry whore to the list of my qualities isn't too far a stretch.

"Is it?" he asks instead, his voice a low rumble. "That's all it was, hmm? I suppose that makes sense since you were never one to be pushed around." His brow rises in a challenge, waiting for me to contradict my previous words.

Instead, we end up in a speechless showdown, our eyes doing all the talking.

Me: *I hate you. Why are you here? Go away and don't look for me again. I miss you.*

Him: *Tell me now.*

Finally, he loses and steps back, nodding, though it seems more to the ground than me, and I breathe normal, once again, thankful he'll leave this alone and get the fuck out of my life.

"All right, Teagan. You chose your side. I understand what you meant when you told me bad things break people apart." His head shakes slowly before adding with a crooked smirk, "Thanks for the dance."

Then he leaves, shutting the door behind him.

Seven

BRENT

"I'M happy we're doing this."

Teagan smiles, but it doesn't quite reach her eyes. Lately, something is going on with her, but I don't know what. I hardly see her anymore though, and even Mom has been noticing her absence. According to her and Dad, I've been grumpier than usual. It's difficult to be cheerful when my best friend is upset.

"Yeah," she agrees. "Feels like forever since we've chilled with a movie marathon." Her words sound good, but her attention is diverted toward her phone.

I sigh. It seems like she spends more and more time on the damned thing. "Cherry-Girl, what's going on? You haven't been yourself lately."

Her attention whips up and she slides the phone into her pocket as red paints her cheeks and neck, highlighting my exact point.

"I'm fine," she rushes to say.

She's not. Something's up, and she usually tells me everything going on with her—good or bad. She's holding secrets, but I don't want to piss her off, so for now, I relax against the couch and lift the controller.

"All right then. Just remember I'm here for you. Always."

Always. It's been a month since she rejected me, and while it was weird at first, I forced myself to shut my heart off to any romantic feelings and simply be her friend because it's what she wants, and I won't lose her over stupid self-pity.

"Thanks, Brent." She smiles, and this time, it appears easier.

Right as the movie begins to roll, the front door flies open and Mom stomps through, a huge gathering of shopping bags with her. I leap to my feet to assist, and I hear Teagan pause the movie and follow shortly after.

"Hey, you two." Mom smiles, barely glancing at me to study Teagan. Mom adores Teagan. She feels bad for her life, and insists Teagan spend as much time here as she possibly can. I'm sure if Mom could adopt her, she would.

"Hi, Annie."

Because these two are long past the formalities of Mrs. Thorne.

"Hey, Teagan. Staying for dinner?" Which is Mom's subtle way at insisting she does.

Which Teagan's well-aware of. Her chest deflates slightly with her easing sigh. "Yes, please. If you don't mind."

"Nonsense." Mom waves her hand before re-hoisting the ones by the door back into her arms. "Now you two watch your movie while I cook and find your father."

"If you're sure..." Teagan bites her lip, ever the polite one. "I can help."

I want to kiss her. I've always wanted to, but seeing her now, biting her lip as she's being polite to my mother is yet another realization of how much I want her.

If only she'd have me.

"Goodness no. Thanks for the offer though." Mom rushes off before Teagan can say more.

She doesn't move from where she watches Mom head to the

kitchen. Her body leans forward, her feet remaining stuck, and I know her enough to recognize it's Teagan's way of debating to still help or not.

"Cherry-Girl, let's continue the movie." Amusement lightens my tone and I pat the couch beside me. "She's already said no. Give it up."

"Still, I feel bad. Not only do your parents feed me, but they won't let me work for it." Regardless, Teagan plops back onto the couch. I fling a nearby throw blanket over her body, aware she enjoys being cozy when watching TV.

"You know Mom thinks of you like a daughter."

While Teagan's foster family royally sucks, it's Mom who picks up their slack. Each birthday, Teagan gets a cake and presents from my parents. She has a permanent spot in our house for Christmas. Mom's even taken to leaving extra blankets and pillows in my bedroom closet, so we have easy access to them in case Teagan chooses to stay over. Of course, when that happens, it's me who takes the floor while she sleeps in my bed.

Teagan shuffles across the couch, bringing the blanket with her. She continues until her arm presses against mine—cold compared to my temperature—but she feels amazing. Her head falls on mine and it takes everything to keep my arm from going around her body and hoisting her against me.

"This is perfect." She sighs.

Agreed.

"I wish we can stay like this forever, Brent."

"Why can't we?"

"Because it's not how the world works. Sometimes bad things break people apart."

That would never happen to us.

Eight

TEAGAN

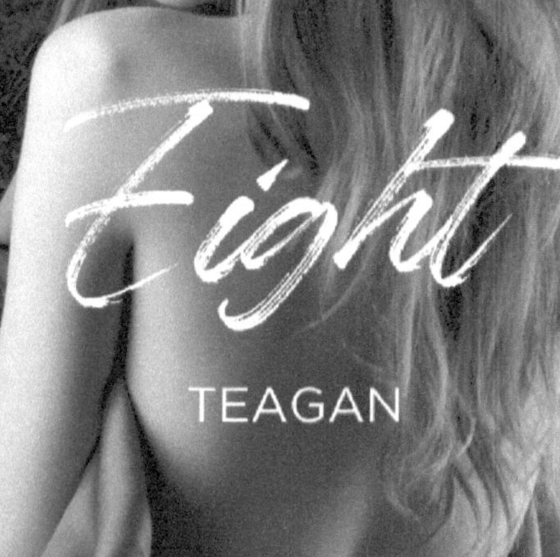

IT'S THE NEXT MORNING, and no matter how much time I let pass after my initial read of the text or how much coffee I've used to wake myself up, his message makes no more sense than it did the first time I read it.

Luckily, another one soon follows.

Right away, I respond back with, *Okay*, despite my numb fingers begging me to throw the phone away. Alex doesn't typically need me so soon after the last time and his message is cryptic at best.

I go about my day, barely doing anything productive, until six rolls around. Usually, the sight of the black town car fills me with dread, but today, it eases a bit of the discomfort in my veins. At least soon, I'll know what Alex was speaking of.

Billy silently opens the door for me, and I slip inside. He never communicates with me. Merely opens my door and delivers me to Alex.

This time, Alex isn't in the car, so I enjoy the peace the drive alone brings, with curiosity knocking at my thoughts.

I shut my phone off, slipping it into my purse in time for Billy to pull up outside Alex's mansion. Within a minute, he has my door open. "Mr. Miller says for you to go on in. Leave your purse."

Of course he does. The sight of the mansion, and the unknowns about to occur, have a knot forming in my stomach. I wipe my damp hands on my jeans before striding up the massive steps, each one heaving more dread upon me. Maybe this will be fine. Maybe his text was a misunderstanding.

Because I have no company I keep—no friends. There's no one I'm close to that he'd find "interesting."

Elena Sparks, my high school friend, was another one I left in the past and didn't dare to ever look in on after Alex threatened both her life and her mother's law career.

I haven't spoken to my last foster family since I was eighteen and before I took off. But they can rot in the fiery depths of Hell for all I care, considering how not only was I a paycheque to them, but it was also easy for them to turn their back on me when finances were involved. When Alex needed a way to ensure they wouldn't tattle on him, he paid them off for their silence.

The front door swings open, revealing Alex standing there in his usual tie and jacket. His arms are crossed over his broad chest, and he looks pissed. Anger lines mar his face, deepening his expression to the point my feet want to take me backward, return to the vehicle, and beg his driver to take me home.

I flinch and don't move. My chest gets heavy with the breathless pants. My feet are bricks as I step into the house, approaching the monster who holds my chains. I glance behind me, playing with the concept of running, but know it's a dream I'll never make a reality.

"Alex."

"Come," he orders, spinning on his heel and striding toward the long hallway.

I follow him, keeping up with his brisk pace as he leads me to what I know to be a sitting room. Except, as I enter, I notice there isn't any place to sit; all the furniture has been cleared out.

He slams the door shut behind us and then I realize what he's brought me to—a goddamn jail cell, one of his own design.

"Alex—"

He throws his hand up, stopping my words, and in it, is his phone, a video cued on the screen.

My feet drag me a hesitant step closer for a better view, eyes narrowing to focus on the video as he clicks *play*. Two people in a darkened room filled with a red light begin to move. A room, unfortunately, I know all too well.

I recognize myself and my red bikini, and the stiffness in my back as I watch Brent stride closer to me, lashing me with all sorts of words I still recall. Alex's video isn't playing any sound, but it's obvious from the angle, it's me in the video. The position Brent keeps his head at hides it from sight, flashing only the side, as if he knew exactly how the camera would capture him, even before enquiring about its existence.

"Why do you have a video of me at work?"

Instead of answering me, his finger jabs in the direction of his screen, demanding, "Who is this, Teagan?"

I shrug, feigning innocence. "A customer, Alex. You make me serve them all the time and this one isn't any different."

The words leave my mouth before my brain can catch up to the attitude I shot at him. No doubt I'll pay for that.

His body seemingly grows larger, narrowing the space around me. "Do not fucking lie to me, Teagan. According to Mason, this is the second time this guy has come into the club seeking *only* you. He does not visit the bar or enjoy the other dancers. Just you and only in private rooms. Therefore," he tucks away his phone, ending the video, "tell me who he is."

Jealousy. I get it now. Someone may have played with his toy, and he doesn't like it. I need to act as though this is nothing.

Why? the devil on my shoulder whispers. *What happens to Brent isn't your issue.*

But it is. Alex has threatened many times it'll be Brent who pays with his life, so no matter the years that have passed, the deal I made with myself remains: *Brent will never know the truth. He's saved me so many times, but this time, he is unable to.*

"He's just a customer, Alex. I work at a strip club. I guess I became his favourite and that's all there is to it."

Alex's already cold eyes freeze into ice. "Mason says before the other day, he's never seen this guy. And the footage I have of last night clearly shows you two talking, not dancing. So, before I ask again—"

"He's no one." I shake my head weakly, dread deepening my tone because he doesn't believe me. Realization slams into me of how this will end. "Before the other day, I never even met him. It's whatever, Alex."

Deadly silence fills the room before Alex moves. But it's not his body that does; rather it's a single muscle twitching in his cheek. He doesn't believe me, and I feel it in the depth of my stomach as disappointment soon shifts into fear. My chest grows weighted, caving in from the dread. I lower my eyes, thinking how nice it'd be to fight like a normal couple where I could safely leave and later return, when we could rationally chat about this.

A solid minute passes before Alex takes a step, bringing his darkness closer. He stops an inch away, looking down at me without moving his head. His teeth bare and a blank expression falls on his face.

"Remove your clothing."

He doesn't believe me...

This time, my thoughts trail off, taking my mind with it to a place where I'll be safe. I know what's next; these moments are scarred into my mind and body with the frequency he's felt the need to punish me over the years.

My clothes pool at my feet and I kick them to the side and out of the way where they won't disrupt his process. This entire thing is a well-practiced event we've done too many times.

My arms quiver, wanting to cover myself from his sickening gaze, but I don't. Hiding only angers the monster more. Something I've learned over the years. He strides forward and roughly grabs the skin of my cheeks.

"Listen to me, you little whore," he hisses, his bared teeth less than an inch away. "You. Are. Mine. And whoever it is you've been seeing better stop, or else he may find himself six feet under. Do I need to add him to the list of people you care for? The people I can hurt." His hands release me with force, and I stumble back but quickly drop my eyes to the ground again. My teeth grit, hating every moment of this part.

The part where he regains power over me.

And I do nothing. I hate doing nothing. Hate being weak—a body to be used and abused. If only I had a weapon and could fight back. A dream I consistently have before the worst comes.

His belt coming undone echoes through the empty, silent room, reminding me of the cage he's created here—prettier, but still as grim as the one he keeps below.

"Now you've made me do this, Teagan. You think I *want* to?"

He's putting it all on me to remove his fault, so when I think about this later, it's me I'll hate and not him. The difference between myself and other women in shit situations is that I'm fully aware of what's happening. Of how I've become meek in his presence to not spook him into negatively reacting, when all I'm truly doing is reinforcing his power.

The issue isn't being unaware—it's being trapped. No one is here to help me, and Alex is too powerful. No matter which cops I find, no matter how far I run, he's one step ahead of me. I've tried it all before and he's still come out on top, so what's the point anymore?

Then he touches me, and I float, allowing my mind to leave my body, leave this room, and even leave this world to find a new place— one that's peaceful and filled with rainbows and damn butterflies. It's a place I try to envision every time, but it never works.

And like every other time, reality slams back into me as his hands find my inner thighs. He wrenches my mind to the place this all began.

"Alex, I'm sorry, but I'm not ready."

Alex huffs, leaning back on his bedframe and crossing his arms. "Teagan, we've been going out for months now. Don't you think you owe this to me?"

His terminology is slightly off, considering "going out" implies being public. Instead, Alex thought it better to hide our relationship from everyone. We meet in secret, sometimes during school to sneak away for our own little moments, or after school at his place. Never mine, which I'm fine with because mine isn't exactly warm and welcoming.

It's whatever though. Elena and Brent are the only people I'd care to tell, and of the two of them, Brent's the one I feel guilty over not saying anything to. He's always known everything about me, but now, I'm hiding a part of the truth from him. In the end, I get it—Alex is popular and doesn't want the questions and I'm simply pleased to be with him, so who am I to complain and go against his wishes? This will all work out in the end.

"I guess." My shoulders lift in a weak shrug, agreeing with him despite the knots forming in my stomach. "But I don't know... I guess, I

think I need a bit more time before we do that." The word sex *refuses to leave my lips, remaining a taboo subject.*

Alex nods once, sliding off his bed, and leaves his room without another word. It takes me twenty minutes before I realize he's not returning, so I let myself out.

Alex's painfully firm grip sinks into my skin at the same time I feel his cock push inside me, ripping through unwilling muscles. My back against the wall should be cold, but instead, I'm numb to the temperature. Numb to the feeling of him inside me... Numb to it all.

Like I've become so proficient at being.

It's ironic that every time he takes me, my mind travels back to the first time he raped me, rather than to a constructed safe space. Maybe it's the regret that I hadn't seen the signs sooner, which could have saved me from a lifetime of misery, or maybe it's something else entirely. Either way, it's where I go, and as he pumps into me again and again, groaning hateful words in my ear, I allow myself to leave once more.

It's late in the evening the next day when the bang on my front door echoes through the house. I'm home alone, so I go downstairs to answer it.

"Alex?" Is it weird my boyfriend is at my front door? Yes, because he never comes here.

He pushes through the doorway, barrelling down upon me and shoving me against the nearest wall.

"Alex?" I try to catch his gaze, but he's focused downward, on my breasts peeking out from my tank.

"Do you know how many fucking girls would die for the opportunity to ride my cock and you dare deny me?"

My stomach flips. Oh, that's what this is about.
"Alex..."

He pushes away then grasps my hand, yanking me up the stairs toward my bedroom.

Okay, maybe I can do this. *I mean, I've seen him shirtless, and it certainly makes my core tingle.*

Alex throws the door shut behind us and grabs me, forcing his fingers through my hair until he has a firm grip that he uses to bring my face closer to his. My scalp burns from his rough touch and it shoots liquid to my eyes. I want to cry with how much this stings. My hands fly up, linking with his, and attempt to remove my hair from his grip.

It doesn't work. Instead, he captures my mouth in a bruising kiss. I've always enjoyed Alex's kisses and our make-out sessions, but right now, he feels different. Meaner...

He finally releases my hair, only to rip at my shirt, pulling it off my body and throwing it to the floor. My self-respect lands there as well. We've done under-the-shirt stuff, but he's never undressed me like this.

Then he grabs my jeans and begins to undo them. Finally, instinct drives me to push at his hands.

"Alex, no, I meant it."

My words seemingly fly over his head, and he nudges my hands away until he manages to get the button undone. I step back, throwing my arms around my body to cover myself from his cruel gaze.

His face twists into an expression I don't recognize, though it's one I've seen aimed toward other classmates when they've pissed him off.

"You think I was giving you a choice?" His humourless bark of laughter makes its way down my spine, and I shiver. "You lost your opportunity to say no the moment you denied me what's mine."

I never believed myself to be a weak girl, but in that moment, I realize how powerless I truly am. How when I throw my body away from him and kick out, pushing him away with my arms, it does nothing but cause him to come at me harder.

I blink, and I'm on my bed.

I blink, and my panties are ripped off.

I blink, and his legs are freed from his own pants.

I blink the final time and his weight is pinning me to the bed.

Dread—cold and itchy—fills me. Dread is much too tame for the realization I now have about Alex, knowing he's far worse than I believed. He's popular; a guy who's used to getting what he wants, sure, but forcing me...

His hands wrench my thighs apart at the same time he meets my gaze, no apology in their depths. "Remember, you brought this on yourself."

I wish I could say I went somewhere else mentally, for the time being. That I lost myself in the depression, the hatred, and floated to a better, more peaceful place for me to survive in.

But that would be a lie.

I feel as his cold hands stroke me once, then again, trying to get me wet for his pending entry, but nothing can overcome the fear keeping me dry.

I feel as his weight prevents me from bucking him off me.

I feel as his cock—a part of him I've only seen a handful of times when I've touched him—braces against my core.

I feel as the worst pain I've ever felt, and ever will, rips—breaks— me as he shoves into my body, rupturing through the blockade my dryness created, uncaring in how my insides burn in response. I gasp, eyes clenched tightly as I work through the pain his invasion brings.

I wish I could say I continued to fight him, but that would also be a lie. Rather, I lie there, waiting for him to seat himself so the pain can lessen, even by a little bit.

Instead, it explodes. Entering me dry wasn't the worst. No, destroying that barrier I've heard other girls mention feels as if death itself has come to take me away. He doesn't slow, doesn't ease in gently, but rather thrusts past it and then continues to move inside me, even as I scream, begging my insides to cry, if only to add moisture to the insurmountable pain.

"Fuck you, Teagan. I could have made this good for you, you whore."

I'm a whore because I didn't spread my legs willingly. I'm a whore because he was forced to take it from me.

I suppose I'm a whore then.

It goes on forever, him pulling back and then pushing in again. Each time, it feels like he gets deeper and deeper, and I'm sure at this point, death is a real possibility. If only to prevent me from feeling the ending of this.

But then he goes faster, his knees shifting him to a position with better leverage, allowing his speed to increase and his hips to slam harder into me. His hand finds my throat at the same time, but this, I don't fight. I welcome the sensation of his grip, hoping he'll end me right here and now.

"Fuck, fuck, fuck," he continuously curses, as if it's his world ending and not mine. He has nothing to complain about.

He won.

He took me, leaving me as a corpse on my bed.

It could be minutes. Maybe hours. I suppose, eventually, I do block out the horror, and when I come to, he's pulling from my body, leaving me empty but pleased it's over.

He gathers his clothing and silently leaves, saying nothing—Not. A. Single. Word. It's there, hours later, with dried blood caked on my thighs and his cum still staining my insides, my foster mother finds me. She casts me a scathing look before walking away, shaking her head.

Exactly like that moment, time passes differently, and by the time my memory is coming to an end, so is Alex's revenge. Perhaps this is why I choose that memory to consistently recall, because it fills the entire time Alex spends destroying my body.

In some ways, it's worse. Worse because the more time that passes, the more I discover everything fucked-up about him. How I missed it all as a naïve girl who only wanted the hot, rich, popular guy and didn't see the psychopath within.

Perhaps it truly is my fault. I denied him then, and somehow, it triggered something in his head. Something that made him want to hurt me. Maybe it was me who created the cravings he's come to have so often, and why he hires the secretaries he chooses, all to hurt them.

It's then he rips his cock from my body and zips up his suit pants before striding away. On his way out of the room, he scoops up my clothing, taking them with him when he leaves me to slump against the wall and fall to the floor below, his cum still dripping from my body.

The only saving grace is the IUD Alex paid off a doctor to implant—against my wishes at the time. In hindsight, I'm happy he did it because I wouldn't be able to endure bringing a child, with Miller genes, into the world.

"The next time you think about entertaining another man the way you have been, remember all the ways I can make this worse for you. I should note, I saw Elena Sparks the other day. Offered her a job," is the final threat he snarls before slamming the door shut and locking me inside the empty room, his threat hanging heavily in the air.

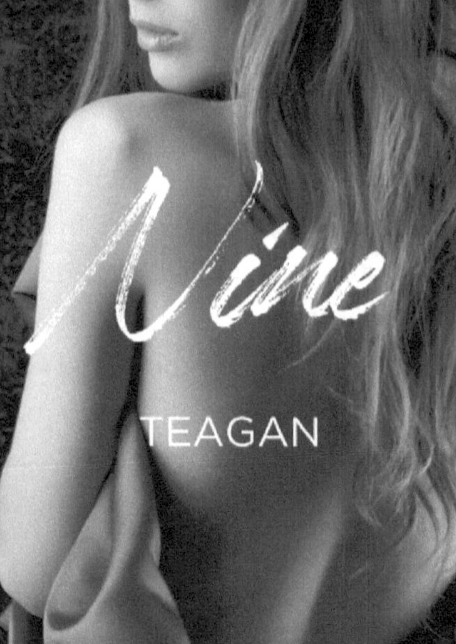

Nine

TEAGAN

TIME PASSES DIFFERENTLY when you're in captivity.

Slower.

Maybe it's been a couple hours since Alex left, or maybe only a matter of minutes. No amount of time changes the fact I've been raped and left behind with his cum drying on my leg. Nothing new to me and yet, it's still as impactful as the first time.

I want to shower. I want to wipe his touch from my body but won't be allowed to until I get home. And who knows when that'll be.

I've never been one to place blame, and I'm not right now, since it was me who welcomed the monster into my life so I have to deal with the consequences. But this round of abuse is due to Brent's insistence not to leave me alone.

My gaze drifts to the floor, mind heading lower, toward the woman I know Alex keeps down there. Brent claims to know something—though I don't see how—and wants more of the same truth, but what he doesn't know is it's better for everyone if he shuts his mouth and lets things continue as they have been.

Remaining silent is the only way I stay alive, though I've thought of all the ways I could piss Alex off to the point he'd kill me. Because death is a more welcome scenario.

But for some reason, I continue to hold on. Hold on until Alex loosens the reins, just as I wait for him to come back and release me from this prison.

It's however long later when the door finally opens, and I manage to slowly lift to my feet, bracing myself against the wall for whatever he'll soon be bestowing upon me. My hands rest lightly at my side, hoping he'll see a meek woman with no fight left in her, and he'll allow me go home.

But when he steps inside the room, the only thing I can feel is dismay, and that casual position a moment ago is long gone, replaced by a sour taste in my throat as my body fights to not puke.

Since last seeing him, he's removed his suit jacket and rolled up the sleeves of his shirt, but the pristine white is now dyed red. Deep red.

Blood red.

His hair is mussed, blood crusting the tips and keeping them upright. Exhaustion draws on his face, his brows low above faded eyes and arms swinging softly at his side. Despite the blood, a person would think he'd just come home from a hard day's work.

But I know the truth.

I'm not religious, but still, I say a silent prayer for the poor girl down below who I'm sure isn't with us anymore.

"Do you see what you made me do? How your betrayal ruins more than my life."

If these actions were taken by another man, I would be shocked, but with Alex, this doesn't surprise me. He's angry and feeling threatened, and now I'm to blame for him taking it out on the girl in his basement.

"I couldn't help myself," he continues. "Picturing you and that stranger..." He shrugs, a meek, helpless expression overtaking his form as he slowly steps closer. "I did all the things to her I wish I could do to you."

A gasp breaks from my lips, and as much as I want to move my hand to my face, to hide myself from him, I keep it by my side, not wishing to give him more ammo than I have already.

I'm sorry, I mentally tell her.

He's made me meet most of the girls. Hell, sometimes I'm here when he lures them in with "work stuff," before trapping them below. This one isn't new, having been here for a few months now. He must be close to his six-month mark, which is when he gets rid of them.

Alex is smart when he hires these girls. Qualifications don't matter. He chooses women without romantic or family ties. People who won't be reported missing when he captures them, after having them work the job they believe they were hired for, for a short time.

"Come with me."

He turns on his heel and leaves the room. I trail behind like an obedient dog, tracking his steps as he leads me down the hallway and toward the basement door.

No... Fuck.

Silently, we continue our trip. As I'm sure any basement in a mansion is built, this one is an entire floor on its own with corridors and sections leading to different places.

The chill of the basement air lashes at my skin, reminding me I'm still naked at the same time the cement underfoot numbs the soles of my feet, quickening my steps if only to get this over sooner.

He'll show me what he's done, and then I can go home and puke in peace.

Alex leads me past the wine cellar and down the familiar darkened hallway no staff is to ever go near. We haven't even made it to the coded door and already the scent of misery is thick in the air. It's a red cloud—red, like the blood Alex endlessly spills—hovering overhead, and when he unlocks the door and gestures for me to walk ahead of him, it grows stronger, casting shadows over the already-dreary basement.

The hallway in front of me is long, but I know it eventually leads to a wide-open room, also known as Hell. Eternal damnation is the theme down here. Not for the girls, but rather for Alex. Every single act he completes down here is a mark on his black soul. One of these days, I'm hoping it's enough the reaper charged with managing monsters' souls comes and retrieves his, to drag him screaming to the fiery depths, where hopefully a demon will be responsible for repeating every act Alex's ever completed onto him.

My slow steps must annoy him since his hand shoves against my back, causing me to trip and realign my feet in time for him to growl, "Faster."

I do, hastening my steps a little, and unfortunately, too soon, we find Hell. The walls are lined with various tools I've seen him utilize to bring death at a more painful rate. In the centre boasts a square, clear glass cage. Four panelled walls and a single-coded door where my eyes fall on the person in the centre.

She's curled up, her arms loose around thin legs. I see nothing identifiable about her past her long, bleached blonde hair that falls around her body and covers her face. Blood mats the edges, and I see the trail dripping from her thighs.

I gag. Bile rises to the top, and I shut my eyes to hide the image from sight, but it's not long before I peek again, strangely compelled to examine her form, searching for signs of life.

"Do you see how I hurt her?" the devil murmurs in my ear. "How she's lying there, wrecked from the pain *I* brought her?"

He revels in his power trip.

"Her name is Willow," he continues. "She was a damned good secretary. One of the best, if I must say, and a beauty on the eyes. Lit up my office every day for those couple months. Of course, each time

I saw her slight form and perky breasts teasing me from those demure tops she'd wear, I got hungry."

His hands land on my hips, eliciting a flinch while I unblinkingly stare at the girl and listen to his horrible recounting of how she found herself here.

"I imagined breaking her over and over. A girl like her, she looks like a fucking princess, and I needed her in my dungeon where I could be her king. You know," he purrs, leaning in closer—enough his blood-crusted shirt brushes my spine, "I nearly debated putting you in her place and keeping her as my permanent woman, but in the end, I don't believe she would understand the arrangement as well as you do. You and I, we have history."

I bite down on the wish that he did swap us. My life would involve more pain, but it would be short-lived with an expiration date, while she would experience entrapment in its worse form. Being the devil's girlfriend isn't the most terrible; it's this part. The gloating he enjoys as he dangles his other victims in front of me.

I haven't seen the outcome of them all, but I've seen enough.

Through a hazy gaze, I spot the subtle rise and fall of her body. She's breathing.

"She's still alive," I whisper.

"Of course. I haven't quite finished with her. She's too delicious for me to get rid of quite yet."

Poor girl.

My teeth dig into my lip, preventing the words from coming out. The words where I beg to help her—to clean her up at the very least. But I know better. The last time I tried to help one of his girls, it broke us both.

It crushed my insides to powder. I then realized the only person to save me would be myself, but that would only happen when Alex tires of me and finally does me in. When it happens, I'll have saved myself because I'll have *survived*. It's all that matters.

But the girl I tried to assist... it killed her. That day, he left for work, and I was still at the house. I snuck down here, having known his code—watching when he didn't think I was memorizing it—I was easily able to get into the room, and even the box. I had the woman in hand, was nearly out of the basement, when he found us through his fucking cameras.

In the end, I learned it was a pipe dream to believe I could get her out and she'd be saved from the horrors within.

Over the course of hours, he brutally raped her. First with his body, and then with every item I ever imagined using on a person. He cut her, chained her... Everything else I've blacked out. Memories I will forever have carved into my mind, but I've shoved so far down behind walls and barriers of self-defence. She was the second one he ever took, and after the first girl, I knew what her ending would be and didn't want that for her. I tried to help but only made it worse.

I was forced to watch it all while being tied to a chair. A fucking horror movie brought to life. A documentary about a psychopathic serial killer acted out in front of me. It was my punishment for doing what I did.

For that reason, I don't open my mouth now.

For that reason, I've stopped trying to save them. Remaining silent *is* to save them. It's why I warned Natalie away from him. At least with her, I had a better shot.

"This is your fault. You made me so angry, Willow had to pay the price."

I wish I could feel something other than numbness, but it's all his words elicit. Again, he's blaming me by justifying his actions.

"She's beautiful, lying there, broken and bloody, because of *you*." His hands skim my hips, trailing his blood-soaked grip up my side until finding my neck. His fingers dance along the base in a way that could elicit tingles if he were someone else. "I told her that over and over too. That everything I was doing was not because of something she did." His hand clamps down on my neck, his long fingers wrapping the column but still remaining light.

I stop moving, completely still, hoping he releases my neck and takes me away from this place and the guilt he's trying to make me feel. I can't be guilty because this is *his* doing.

His other hand goes to my thigh and spreads my legs, his fingers stroking back and forth over my clit. The urge to fight him and push his hand away is strong, but I clamp down on the compulsion.

"You're supposed to be wet, Teagan. The sight of her has me craving you, and you're not ready." His hips jerk, the hardness of his cock straining behind his pants.

Fuck.

I won't get wet. Not from him, and certainly not from the image in front of me. When he takes me—because no doubt he's about to —it will hurt again. It'll burn when he shoves his way into my body, but there's nothing I can even think of that'll make me wet. Alex was the first and only man to ever enter my body, and I know nothing of what it's like to be with someone else. All I know is the pain Alex forces into me each time.

His hand slaps my clit once, and he grunts, "Well, so be it then." His zipper descending rips through the silence; it's loud over the increased beating of my heart.

He thrusts his cock into me, driving it through the barrier of dryness. As he moves inside me, like a knife stabbing my insides over and over, my eyes clamp shut and my mind readies for its journey back to the first time again.

But before my mind goes to its semi-blissful escape from reality, he speaks, keeping me in the present. "You won't tell me who your visitor is, but perhaps you can think of him. I'll allow your mind to have him, to wet your fucking cunt, so it'll be *me* who takes your body."

Brent. He wants me to think of Brent.

Brent, who was my high school best friend.

Brent, who's filled into his body, replacing fat with muscle, giving his wonderful soul a beautiful outside to match his inside. In the silence of my mind, I appreciate how striking Brent has become.

How, despite the hate filling Brent's expressions and his plea for information, I'd be happy to have him hold me again, like he's done so many times in the past. To have him love me like I know he used to and for his hands to stroke away every ounce of pain Alex has ever wrought from my veins.

Suddenly, Alex's cock glides smoother inside me and hate joins the lust my body apparently feels. Hate, because Alex got what he was aiming for—confirmation my visitor is more than simply a stranger.

"That's it," he murmurs, increasing his pace. "If thinking about him is what gets your pussy wet, I understand, Teagan. Sometimes, I seek excitement elsewhere too."

My gaze falls on his "elsewhere" still lying unmoving inside the glass cage.

Then his grip on my neck grows tight, reminding me he's there. I gasp, his hand stealing away my breath. "But make no mistake," he growls in my ear, "that's the *only* place you will ever see this fucker again. Mason will be blocking him from the club, and you will not *think* about betraying me or it'll be you inside this cage instead of Willow. Understand?"

Despite my weak nod, his grip tightens, and I stop breathing. As much as I hope this is the end for me, I know it's not. He'll release me, exactly as he's done so many times before, keeping me barely alive and dangling on the tempting edge of death. Now, it's a matter of when he'll let me go.

"Good." With his simple word, his hand against my throat goes heavier and his pace increases.

It hurts still. Emotionally and mentally especially. A bit physically too, since he's rougher than what I want, but for the first time ever, it's bearable because I'm wet. I allow my mind to imagine Brent behind me, taking Alex's place. His languid strokes would drive me to the edge of pleasure rather than pain. His touch on my neck wouldn't be choking and possessive, but rather gentle and caring as tingles coursed down my spine. If it was Brent, my mind would be on him instead of elsewhere. And when I came, it'd be with the knowledge he genuinely cared for me.

That's when I realize my pussy grows wetter and clamps down around Alex's cock. And despite the breath he's taking from me, I still manage to find some to sigh through my orgasm.

The first I've had in years. Alex got me off a few times in high school when we fooled around before having sex. After our first time together—the first time he raped me—I've never orgasmed since. No matter how many times I've tried to pretend Alex was gentle on my insides.

Alex hisses in my ear. "You have no idea how fucking jealous I am that it's thoughts of another guy having you orgasm. I'm feeling very murderous right now. But," he pauses, his hand loosening around my throat, and I suck in gulps of air before he undoubtedly takes more from me, "it's still *my* cock you're coming on. Not his. Never his."

He pulls from my body, leaving his own sticky mess behind. Beneath his final words is the clearly implied threat and I'd be stupid to act on it. Like he said, Brent will remain my mind's secret, nothing more.

Only when I hear the zip from his pants do I lower my hands from the wall, eyes falling on our unknowing audience. Shame is heavy on my shoulders. Shame for everything.

For being at fault for harming this girl. For orgasming just now. For speaking with Alex that day in school.

Just before I turn away to follow Alex out of the room, the

woman moves a fraction. Enough her blonde hair falls away from her face, revealing the most gorgeous pale green eyes I've ever seen. She meets my gaze, understanding passing between us as she blinks once in recognition of what she witnessed.

Beneath the understanding though, there's something else. I wish it was determination, life, or even misery—some emotion to indicate she's still mentally stable. But it's none of those.

It's emptiness.

Blank and lifeless, as though she's barely holding on.

Ten

BRENT

"I'M SORRY, but you have been banned from the premises." The bouncer crosses his large arms, giving me a once-over. Impressive considering the kid's, like, eighteen and barely out of high school.

"Why?" I straighten, giving him my own look of intimidation, aiming to become larger and fill out more of the immediate space.

I'm not sure it works though because his brow only lifts in mild amusement. "Sorry, boss's orders. Can't let you in."

"Just me?"

"Yep."

Without saying goodbye or anything, I spin on my heel and stalk away back to Hawke's car, where he waits. I climb inside, throwing myself onto the leather seat and growl.

"I'm banned from the club. Ten bucks say this is Miller's doing."

Hawke slowly nods and takes his bottom lip into his mouth, nibbling on his lip ring. "Want me to try and see if I have any luck?"

"No." If it's not me, it'll be none of them. Only I will be able to get through to her. I saw it the other day. The mere mention of our past sparked something in her gaze and now I simply need to continue the path I've began paving.

"It's weird," he comments after a long second. "He must be watching her if knows to ban you specifically. You think he knows who you are?"

I shrug. "I kept my face tilted away from the camera once she pointed it out, and it's not like the club has my ID."

"I've pulled the club's paperwork. Place is owned by a Mason Ford. He's legit. Keeps the place up to standards and passes all his checks each month. I've uncovered no hidden paperwork or mention of a partner; everything about this guy's business is open. Alex has no affiliation to him."

"No, but rich guys don't need to own the place to control it." I throw my back into the leather seat, frustration picking at my nerves.

"What now?"

"Now we go back to your place and get the others. I'm pulling a Tristan and waiting her out. I'll get her to talk to me, even if it's through a bit of force and fear."

Hawke whistles and starts the car before pulling away from the club. "And they say I'm the fucked-up one."

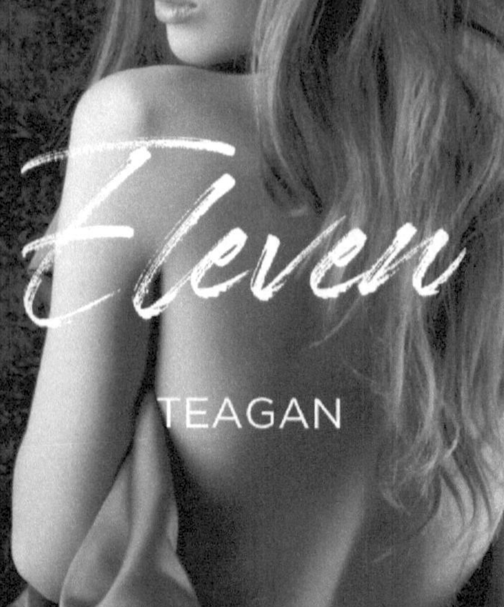

Eleven

TEAGAN

ALEX DOESN'T GRANT me a shower before sending me on my way with Billy, back to my "normal" life and away from his house of horrors and Willow. He said he's not through with her, but how much longer does she have left on this planet?

Even though his driver takes me farther away from Alex's mansion, we never quite reach safety. I've learned no matter how far he drives, it's never enough.

I've tried once.

Right before graduation, Alex was put into the hospital, so I took off, leaving behind a family that didn't care about me, and not even mentioning my plan to Elena or Brent, two people who did care for me. Brent was the hardest to leave, but I had to choose *me*—for my own well-being. I ran and ran, hitchhiked when I could, and made it to the other side of the country with the firm belief I was finally safe from Alex's tight clutches. I hoped by the time he was healed and released from the hospital, graduation would have passed, and real life would kick in and he wouldn't care about whatever fucked-up relationship we had. He could go on destroying the lives of others.

But his daddy's money reaches far, and he found me, dragging me home kicking and screaming the entire way.

That was when I truly learned what a psychopath he is.

Everything he's ever done to any of his secretaries, he first practiced on me. Over and over. To the point of death, but he always pulled back at the last second. I'm not entirely sure why he wants me alive so badly. At first I was grateful, but now I wish he'd kill me and end this nightmare.

After a few months, Alex grew bored, but rather than releasing me, he lured his secretary into his home to continue more of the same with her. She was his first kill. I'm unsure if it was an accident he went that far or if he did it on purpose, but whatever the case, something awoke in him that day.

That's when he made me a deal. Well, it's what he refers to it as, but really, it was an order. Alex is smart; he's aware a man in his position is very publicized and requires a woman on his arm. He can't risk dragging his captives out of his basement, but he also won't chance letting the truth of his treachery slip out. Because, no doubt, if he got a different girlfriend, his darkness would seep from the edges at some point and any unknown factor is a gamble.

I was the ideal solution. All I had to do was be his fake girlfriend for any function, dinner, or meeting he deemed required my presence, and my life would be paid for. I soon learned, though, there was more to it and in no way was I free. If anything, he shifted me from one cage to another. My new one required a certain diet, a job he forced me into, and any other way he found to control me.

I always hoped, eventually, I would feel safer this way, but it's not the case. If anything, our situation puts me more on edge because the rapes may have lessened, but they never stopped. If I step out of line, I'm beaten and tortured and then forced to watch as he continues extracting vengeance from an innocent's flesh.

Alex claims he granted me freedom, but all he's done is give me a larger cage to run around in.

"We're here," Billy announces, as the car stops in front of my townhouse. A moment later, he's opening my door for me—an act I've never determined why. It's odd how Alex hasn't forbidden him from being kind to me. "Boss already called the club. You're off tonight."

Wow. Kindness. Why? Because he's aware my insides are still screaming? It's unlike Alex though, since the last time he raped me before work, he sent me there with a chuckle that I'd soon be grinding on a stranger while my pussy was full of his cum.

Breathing a relieved sigh, I emerge into the cool night air and finally turn on my phone for the first time in hours. Disappointment curdles my stomach when only the time lights up my screen and not a dozen text messages. I wish I knew why that feeling assaulted me at that fact.

I quickly skitter away from Billy, pleased at the sight of the plain white door signalling some semblance of safety. When I make it past my entranceway, the weight of the entire evening drops onto my body, making it heavy and fatigued. The only thing I want is a shower to scrub away the two rounds of his cum dried to my legs, and then a hot bath where I can drown myself into oblivion with a glass of wine, before passing out and pushing this day into the millions of nightmares constantly plaguing my mind.

My hand hooks on the door and I toss it shut behind me, uncaring to turn around and close it softly, simply waiting for the sound to reassure me I'm safe enough for the remainder of the night.

Instead, there's a scuffle and I look up, eyes searching through the dim lighting a lamp left on from down the hallway provides. There's only a blur and my front meets the door, a set of hands pushing on my back to hold me there—one at the base of my neck and the other on the middle of my back.

Alex? Has tonight not been enough for him, he needs to further harm me?

Somehow, the hands on my body don't leave, but suddenly, my own arms are yanked behind me. Rough rope—a feeling I'm unfortunately too familiar with—wraps around my wrists, pushing them together tightly, the bones crying out in agony.

There's more than one person here.

I wish some sort of instinct allowed me to fight this. To drop to the floor and kick out, to at least try to get free, but years by Alex's side has my muscles going slack. If this is something Alex concocted, it'll only worsen when I harm his men. He's rewired my instincts.

But then the hands on my back dig in deeper as a body pushes forward, a back pressing into mine, and a familiar voice becomes warm velvet in my ear. "You brought this on yourself, Cherry-Girl," Brent whispers. "We had to, for the sake of everyone else, and you know it."

"You fucker," I hiss, jerking my shoulders to free myself. I suppose, there is some instinct in my body now that I'm aware this is not Alex's doing. "What the hell is wrong with—"

My speech is cut off as a cloth is shoved in my mouth, pushing my tongue down, flat and useless.

Seriously? He's kidnapping me.

"She's good," another voice speaks low. My mind scrolls through its memory bank of who it can be—who Brent would be working with or for—but I come up blank. "Let's go."

Go? Go where?

Brent keeps me facing forward as a hand darts in my vision and opens it, but whoever is attached to the arm remains out of my view.

A black car, engine idling, is parked by the sidewalk, right where Billy was last. There's a person in the driver's seat, but from the distance, there's nothing identifiable about them.

You're an asshole, I wish I could tell him, while hoping Brent has become a mind reader over the years and he can hear me regardless. The vehicle's door is opened, and Brent shoves me forward.

With my arms tied behind my back, I have no control and end up partially on my side, grunting and huffing as I fight to fix my position. By the time I'm upright, Brent slides in beside me, grinning, despite the death look I shoot his way.

I quickly glance away, focusing on the front seat and the figure in the driver's seat. He's twisted around to face the back seat, his grin wide and familiar from beneath dark hair. I should be surprised to see him, but it's obvious that Brent has retained his high school friends.

Tristan Pence.

"Teagan Faber. Never thought I'd see you again."

I could say the same about you, buddy. Instead, my grunt is muffled, restrained by the cloth, and I tell him everything with my glare.

The passenger door opens, and this time, I'm not surprised at who gets in. If anything, it makes sense.

Ryker Ames.

He's filled out since high school—since he sent Alex to the hospital. Ryker is both my hero and villain. The injuries he gave to Alex was the last time I truly smiled, aware the dick got everything he deserved. It gave me the chance to run away and pretend I could be free from him, even for a short while. At the same time, if Ryker never hurt Alex, I would never have had the opportunity to try, and Alex wouldn't have hurt me as badly as he did upon finding me.

Wait—he should be in jail.

Oh. My. God. I'm sitting with a bunch of convicts.

He grins as if he knows what I'm thinking, in time for Tristan to start the car and pull away. But instead of looking at them, I twist my body the best I can, to keep Brent in sight. As much as I appreciate the way his form is relaxed against the cloth seat, his arm balanced on the window's edge, legs spread and obviously relaxed, I hate him. My gaze narrows on the smirk playing on the edge of his lips, hoping he can hear everything I'm silently shouting at him.

What the fuck is happening?

What is wrong with you?

Alex will learn I'm gone.

Why are you doing this?

Who have you become?

"Remember, you brought this on yourself," is the final thing he says before directing his attention out the window and on the passing city lights.

When the city lights fade into trees, I examine the passing highway. The highway? They're taking me away from Cortville? My disgruntled sound drags Brent's attention back to me, but he merely shrugs before looking out the window once more.

With nothing left to do, I remain still and wait until our destination approaches. When it does, nearly an hour later, we pull up to a residential street and a pretty house. A fucking house in suburbia is where they're taking me?

The doors unlock and Brent immediately clamps down on my upper arm. With his free hand, he flicks the door open and steps out, dragging me across the car's bench seat with him. The other two follow behind, and the car beeps when it's locked.

As Brent nudges me forward, my eyes skirt the neighbourhood, searching for any curious faces that may be choosing now to glance out their windows. Unfortunately, as it's nearing eleven at night, everyone is tucked away in their wonderful lives involving normal jobs and children. No house is lit up; everyone blissfully unaware of the kidnapping occurring right outside.

Brent walks me to the front door, where Tristan opens it and Ryker takes up the space behind us. In high school, his attention was all on Elena, but even then, he was a scary motherfucker. Now, he's downright horrifying and could, no doubt, cause a lot of damage.

The house opens into a foyer, a living room to my right and a staircase to the upstairs on my left. Past Tristan's shoulder, down the hallway, I spot a kitchen. The house—whoever's it is—appears to be a standard one. Nothing malicious that I notice.

"Girls are gone," Tristan comments.

"Good," Ryker rumbles from my back.

Girls? There are more people involved in Brent's chaos? The only girl Ryker would ever want still in his life is—

I twist around, putting Ryker in my sight, and his grin tells me exactly what I guessed.

Elena is involved.

The mere thought has my stomach flipping. Alex deactivated my old cell phone, but I committed her final text message to memory.

ELENA

> I know you won't respond to this since you haven't with all the other ones. You clearly want to be alone but know how much I love you. You've been an amazing friend and I always dreamed of walking across that stage with you and celebrating afterward. It'll be the one party I'm willing to go to but only if you're with me. I can't lose you… not after I'm losing Ryker. I'm sorry if you've been going through things and I haven't been the greatest friend. I'm here now and begging you to let me know you're okay, wherever you are. I love you.

Times change people though. I'm evidence of that, and I suppose Elena is too, if she's involved in this. Whatever *this* is.

Brent shoves me forward while Tristan swings open a door beneath the staircase. After a quick, wicked grin toward me, he disappears inside it. Long-crushed down instincts arise in time for my heels to dig into the hardwood flooring beneath my feet.

"Nnn!"

"Keep walking." Brent pushes me through the doorway and toward the dozen wooden steps leading downstairs. Shy of being pushed down them, he'll make me descend either way, so it's what I do, keeping my eyes pinned on that opening down below.

If I see a fucking glass cage…

Instead, what I do see has me freezing in place, but of course, Brent is right there, his hand immediately clasping my arm and leading me to the single chair in the centre of the basement.

Seriously?

But it's not the chair I'm focused on. It's the room. A table is pushed to the far corner, out of the way. Corkboards and whiteboards are hung on each of the walls, notes and images pinned to them, but with how Brent's moving me, my eyes can't focus on any one thing.

Beside the chair, Tristan stands, his arms crossed over his chest. He looks pleased, like this is amusing to him.

Behind him is someone else, and certainly someone I'd remember from school. His arms are also crossed over his chest, but he appears bored rather than amused. Black inky hair hangs over his bright blue eyes. He's beautiful, reminding me of the goths I used to see around school. But more noticeable than that are the tattoos lining his arms, disappearing beneath his shirt, and the various piercings all over his face. His nose, his lip, and his brow.

Brent pushes me in the direction of the chair. His hands go to my shoulders, and he drops pure muscle onto the bone, buckling my legs until my ass touches the seat. The rope loosens for the briefest second, but I don't bother attempting to escape. With Tristan and the goth staring at me, and Ryker likely guarding the stairs, I wouldn't make it an inch before they stopped me. The rope is quickly retied, this time looped around the chair. I jerk my arms, but they don't budge.

"Want us to stay?" Tristan focuses his attention on Brent, still behind the chair. His intimidating stance becomes a shadow over me.

"No. Teagan and I have some history to catch up on," Brent says. His feet take him to my side, back into my sight, but it's no longer Brent Thorne staring at me. The guy pinning me with his eyes, causing my back to hunch and a tinge of sadness to mask my anger, is a stranger, and that's when I realize how fucked I truly am.

Even the guy who was always my hero is now my villain.

"We're taking a trip down memory lane," he finishes, a promise heavy in his tone.

Twelve

BRENT

FIVE YEARS AGO

TODAY IS THE DAY.

I've done my waiting, I think.

I've been the friend Teagan's needed. The shoulder to cry on when she was sad. Her meal card when her shit family forgot to send her to school with food. Her protector when other guys made her their bully victim—not that she ever needed a protector. She proved that the very moment we met, saving me from a parallel fate.

Similarly, Teagan's been there for me in ways she doesn't realize. She's made me feel better. Unlike so many others, she's looked past my exterior to get to the person inside, and she cares about me. She's the one to make me laugh when I need it. The first one to shoot back at someone's negative comments. Some days, I swear her heart could explode with how much goodness she keeps in there.

I'm sure I've loved her since the moment we met but buried the emotion beneath friendship. It's been reined in, but now, I need to shout it from the rooftops. I'll ask her out and she'll say yes and then we'll be together.

Tristan and Ryker convinced me to try. They don't know we're friends, simply because it was Teagan's idea to keep our relationship quiet. "We have each other, but we should try to also have outside friendships too. We need to vow to try, without the influence of one another," is how she worded it.

Ryker continues to bitch about how I have a girl on the side I won't tell them about, and finally, Tristan exploded earlier with, "She'll always say no if you never try."

I sidle up to her in our shared gym class. She's panting from the latest round of running, her chest heaving beneath the shapeless gym shirt.

"Hey, I have something I wanna talk to you about during our walk home."

Most girls would be curious, but Teagan only smiles. "Sure." When the teacher blows his whistle, we begin running again, and Teagan takes off. She's quick. I've tried to convince her to go out for track, but she hates the concept of running for sport.

As I take a turn around the gym, my eyes settle on the clock on the wall. Thirty more minutes and the final bell will release us from this day.

MY NERVES ARE BOUNCING beneath my skin as I wait by our lockers for her. She never takes long to get cleaned up from gym, but today, it seems like forever. I study each person passing by me, wondering if my nerves are obvious.

Lost in my head, I miss Ryker and Tristan coming to a stop beside me. Tristan leans on Teagan's locker while Ryker remains in the middle of the hallway, uncaring that he's in others' way.

"So," Tristan begins, "what'd she say?"

"Haven't asked yet. Didn't want to do it in class."

"Pussy." But he's grinning. "Good luck."

"You won't need luck," Ryker comments. "You'll..." He trails off, his attention diverting down the hallway. I follow his sight, spotting Elena Sparks chatting with another guy. "Excuse me."

By the time I blink, he's already gone, pushing through the crowds of over-eager students, readying to leave for the day.

Tristan smirks and lifts himself off the locker. "I better follow and make sure he doesn't kill the guy for daring to look at Elena. Excuse me."

He leaves too, just in time for Teagan to break through the crowd, a relieved look on her face. Relieved, because she despises crowds so finally getting through them is pleasing for her.

"Hey," she says a bit breathy as she unlocks her locker. "Damn, end of days suck."

To someone who barely knows her, they'd think her thoughts are due to the crowds that loiter in the hallways. Only I know it's because the end of school means she needs to go home to a family that doesn't care for her.

"What did you want to talk to me about?" she asks, pulling her bag from inside the locker.

At the same time, a screech comes down from the hallway, pulling everyone's attention down there. I spot Elena with her hand on her hips as she screams at Ryker.

I shake my head at their weird-ass interactions. I'll never understand Ryker.

"Outside," I say. "Where it's quiet."

Teagan nods and gets to finishing filling her bag with whatever school work she requires for tonight. On top of everything, she's a damned good student. Always almost topping the class. She's determined to get a scholarship for university, that way she can afford to go.

She finishes her task, and we head toward the front door and get outside, setting our pace in the direction of her house. I walk her home every day before turning in the opposite direction and going to mine. Mom says it's adorable. I see it as simply being kind.

My hands curl and flatten three times, creating more moisture to accompany what's already there. Suddenly, everything is real. This is it and before I pussy out, as Tristan would refer to it as, I spit it out in a jumble of words I can only hope she understands.

"Teagan, I... I—Um." I swallow through the lump and retry, "Teagan, I know we're only friends, but would you consider going out with me? Like, on a date? Like, romantically?"

Have you ever heard of loud silence? I haven't until right this second, but her lack of speech, breathing, or anything identifiable indicating she's heard me is so fucking loud, I'm sure people down the road could hear her shock.

I shouldn't have done this.

Everything inside me cries to curl up and die. I'm an idiot for coveting this. Once a friend, always a friend. No doubt she has someone better in mind. Someone who doesn't look like me.

After a few agonizingly long moments of silence, my eyes cut toward her, spotting a tear falling from her eye and creating a slim, wet line down her cheek.

Fuck, I've made her cry, and we're stuck with it out in the open now, unable to be taken back.

After another long minute of her not speaking, I mutter, "Sorry. I shouldn't have asked."

For a brief second, I debate turning around and going home. The only thing worst than being friend-zoned is continuing to do all the same friend-like things while fighting not to show how her rejection affects me.

"No," she finally whispers. "It's fine you did, but I can't."

Can't. Because she can't be seen with me romantically when there's better options out there for her.

"Okay." What else can I say that won't end up with me tearing out my heart to lay it at her feet?

When we arrive at her house, I nod once before turning and striding away. Only when my back is turned do I allow myself to cry those tears my body has been craving to since the moment she rejected me.

THE NEXT DAY, the one after that, and the one after that... all the ones after it, we never speak of that moment. Not even as she begins to change but won't tell me why. When she grows distant and sad, but never wants to speak about what's making her feel that way.

For the rest of high school, I believe my question broke something between us. Whatever she's experiencing, she doesn't confess, but I suspect it's something she would have once. Clearly, she's no longer comfortable.

One day, she disappears without a word. Her family, Elena... no one knows where she's gone. Not even me. It's then I realize, I was never for her what she is to me, and it's a hard truth I need to accept.

Thirteen

TEAGAN

LONG AFTER THE others clear out of the room, Brent remains unmoving. His jaw is locked, his frosty gaze narrowed down on me, unblinking as he studies me. His back is rigid, spine straightened while he prepares himself for his next step.

I return the look, biting down on the cloth I'm praying he'll remove from my mouth soon. If only so I can tell him what an idiot he is being. How, if Alex learns I'm gone *and* finds me here, he'll be dead. Him, Tristan, Ryker, and their new goth friend won't make it out alive.

"Fucking shame," he finally murmurs, stepping closer. His hands work at the back of my head and the cloth falls away, landing on my lap.

My mouth flexes, opening and closing a few times to work sensation back into my cheeks.

"What is?"

"You."

Whatever that means. "What is *wrong* with you, Brent? This is taking things a bit far, don't you think?"

He shrugs lazily, lifting and dropping one shoulder as he comes back to face me. "You wouldn't talk to me, and I need information you have."

"I still won't talk. You're a moron if you believe kidnapping me will change my answers."

"We'll see," he says darkly, crossing his arms.

He thinks he's showing me darkness. Cute. Being macho and alpha and all that shit. He has no idea how far away from the real thing he is.

"Nothing else to say?" His brows lift with his question. "You've changed, Teagan. Once, it was impossible to shut you up."

When you talk, people find reasons to hurt you. But instead of telling him any of the truth, I school my features, even rolling my eyes to further indicate his idiocy. *Anything* to get him to drop the charade and release me.

"You haven't. Still panting after Ryker Ames and Tristan Pence, I see." I know I'm hitting below the belt with that one. He was terrified of them at the start of high school, and I was the one to encourage him to speak to them. They became real friends to him and then he never spoke a bad word against them.

"We have a common goal."

"Involving Alex."

"And you. Apparently."

Not me. I'm not involved in Alex's treachery.

Brent's providing me an opportunity, I realize. I speak, and they can get me out of there. I can be free.

And then I chuckle to myself, out loud and uncaring if he's witnessing my breakdown. It's laughable to know, for the briefest second, I considered giving him what he wants, letting him save me in the ways he believes he can. No one can though. He won't win against Alex. Alex's hold on me is too strong, too tight, and only he'll be the one to untie the chains and release me when he's finally finished.

"How did you find me?" I ask.

"That's not your concern."

I huff, shaking my head lightly. "You want me to admit all my secrets, but you won't tell me anything. Fair's fair, don't you think?"

"Difference is you're the one tied up and I'm not, so if there's anyone making demands, it'll be me." As if reinforcing his freedom, he drags over another chair from the corner, the metal legs scraping roughly against the cement floor. "And I have an endless amount of time to wait you out." He drops down in the chair, hoisting one leg over his other, balancing his ankle on his opposite knee.

He doesn't, because at some point, Alex will realize I'm not at home when I don't respond to his text messages, and he'll search for me. He has all local police departments under his thumb, including Bridgetown's force, along with his own staff, so eventually, someone will find me here.

After a long moment of stuffy silence, Brent speaks, "Why did you run away at the end of school?"

"I needed out," I say truthfully.

"Out from what? What were you running from? Alex?"

I look away, focusing my attention on his shoes instead.

"Fuck, Cherry-Girl. I'm trying to help you." His words are more of a frustrated growl, and I bite down on my tongue to prevent from smiling. Even though four years have passed, he's as easy to get to now as he was then.

For someone who claims to be the one to break me, he's certainly not doing a good job.

"Why are you working with him?"

I shift, clenching my thighs together. I wonder what he'd think, knowing I'm sitting here with Alex's cum drying inside me. Would he look at me with stronger hatred or simply disgust?

"Give me one truth," he demands. "Are you working with him? Unwillingly, perhaps?"

It's one simple truth, and nothing that'll give away the rest. The desolation in his gaze does something to me. Makes me *want* to tell him at least this... So, I do.

"No."

Surprise flickers in his eyes because he obviously didn't expect me to respond. His leg falls to the floor along with his sigh, and he leans forward, positioning his elbows on his knees. "Then you're working *for* him?"

I snort, countering with, "That's not one truth."

"Teagan, we need to know where he's keeping the girls. I'm simply trying to get to the bottom of it." He stands, pushing off the small chair as he heads toward the other side of the room and stops by the table. From it, he gathers a file folder and returns.

He opens it and lays out the entire truth.

Images of every secretary Alex ever had trapped in his basement.

Torn, mangled, and bloody. But I know what got them there. How the rapes made them beg for death, how the knives carved up their skin, how the ropes burned into their throat, causing breathing to be impossible, right down to the last second as he fucked them into death.

Carmen. Mia. Anne. Gemma. Zoey. Rachel. Charlotte. Scarlett.

They're all there. Every single one of them.

And soon, Willow will be joining the lineup.

"Hmm," he hums before shutting the file and dropping it to the floor at our feet. "Teagan, why the fuck do you not look surprised by these images?"

I stare at the folder on the ground. How they got those images, I'm not sure. Alex doesn't discuss how he disposes of the bodies, but clearly, they're being found and not linked to him.

"Because I'm not," I whisper, throat thickening, eyes locked on the tan folder. "You said so yourself, I already knew about the women." He implied it at his last visit to the club.

"You certainly never indicated you knew every little gritty detail of what happened to them."

I more than know. I've seen it.

"And you're okay with this? Okay with these girls losing their lives to a psychopath?"

I don't move my eyes away, not as he throws question after question at me. They slash at my insides and my hands fist behind my back. My eyes fight to remain open, but I won't show him how his words affect me. How they make me want to cry because I *hate* Alex for what he's done to these innocent women.

"You claimed you're not helping him, but is that a lie? Are you luring the girls to his house? Is this your own willingness or has he created some little fucked-up cult you've become a part of?"

"Why do you think so little of me?" I ask, my tight throat not loosening at all. The words hurt to speak, but I add, "You actually believe I have a hand in this."

I've only ever seen Brent angry once, but never like this. Not in the way he explodes, his face growing red, his body extending beyond my form, the chair getting thrown out of the way.

"Because I don't know what else to think!" he roars. "Because you won't fucking *tell* me anything. You disappeared from my life four damn years ago and now you pop up, associated with Alex Miller of all people. Alex, who's leaving a trail of bodies in his wake. Alex, who's tried to harm his own fucking sister. Tell me, Teagan... Cherry-Girl," his voice softens, lowering to an almost-whisper, "how else does this look to you?"

I look away from his agonized eyes and his fists clenching his hair, instead focusing on my lap. My shoulders hunch in an attempt to curl into a ball. The last time someone was this angry at me, I didn't sit for three days, being bruised all over. The only thing I could do was lie in a hot bath.

His legs come into my peripheral vision briefly before he

crouches, his face replacing where his legs just were. Still, I don't look at him. Not as his hands land on my lap, covering my own.

His touch feels *good*. Warm. Like home.

Like someone who's wanted *me* for me. To protect and love me, yet I sent him away. The day he asked me out, I wanted to say yes. I craved it more than anything, but Alex already had me in his web, and I couldn't admit what Alex was doing to me and risk his family coming down on Brent's.

That's when I feel it. A lone tear escapes from my eye and slides down my cheek, leaving a streak in its place.

"I know." Because I do. If I was in his place, I would blame me too.

Hell—I'm in *my* place and I even blame me. Countless times I should have called it into some faraway police force, but I know all they'd do is contact local authorities. And who else could have told the truth but me? Alex keeps his staff in the dark; I'm the only one trapped in his secret.

Brent's hand moves more into my line of sight and before I realize what he's doing, his finger tilts my chin up, my eyes unwittingly going too, landing on his soft, round lips as they speak quiet, gentle words.

"You're crying, Teagan. We are only trying to help these girls. We'll help you too."

"We" being him and the guys? He thinks they can protect me from the devil? It's these beliefs that'll get them killed and exactly why I need to keep my mouth shut. They won't win. No one does.

"I thought when I found you, I'd be angry for the way you left without a word. You never responded to any message I sent you. You never returned." His eyes flicker, reflecting my own misery back at me.

"If not angry, how do you feel instead?" I find myself asking.

"Sad as fuck." His lips twitch into a small smirk. "I loved you. I realize we were never together romantically, but it doesn't stop the feelings I had for you. Now..." His head shakes once, desolate, with a lack of energy. "Now you're a stranger and it's destroying me inside."

I examine his face, searching for that anger I saw a few moments ago, but sure enough, there's only sadness.

"I'm sorry," I whisper. "It'd be safer for you to hate me."

"What does that mean?" Brent's brows scrunch, and my insides twist with his obvious care.

"It means you need to release me and let me go back to *him*."

Brent gets taller then and I realize his new position puts him a fraction closer to me. His face lines up, the dark specks of his eyes flicking in the dim basement light, growing brighter somehow. He's beautifully forbidden and I need him to return to being only a past memory before we both get into trouble.

"Never."

And then he does something I've only ever dreamed about.

He kisses me.

Fourteen

TEAGAN

HIS MOUTH CONSUMES me in ways I've only seen in movies. Like his whole body—his entire soul—is throwing himself into the kiss. His tongue dances along the seam of my lips while his hands find my jaw, and he tilts my head, positioning in an angle he finds suitable. His hands lightly touch my neck, bruised from where Alex gripped me mere hours ago, but it's so gentle, I hardly even notice.

He swallows my shocked gasp as his tongue tangles with mine, taking the kiss to a deeper place. A place he's been wanting to go for a long time, and I've wanted to follow him to. My thighs clench, reminding me that only hours ago, imagining his touch had brought me to orgasm during a situation I shouldn't have enjoyed.

This is stupid and will likely get us both killed, but for this one moment in time, I allow it. He's kidnapped me and now I let him annihilate the rest of me. I return his kiss and push the rising darkness away, letting Brent's light momentarily cover it.

His hands go behind my back and I feel the rope loosening. *What. Is. Happening?* It falls away, and once my hands are free, I'm able to touch him, to hold his shoulders in a way I never thought I would.

A tidal wave of emotions threatens to wipe me away, but before it can, I cling tightly to him, unwilling to lose the connection. This is—It's a lot, but it's the kind of *a lot* I want. His lips move under mine, soft, yet demanding, but not rough. He's not here to hurt me.

Brent would never hurt me.

With me freed from the ropes, his hands come around my waist and he lifts me as though I weigh nothing, until I'm standing on my own feet. His hand, still on my neck, gets heavier as realization crashes around me.

I'm kissing Brent. I'm kissing someone who isn't Alex. And though Alex has left stains, it's easy to pretend they're not there and to simply *feel*.

I moan, a deep noise in the back of my throat.

"That's it," he murmurs. "You're so fucking beautiful, Cherry-Girl."

I *feel* beautiful because that's who Brent is. He makes a person feel better, even when they don't deserve it.

And I don't deserve this—this heaven he's granting me. For a moment, I forget about everything—why I'm here, how I've gotten here, and who my true captor is. For a second, before Alex rips me away, I can enjoy what I never will again.

Because after this passes—and it will pass—after reality sets in again and Brent realizes this beautiful kiss is too dangerous, we'll return to being enemies. I need him gone; far away from Alex before he gets hurt. If it takes a million stupid lies like the one I gave him regarding Natalie, so be it.

It doesn't stop me from tilting my head and deepening the kiss. His hand lifts from my jaw and rests lightly on my hip, testing the touch. His hand is lighter than anything Alex has ever done, so I don't move him away, and even step closer .

"Is this okay?"

"Yes," I whisper, giving him this much of the truth. *I've always dreamed of it.*

"So truthful now."

Because I have no reason to hide this from him. If he wants to risk his life, who am I to stop him?

"Tell me where he's keeping the girls," he murmurs, almost soundlessly against my lips, before capturing them again.

But his words are a bucket of water to the moment, and I jerk my arms, wrenching them from his grip, so I'm able to shove him away completely. Unlike Alex, he listens and pulls back.

I can't *believe* we did that, when it was all just a sick game to him. His treachery is no different than Alex.

"Fuck you and your emotional warfare," I hiss, backing away.

Brent's responding smile is malicious. "Maybe it wasn't a trick. Maybe I truly loved you and wanted that."

"I believe you," I tell him honestly. "*Loved* being the key word. Past tense. But no more, right?"

"I don't love murderers."

My nose lifts, and my lips form a sneer. "Is anything you just said to me true?"

"Every word. I loved you. Anger is too tame of a word for what I feel toward you right now. Hate is more like it. I *hate* who you've become, hate you're not helping us, and I hate you're hiding the truth from me, but it also makes me sad."

"Fuck you," I curse again. "Fuck you because you'll continue to be sad. I'm not giving away the truth, and no, you're right, I'm not helping." Accepting I'm being dramatic, I fall into the metal chair I was previously tied to. My arms spread wide and my own sly grin stretches my lips. "So, what now, Brent? What do you plan on doing with me?"

He doesn't miss a beat, crossing his arms and leaning against the cement wall. It's obvious nothing we did had any lasting effect on him. "Now, you'll remain here until you find it suitable to give us what we need." He shrugs lazily and heads for the staircase, plopping down on the third step and guarding the only way out of here.

"And if I never?"

He shrugs again, an action seemingly becoming his favourite. "Then I suppose we die down here."

I ONCE SAID time passes differently when you're trapped, and for the second time today, that seems to be the truth. Although, I suppose it's the next day by now. Curled up on the chilly, cement ground in the farthest corner away from Brent and his emotional games, my ass is going numb. After about an hour in the chair, it became too uncomfortable, so I moved, but my new bed isn't much better. To top it all off, my bladder has been burning for at least an hour. The wall behind me is no pillow, but it's serving as an effective place to rest my head at least.

"You could at least get me a blanket."

"Murderers don't get blankets."

I huff, rolling my neck until he's in sight. "I'm not a murderer."

"You're certainly an accessory to one. Prove me wrong." His brow lifts, attitude reaching me even from across the room.

He's not wrong. I'm sure it's exactly what a judge would find me. I left Alex's mansion regularly; I wasn't trapped there. Went to work and spoke with other people—people I could have had contact the police in my stead, if I wanted, but I never did. A jury would convict me right alongside him.

I'm already living an imprisoned life, so if I have to be locked up in federal prison just so he can too, so be it.

"I beg you to prove me wrong, Teagan. Natalie believes you're in trouble, but you're claiming to be perfectly fine. Until you tell me you're on the right side, you're a murderer as he is."

His vicious hate zings in my stomach and head and though I want to react to them, I push the feeling aside to state, "I have to pee."

"I'll get you a bucket," he shoots right back.

I narrow my eyes, searching his form for signs it was a joke. "Seriously?"

His own eyes crinkle and he stands, brushing his hands along his shirt. "No, come on."

Freedom! No doubt it'll be short-lived, but if we're going upstairs, it means I'll also feel the warmth of a home rather than the harsh chill of a basement. With more energy than ever, I follow him up the wooden steps and into a darkened house. Warmth is an instant blanket and I shiver from the differences my body gladly accepts.

"Is this your house?"

"No," is all he supplies as he leads me down the hall and toward the kitchen. A quick right turn before the kitchen entrance reveals a small bathroom. "Here."

"Thanks." I slip past him, eager for the relief a toilet is about to bring me, uncaring he remains right outside, listening.

When washing my hands, I manage to utilize the water and wipe some of Alex's cum still staining my legs. That alone makes this bath-room visit worth it.

When I exit, Brent's leaning against the wall outside the room. His eyes find me instantly, but the emotions in them are unidentifi-able. "Better?"

"Yep. Thanks."

He starts down the hallway, stopping in front of the basement door again, but I glance behind, at the living room with the warm, comfortable couches.

"Keep walking," he growls, pointing to the cold downstairs.

"Dick," I say haughtily, ensuring I toss my hair over my shoulder as I pass him, whipping him in the face. It makes me feel a tad better.

"Yep."

Back down in the dreary, cold basement, I immediately go back to my corner, dropping back to the ground, scowling with the knowledge I'll need body heat to rewarm my spot. My legs fold, arms looping around them and tying them around my body.

I've experienced worse. This isn't *that* bad.

Brent adopts his position on the stairs again, this time with him leaning on the wooden post connecting the stairs to the house. Weariness deepens his expression but no doubt, he'll do anything to hide it from me. As if he hears my thoughts, his hands wipe at his face, and when they lower again, his apparent exhaustion is gone.

"I'm not telling you anything and I'm fucking exhausted. Could you turn off the light so I can at least have a nap? You have no idea the evening I had."

"I'm sure it was all sorts of evil." Despite his rude words, he flicks off the light, casting the entire basement into darkness. The barely-there moonlight shines through the single window, but it provides no light, only offering me something to stare at as I drift off.

Minutes pass of absolute silence and before my body does indeed nod off, something compels my next words.

"I'm sorry, Brent."

"For what exactly?"

"Everything." I sigh, tightening my arms around myself. Hidden in the darkness, it's easier to be truthful. "I didn't want to run away in high school, but I had no choice."

He stills—I hear it rather than see it. He's always been a part of me, so I know when his heart momentarily pauses beating as he listens to my words.

After a long second, he says, voice deep and gruff, "I don't know what that means."

"I know. You're not supposed to." I hesitate, rolling my next words around my mouth. "When I took off, I thought it was for the best. I didn't realize it'd only make things worse."

Brent's next low, pained, *"Teagan,"* nearly does me in, but instead, I bite down on the emotions he is working to elicit from me and shut my eyes, catching what sleep I can before morning comes.

WHEN I OPEN MY EYES, everything hurts. Most of the aches are normal—my thighs from Alex's treatment, my neck from where he gripped me. Some are new though, such as a cramped neck from where it's been bent in sleep and my numb, sore ass from sitting on the cement ground all night. In hindsight, I should have laid down and stretched out.

It's morning. Daylight streams through the window, lighting the basement and the sight of Brent sleeping, slumped against that same wooden post. Carefully positioning my feet on the floor and using the wall as a brace, I stand, vigilant not to make any noise. As a child, he was a deep sleeper. I can only hope that hasn't changed.

Keeping my steps light, I make it across the floor until I'm standing in front of him, studying the space beside his body. If I can stretch my leg past him and lift myself onto the stair beyond his shoulder, I have less chance of brushing him than if I used the step he's sitting on. It's not a lot of space, but in the end, he has nothing but a chair and a rope down here, so whatever way he chooses to punish me will only be a fraction of what Alex would do. Therefore, it's worth the risk.

I lift my leg but make it no farther than that as he moves, his arm striking my leg. His hand wraps around my calf and he lowers it, his brows going the opposite direction.

"Going somewhere?" he asks, voice lined thickly with sleep.

"Away from here."

He shakes his head and nudges me back, making room for himself to stand. "Cherry-Girl, you seem to be misunderstanding, you are n—" Whatever he's about to spout freezes on the tip of his tongue as his eyes study my neck, his mouth falling open with every passing heartbeat until his horror-filled eyes meet mine.

I swallow because I believe I know what he's found. The last time Alex strangled me as hard as he did last night, I awoke with purple bruising on my neck the morning after.

"Who the fuck hurt you?"

Fifteen

BRENT

DURING ONE OF my visitations to Ryker when he was in prison, I once asked what was in his head when he reacted to Alex's comments about Elena. He told me he saw literal red. *"Seeing red is more than an expression people say when they're angry. It's a feeling—an overwhelming sensation that consumes the mind, body, spirit, and most importantly, the senses, until there's nothing remaining but pure, blinding, red fury."*

I think I know what he felt like.

It's the exact thing coursing through my veins, masking over my vision, and consuming my soul. Hunger for blood—Alex's blood. To watch him pay for what he's done to Teagan. To be the one to extract vengeance from him one scream at a time.

Oh my God.

Everything—every damn realization hits me so strongly in that moment.

"I didn't want to run away in high school, but I had no choice."

"When I took off, I thought it was for the best. I didn't realize it'd only make things worse."

She ran from Alex. She's *been* running from Alex. She's been fucking *surviving*.

It all makes sense now.

Which means Natalie was right, and I'm a moron for not believing her.

My gaze goes past her, to the folder still lying on the floor between the two chairs we sat on yesterday. Whether she helped him lure those women or not, no longer matters because she's as much a victim as they are—were. How much longer until she was one?

"Oh, God."

How much longer until it was her body we identified, in which she was lying mangled and bloody and...

My attention falls to her thighs as fresh realizations form real horrors in my mind. "Oh, God."

Fuck.

Fuck.

Fuck, fuck, fuck.

I pace in a circle, fists clenched in my hair. My fucking Cherry-Girl has been *only* an hour's drive away, suffering while I've spent years despising her for leaving.

"You're not working *with* Alex." As she's admitted already. "Or *for* him. You've been his damn prisoner."

Her next word seals Miller's fate. He won't see the inside of a jail cell because his ass is going six feet down, where I can lock him inside Hell for the devil to swallow him whole.

"Yes."

Sixteen

TEAGAN

THINKING about admitting the truth to Brent and actually doing it are two entirely different things. When Brent's eyes narrow on the bruise on my neck, they darken with a ferocious viciousness I hadn't known him to be possible of.

This is death.

It's from an over-eager customer.

The lie flits through my mind and exits just as quickly. Instinct demands me to feed him another lie and get Brent off Alex's trail... but I blink. And the Brent sitting in front of me isn't this new version.

It's the one I loved. The one whose face falls, his expression becoming pure agony and genuine care. It's the very expression he'd give me when we were kids and he'd hug away my hurt and worries. It's one from my friend.

Maybe it's my stupidity. Maybe it's the hunger from my grumbling stomach, or the lack of energy from being locked in this basement, but I can't—*won't*—stop the word from dropping from my lips.

No doubt, I'll regret it soon. When Brent tries to react in whatever idiotic way he's planning and attacks Alex, I'll lose him all over. Sure, my admittance wrote his death sentence but...

For the moment, I let my nightmare pause. I'm no longer Teagan Faber, captive to Alex Miller, who's surviving within the lies I feed myself. I'm Teagan Faber, best friend to Brent Thorne, who wants this over with.

"Yes."

Yes to everything he's assumed so far. Yes to his deduction I'm not working for or with Alex. Yes to Alex's own grip that secured this admittance from me.

Brent's eyes harden, the blue reverting to a darker colour than I've ever seen on him and he comes closer, walking into me to the point I step away again. We continue this dance, as he stalks me in a circle, his manic eyes searching mine, fists clenching by his sides.

"Teagan, you *have* to tell me. You can't-you can't protect him any longer."

I'm not. I'm protecting me. I'll do so until he kills me. Alex will destroy me, and murder Willow, if has hasn't already. If it's not her, it'll be another. He'll take Brent away and force me to witness as he rips him apart too, as he's threatened when he captured me back when I ran away.

"Think of the girls," he whispers, his steps slowing, as though his energy is depleting.

It's all I've ever done.

"I *am*." My words slash in the cold air between us. "If it gets out I said anything against him, he'll double his efforts on them. When I piss him off, he takes it out on me *and* them, and I won't—I can't—I won't..."

My mini rant crushes my chest because I've already said too much. Brent doesn't get it. He hasn't *lived* it, so he'll never understand why he can't have the whole truth.

"Teagan." His arm stretches toward me, but he drops it at the last minute, indecision filling his expression. "We will protect you, I promise. He won't get near you. Help us."

His words jolt me. *"We?"*

Brent's eyes cast to the ceiling and back down. "Tell me everything you know, and I'll do the same."

For the first time in my life, I'm holding the reins and I'll continue to keep control while I can, so I shake my head. "No, you first. Then I'll talk." I pause, nibbling on my lip for a second before agreeing to the rest. "I'll tell you everything about the past and the present."

He sighs, his jaw jutting, but after a long second, he finally grunts, "Fine." He whips out his phone from his back pocket and types out a quick message. "They're all upstairs, waiting for news."

A moment later, a herd barrels down the stairs and soon, five people come to stop in front of me.

Ryker, Tristan, that goth guy, and—

"Elena," I breathe.

My skin itches, excitement making it jumpy as I am dying to react. It's been four long years without her and until this second, I hadn't realized how much I truly missed her. Tears stream down my face instantly, but my feet refuse to budge. It's way too surreal to move, and honestly, given the circumstance, I'm uncertain what to do even if I were to go to her.

She's clearly not a mind reader though because she flies at me, squealing, her arms wrapping around my body, squeezing me tightly. Blonde hair invades my senses and her grip on my body is familiar—and pleasant.

"Oh my God, girl, I still can't fucking believe it. You're here!" When she pulls back, her face is red and blotchy, the evidence of tears forming. "When Ryker told me you were involved, I couldn't believe it. And then to learn you're still *here*, in the area..." But then her attention falls past my shoulder, to the chairs and the rope on the floor, and she spins on her heel, finger pointed toward Ryker. "You dick, you said she wouldn't be hurt. You—"

"Dolly," he reaches and clasps her close to him, "shut it."

"But—"

He growls and, strangely, it feels right. Like Elena's entire past has come to a happy conclusion.

The figure beside Elena moves, coming into my line of sight and my heart stops. A name Brent has already mentioned knowing but seeing her *here* makes everything come to the forefront. Like, my worlds are colliding in the worst way possible, and I don't know what to think.

Natalie Miller, Alex's sister, steps forward, hand bracing toward me as if I'm a rabid animal.

"What the fuck is going on here?" I ask the group, but only address Natalie. Warning her becomes the stupidest thing I've ever done because I deduce, "You told them about me."

It all makes sense now. How Brent was able to find me. Why he knew about Alex.

"You're his *sister*."

Natalie looks away, staring at her feet, and when she faces me again, the hurt in her eyes is obvious. "I know," she whispers. "I wish I wasn't, but more than that, I wish he wasn't what he is. I wish this could be different."

"So you knew, when you were in his office?"

She nods. "Your behaviour confirmed it. And then when you tried to warn me away."

I look toward Brent again, whose brows lift in a knowing expression. Of course he was aware of my lie the entire time. Using money as the reason probably wasn't the most convincing, but it worked in the moment, or so I thought.

"This is so fucked-up."

Ryker pushes past Elena's grip on his shirt and shoulders Natalie out of the way to bear down on me. His size towers over me, but he stops short, growling, "And what Alex is doing isn't? The moment he muttered Elena's name that day at the party, he slipped up, giving us the biggest clue to his villainous acts."

"And?" I scan the group. And then I laugh, my hand clenching my tightened stomach muscles. It's unattractive, loud, and bellowing, but it gets my point across. "If you all think you'll be the ones to stop him, please tell me how you plan on doing that." My sarcastic disbelief is loud.

Brent steps forward to, cutting in from the side. "We won't until you tell us everything. Where is he keeping them? You know, obviously."

They're all morons. Even Elena, but as I look toward her, there's no animosity in her gaze. Only sadness. As though she's dismayed by this entire thing. She stares at me, silently begging me to respond. Then I glance at Brent, whose direct focus reminds me of our previous deal.

My hand flutters to my neck, stroking the bruising there. Alex will beat them. He always wins. My next words will sign my death warrant when Alex discovers what I've done.

But I open my mouth because perhaps—just *perhaps*—there's something to this entire thing they've planned.

"This is everything." My eyes briefly rest on Brent before moving to Elena—the two people most affected by my past. "From the very beginning." With a ramrod straight spine, I pull in air once more and begin weaving a tale that will make all their hairs stand on end. Because understanding true evil is more than acknowledging that your crush is a bully.

"It started the final year of high school. Alex asked me out one day, and I didn't say no because, well, why would I?" A noise escapes my nose—a sort of half-snort, half-huff. "He was hot, popular, and everything I assumed I wanted. Our relationship was on the down-low, which was fine." I shrug weakly, spine bending with the weight of old shames and missteps. "I mean, he was a *Miller* and I was a poor foster kid, stuck with a family who couldn't care less. I didn't blame him for not wanting a public relationship."

I look at Ryker. Rumours deemed him also from the foster system, but for different reasons than me. When I was three, I was abandoned and found by a neighbour who heard me crying. No one wanted me and I bounced from home to home while Ryker received a loving family. Understanding passes through his eyes though and I spot his hand linking in with Elena's. A small rumble of jealously settles in the base of my stomach and I glance away from their happiness.

"That went on for a while and we fucked around some, but I wasn't ready for sex yet. When I told him that—"

He raped me. This will be the first time I say the words out loud. I may relive that day each time Alex forces me, but I've never told anyone my shame—my horror. Never *said* the words beyond the safety of my mind.

"Teagan," Brent prompts, in a questioning tone.

"I told him I wasn't ready, and he got angry and left. But the next day, he came to my house, which is something he never did, and..." A lump forms in my throat and my hands instantly go damp. Years of secrets build underneath my skin, and I can't help it—can't stop them—*won't* stop the tears from falling.

What is happening to me? My eyes land on my palms, not wishing to witness anyone's pity. I don't know why I'm getting emotional over facts I've long accepted. What he did may have hurt then, but compared to how he works now, it was the closest thing to gentle I've ever experienced. I've pushed aside the feelings and the memories, opting to remain in the present because my past can't change.

So why am I crying? Why am I getting this emotional?

Someone may claim trauma, but I know for a fact that's not it. I've managed the past: folded it up and shoved it in a box so it's not an issue.

"Teagan," Brent repeats, this time softer. He steps toward me, but for his one, I take two backward.

"No. I'm—" *Fine* is what my mouth aims to say, but the word is stuck in my throat. I've been believing I've been fine because I've shoved the pain away for years, but it's apparent my insides claim something else.

Through a thick throat, the words finally emerge. "He f-forced me. R-r-raped me. Left me bleeding in my bed."

Ryker curses. "Your family?"

"Couldn't care less." With the admittance out, the lump loosens the slightest bit. "My mother found me and hardly blinked. When Alex's father showed up with a large cheque for them, it basically guaranteed Alex could continue using me. So, he did, over and over." *And over and over and over.*

"Child neglect. Child endangerment. Blackmail. I could nail them for so much right now." The new voice comes from the goth guy at the end of the line. His words spark questions I'll ask another time.

Through this, I'm dying to peek at Brent, to determine his reaction, but I keep my vision focused on everyone else because it's not the time to factor in his emotions.

"We were nearing the end of high school, so I hoped I would be free." I sigh, my absent breath lowering my shoulders a fraction before I focus on Ryker. "And then you sent him to the hospital."

"Good times," he interjects. "Wish I killed him."

"Me too," I whisper, lips twitching with the most amusement I've felt in a long time. "When I heard how bad his injuries were, I took off. I was at the party, you see, upstairs, and once I saw him being dragged out into the ambulance, I didn't think. Didn't go home. I ran, hitchhiking when I could, and made it to the other side of the country with only my phone and the clothes I had on."

My eyes shut briefly, but when I open them, I finally look toward Brent, finding a shadow of a man I knew. It's as though his entire being has darkened, shifting into a demon of my present rather than the angel I knew him from my past.

"I'm so fucking sorry, Brent, for leaving like I did. I-I didn't want to."

Years of pain bubbles to the surface. I've always hated not mentioning anything to him, but I couldn't. He'd demand to know why I was running away, and then would aim to help me. But Alex's father had too much money; he'd already paid off my family, and I couldn't watch as he, somehow, twisted my best friend against me.

"You had to," he rumbles, tone deepening. "You did what you felt was right."

"I thought it worked, but the Millers' reach is far, apparently. He dragged me back home. At this point, it was the summer after graduation, and he was readying to take over his father's empire."

I stop speaking, my mind going over my next words because this is where the story gets dark.

"In his basement, he had—has—a glass cage. He built it when his father gave him the keys to the company and to their mansion. Principal Miller was a dick—" *Considering he hid the truth of his son's behaviours,* "—but he also didn't know the truth of his son's proclivities.

"The cage is where he locked me up. Every horrible thing you imagine being done to a human, it's been done to me. Knives. Rope. Starvation. Degradation. Raped with items and tools that should never enter a human's body. It was punishment for running, you see."

Natalie's eyes bulge as she learns more of her brother. Her mouth opens and closes three times; she finally keeps it parted, as if to speak, but her words are soon cut off by Brent's guttural mutter.

"He's a dead man walking."

Despite the flash of heat in my stomach, I continue, "After a while, I believe he began to realize how much he enjoyed it, but he claimed he'd grown bored of me. Wanted new screams." I swallow, fighting past the tension again. "New women."

This time, Goth Guy curses.

"Alex isn't dumb, and he knew he would eventually require a woman on his arm, given the amount of social and business functions he attends. I was the easy out for him. I would retain my 'freedom,'" my fingers lift in air quotes and my eyes roll, "meaning I would have everything paid for, so long as I did what he told me to, worked where he demanded I do, and attended any function with him. He threatened you." I glance at Brent and then Elena. "Both of you. Your families. It was one more thing he used to break me then, but he enjoyed reminding me often of the power he holds." I centre my attention on Elena. "That job he offered you wasn't a job at all."

With those words, I pause, dropping my gaze with the horrific realization. Sure, Alex mentioned that in the past, but now, it all hits me at once. Elena could have been his next victim. For real this time, and not only a threat.

Elena's lips pinch together and she nods, though doesn't appear surprised. Pushing past the wave of emotion, I continue.

"No wasn't really an option, and I had to make the best of it. I want to run from him all the time, but I don't because the outcome of not doing so is safer."

"A strip club," Tristan comments. "Seems awfully... open... for a guy like Alex, no?"

"He's a psycho," I shoot back right away, shrugging one shoulder. "He gets off on the power. Forcing me to take my clothes off for men who'll never get the chance to touch me is fun for him. He chose a profession that would degrade me, rather than empower me." I shrug again, because, in the end, the entire job is sort of a perk. Mason's a good man, not sleazy at all. I may hate it, but there are worse horrors.

"Have you ever..." Natalie starts, her question trailing off into a bitten lip as her feet shift side to side. "I mean, has he ever... *shared* you?"

The one freedom I had the others didn't. "No. I can't say the same for the other girls though." I don't know for one hundred percent certainty, but it's not totally off the table either.

A collective sigh breaks from Elena and Natalie.

"He's smart though and that's why I'm saying whatever plan you're cooking up won't work. He only hires women without close family connections. They work as his secretary for a short while, until he tires of his current victim, and then he lures them into his house. He's done it too many times." I twist my core, catching the folder in sight from where it still rests on the floor. It's a sign of the quiet guilt I've been burying for years. "I knew them every one of those girls. Everything I say right now is *for* them."

More tears follow at the mere thought of those innocent women being wrapped up in a sickening plot because I agreed to Alex's deal. Maybe if I'd denied him then he would have kept me to punish me further, and he would have learned to hurt only me. Maybe I could have held on long enough to satisfy all his cravings, and no other women would have lost their lives.

"None of them deserved it," I continue. "Sometimes, he revelled in having me there when he trapped them. Other times, I got to see them later when he gloated about their injuries." I think of Willow, of the pretty woman lying nearly dead on that cage's floor, and it's the vision of her desolate, lost gaze I see in my mind when I add, "He has someone there now."

A murmur ripples through the room. Brent shifts a step closer to me, but this time, I don't back away. Ryker and Tristan seemingly grow larger, while Elena and Natalie both shrink back. Goth Guy straightens, his gaze hopping amongst everyone.

"Name?" Tristan asks.

"Willow. That's all I know."

He curses. "I don't recognize it from the missing persons reports."

I jerk my head once. "I told you, you won't. She was probably a loner. No family. Lived alone. Neighbours may eventually pick up on her absence, but it depends how attentive they are. Besides, he has all local and nearby police authorities paid off."

Elena strides forward with a determination in her steps, and wraps her arms around me. The bruise on my neck burns with her tight hold, but for the moment, I don't care. Because as I return her hug, my legs buckle, my body losing the strength to keep going.

I needed this. And I hadn't realized exactly how much.

It's out now. Unearthed, and a weight lifts off my shoulders at the same time my insides grow heavier, burdened by the reality this day has brought. So many hidden truths. So many lies. The horrors I've lived and witnessed all at the hands of a single monster. They're all out for five people to take in.

"That's why I never answered your messages," I murmur into her hair. "I wanted to, but I didn't want you dragged into it with me. Not you, Elena. I loved you too much."

"You've been living this secret for so long, Teag, I'm breaking inside for you." Her hold tightens, as if showing me she'll be keeping us tied together for the time being.

From over her shoulder, Brent moves, coming into my vision, and I open my eyes, returning the lost soul's broken gaze. His body is rigid, fists by his side, and his face an impassive expression when he growls his next words.

"When was the last time he raped you?"

He doesn't want to know. I don't *want* him to know. Why? I

honestly wish I knew, but something in his soulful, pained gaze tells me that admitting this truth will do more harm than good. Everyone's already looking at me as though I'm a kicked puppy.

"They got much less frequent since he had his other victims."

"The last time?" His teeth bare with his repeated question.

Elena releases me and backs away, sensing there's more to come from Brent's demands. I scan the group twice before settling on him.

"When?"

He'll regret this in a moment. After another beat, I speak in a strained whisper, "Yesterday."

Brent turns and walks away, giving me his back.

Seventeen

TEAGAN

THE SIGHT of him abandoning me, now of all times, crushes my insides, leaving me with nothing but thick debris to breathe though. The basement door slam shuts, its crashing sound echoing down the stairs and straight into my fragile sanity.

Maybe he's pissed to hear Alex recently touched me, or perhaps it's due to my story having ended, and now I'm a villain, no less than what Alex is. I may not have trapped the girls, but I certainly never spoke up either.

In fact, if everyone hates me, it'd be no less than I deserve.

Either way, Brent walking away signifies one thing: he's done with me. Years later, he's finally able to do what I've done to him, and I get it. I understand the pain he must have experienced back then.

Then a bang ricochets from upstairs.

Ryker steps forward to drop a kiss onto Elena's forehead. "I better go see him." He nudges his head toward Tristan and they both start up the stairs.

Goth Guy sighs, a sound heavier than I thought someone could make. "This is my house, so before the ravages it, I should go too."

He follows the guys up the stairs and when the door shuts again, it's only Natalie and Elena down here with me.

"When did you realize the truth?" I ask, directing my question at Natalie.

"Recently. I didn't want to believe it, but they made me realize the party he threw was more than it seemed."

"Yeah."

Elena leans forward and grasps my hand again. "Teag, I am in so much disbelief right now. I can't—I didn't know."

"I didn't want you to," I reply simply.

"But still. You were dealing with this shit for more than half of high school and I never knew. I was so wrapped up in Ryker's drama, I hadn't realized what was going on with you. Maybe if I was a better friend, I would have noticed." Her eyes grow wide and watery. "I'm so sorry."

"No." Quickly, I rush to lay my hand on hers, halting her line of self-deprecating thoughts. There's no one to blame but me. "It wasn't as bad then, and I was decent at hiding things. Our lives took different turns, it seems."

"Yeah." Her cheeks darken and she drops her eyes. "There's a lot we can talk about another time, but yeah."

On cue, feet stomp down the basement steps and Ryker and Brent stand in front of us once more. They couldn't look more opposite from one another. While Ryker's expression is pinched, his dark eyes narrowed on Elena and me, and his mouth pressed into a flat line, Brent's attention is pinned to a spot on the wall, past our heads.

I see how it is.

"Natalie, Elena, come," Ryker commands.

"*Please* would be useful." Elena rolls her eyes before she joins Ryker at the base of the steps. His eyes soften at her approach, and he leads both girls away, leaving Brent and me alone.

The silence is painful and numbing. Loud and silent.

Minutes pass and the statue he became never unfreezes. At this point, if he and the wall were having a staring contest, he would win.

"Are you ever going to look at me?" My voice is no higher than a whispered murmur, and I hate what I've became—scared, genteel, and so unlike the girl he found in the club the other night. The persona I created to be for the past few years.

His jaw ticks, so at least I know he's heard me, but he still doesn't look away from the wall.

"Or speak to me again? I get it, you're mad—"

His coarse, booming scoff cuts me off. "*Mad*. Yes, mad, that's it." The sarcasm is heavy in his tone, implying it's not at all that. "Teagan, if you don't realize by now that *mad* is merely a fraction of what I feel, you really don't know me at all."

My shoulders shrug, though he's not looking at me. "People change. I might not."

He scoffs again then *finally* looks away from the wall. "I've never changed, not that much." His lips fold together once before he goes on, "I'm not *mad* because I'm fucking *furious*. Torn up inside. Ready to rip this world apart and watch it burn. I'm fucking pissed at this whole thing, at myself, and at Miller."

"I'm sorry," I whisper, having nothing else to say.

The skin between his eyes furrows. "For what?"

"For," I wave my hand in the air, "everything. All of this. I get it, you're mad I abandoned you."

Brent steps forward, as if coming closer, but then stops again to watch me through hazy, blue eyes. His next words start soft, a murmur he barely wants me to hear. "I went through hell when you left, Teagan. I knew you were always unhappy with your life, but I thought you'd have the decency to say goodbye." He shakes his head, his jaw clenching again as he paces a few inches.

"But to hear that you ran away, in fear—*fucking fear*—makes everything so much worse. I never knew; I didn't see the signs. We were *best friends*." His hands go to his hair, and he starts yanking on the strands, his fingers twining around his light locks. "My first instinct was to be mad *at you*. To hate that you hid a relationship from me."

I understand his anger, considering what he lost that day, but for him to blame me—to rant about being hurt I didn't tell him, rips at my insides. He may have lost me, but dumb male pride is no excuse for what I lost. For how my life changed. He's not angry I was raped yesterday, or that I was tortured, or even about the multiple women.

No. It's all about *him* and his anger. He's so selfish, he's putting his own misery on me. He believes he's angry, but he doesn't know true anger.

True anger is being helpless and alone, knowing I could have prevented this years ago, if I simply ignored Alex the day he took Elena's spot in Math class.

True anger is watching every woman tramp in, confident and pleased to be helping their boss, only to never leave his mansion again.

True anger is living every day in fear he'll show up, toss me in his vehicle, and decide it's my turn inside the cage again.

True anger is recognizing I should report Alex and his evil deeds but remaining silent.

True anger is knowing I was raped for the first time in six months, and it was Brent's fault. He wouldn't stay away when I begged him to and it's Willow and me who paid the price.

True anger bubbles and boils beneath my skin until it explodes, taking him out with it.

"Fuck you, Brent. You're no damn better than he is. You say you haven't changed, but you have." I rake my eyes up and down his frame. "The friend I knew wouldn't sit here, victim blaming, because *you* can't handle your own damn ego. Fuck you and fuck all of this. I should never have opened my damned mouth."

I stalk by him, shoving his shoulder as I pass. I make it to the bottom step, foot hovering, before stopping and returning the blade he's stabbed into me with his cruel, unthinking words.

"So you know, you refused to stay away when I asked you to. Alex received footage of the private room and wondered why I had the same visitor on back-to-back nights, and never danced for him. He was jealous of *you* and acted. So, if anyone should feel angry, it's me because you didn't leave well enough alone."

And then I go. Leave him to choke on his own words and selfish emotions.

Eighteen

BRENT

I NEVER BELIEVED in events that can cause the entire world to shift, but I was wrong. So, so wrong.

I'm at fault.

I do more than see red.

Red. Black. Blue. Purple. The fucking rainbow of any colour that makes up a busted body after I'm through with him.

Your fault.

For so long, I've been blaming her, but now, it's time for me to stare into the mirror at my own reflection. Because all this is *my* doing.

But before the world can take another turn, I rush away from the basement.

Nineteen

TEAGAN

"TEAGAN!"

I slam the basement door shut, effectively cutting off whatever bullshit Brent's about to spew. Five sets of eyes stare curiously from the living room, but I rush pass it, striding straight toward the front door.

"Good luck, guys, and it was nice to see you all again. While you're getting yourselves killed for your plan, I'll be climbing back into his cage. At this rate, it's the only place I'll live out my life."

Stunned silence meets me, interrupted only by the crashing of the basement door.

"Don't run away again, Cherry-Girl. You're done running."

Since he's found me, he's utilized that nickname over a dozen times, but this time, it feels heavier. It drops on my body, making my arm too leaden to reach for the door, so I turn away, fully aware of the audience forming.

Brent storms up to me, stopping short, his heaving chest inches from my own. Frantic strands are a messy mop on his head and his normally peaceful eyes are livid as they scan me. His hands lift, but remain in the air, as though he wants to touch me but won't.

"You didn't let me fucking finish, Teagan. Do you not recall what I said downstairs? I'm angry at myself, and at Alex. I *want* to be mad at you, because for a long time, I was, and it's what I'm used to feeling."

His arm rises, fist resting on the door beside my head, effectively trapping me in on one side. Fighting instincts flare, demanding I shove him away, but I don't.

"But I'm not," he continues, his eyes melting into a pool of agony. "I can't, even if I tried. You ran away for you. Sure, I wish you came to me, but I understand. You were surviving and I'm angry at myself for not seeing it. I noticed you were becoming distant, but I never once opened my mouth, and now, I wish I had."

His other arm comes up on my other side, trapping me fully. As if I would leave right now anyway. "I'm ready to murder his ass for everything he did to you then and now. I'm pissed he drove you away from your home, that you *had* to run. I'm livid he took Teagan Faber from this world. I'm annoyed at him and at myself because you were so fucking close this entire time, and I never found you."

His eyes flick to my lips and I stop breathing yet again. "So, no, I'm not mad at you but at this entire thing. That is, until a moment ago when you gutted me down below with your final words." His arms drop and he backs away, giving me space once more. Then his eyes fall to our feet and it's where he stares as he speaks again. "Sorry won't cut it, I know. You warned me but I persisted and—"

His eyes shut, blocking out the desolation in their depths and, after a beat, when they open again, I'm staring at a soulless man. "When Natalie said you were involved with Alex, the only thing I wanted was to hate you for helping a monster. She tried to counter my thinking and say you needed to be saved, but I chose not to listen to her because I was so focused on believing the worst. Then I found you, and I couldn't think of revenge when all I wanted to do was love you again, except I had a job to do. While I've been a mess of emotions since then, nothing's been remotely close to how I felt below. I—"

He falls forward, onto his knees, as if his body loses all strength to keep him upright. While curious eyes bounce from him to me and back, they're not who I'm focusing on. I've never had a man on his knees for me. Period. I've been on mine for Alex more times than I wish to count, I've crawled on chilly floors toward men who pay me to remove my clothing, but never has someone begged for forgiveness or even looked at me in such despondency.

I don't know what to do. I've never had to make a decision like this, never had to be the one to grant mercy.

"I'm sorry for assuming the worst. I want to say that's the worst part in this entire thing, but," he shakes his head roughly, "it's not. My errors are nothing compared to what you've survived."

My heart dies all over again. If I thought Alex ever broke me, it's nothing to what Brent's words do. And though my legs buckle, and I fall against the doorway, requiring it to hold me up, his apology also changes nothing.

Not the past, but especially not the future. Or even the present. They won't win against Alex, so there's no point in addressing these emotions, all to die in a few short hours, days, or weeks.

As if the others think the same thing, Goth Guy steps forward and into the space between Brent and me. "Look, I know this is emotional for you both, but let's not forget what's at stake here. We need to act now and talk later. That girl you mentioned, Willow, every second that passes is one more he's hurting her."

His logic breaks the spell between us, and Brent lifts himself to his feet, huffing. "He's right. We need to get going." His eyes remain on me though, as if waiting for me to fight him further.

Going. As if... What, they expect me to join their ragdoll gang and help take down the big bad man? I've told them about Alex's basement, and already, that'll earn me a one-way ticket to death. While they're working on whatever insane plan they believe will work, I'll climb back into the cell and curl up with Willow and wait for Alex's punishment, because once he kills all of them, he'll wipe me out next. Alex isn't dumb; he won't let them win. Besides, that's only *if* they can get into his basement, past the coded door. The code they'll need was the very code I used to escape once, only to learn its numbers were my demise. I won't make that error again.

"Good luck," is all I mutter before my hand finds the knob, turning once again to leave. The conversation between Brent and me has long faded away into the recesses of my mind where it'll get through the painful death Alex will grant me. "You'll need it."

Before I can open the door, I hear a soft, "Teagan." Elena.

I don't turn around, continuing to give her my back. My fist tightens on the knob, wanting to escape this house of crazy.

"Teagan, don't go. We need your help."

"Why?" I growl, still facing the exit. "I told you, he keeps the girls in his basement. Good luck."

"Don't you want this to end?" Natalie this time.

Her weighted question shifts the tense energy in the room to desolation. When I don't answer and a few terse minutes pass, I hear them turn away, one by one. Steps echo farther down the hallway until it's only Brent and me again.

I know Brent remains because I feel his energy—his vibe—his essence. I recall the memory of his lips on mine, aware I didn't want it to end.

"The Teagan I met stood up to bullies to save others. Shame how people change."

And then his soft footsteps start up again, until they fade and rejoin the others.

His last statement is much louder than his victim-blaming,

dickish words in the basement, and even his apology from moments ago. Not only do they echo, but they chime. Over and over.

"The Teagan I met stood up to bullies to save others. Shame how people change."

I have changed. I tried to stand up to Alex, and I failed. It's all that ever happens when someone goes against him.

Every single time.

No matter how many cries he rips from my throat or how much begging I do, he doesn't show mercy.

No matter how much blood he sheds, it's never enough for him.

No matter how much the women plead for him to kill them, simply to end their lives—and the pain—sooner, he won't listen.

They'll discover that shortly. When they arrive on his doorstep and attack his sanctuary, they will lose.

"Shame how people change."

Not that much. As a child, I had to survive each home I was placed in. As a teenager, I had to survive parents who disliked my presence. And now, I'm surviving my enemy.

You've changed, Brent. Not me.

He's different because, once, he understood my pains. Now, he blames me for not helping the girls. He doesn't realize I *have* been helping them. Every single time I keep my mouth shut, I save us both from insane bouts of vengeance. Remaining quiet means their pain won't be amplified by pointless anger.

Finally, strength enters my hand, enough to twist the knob, and I throw open the door. My gaze stays front and centre as I exit the house, shutting the door behind me.

Good luck to you all. They'll need it.

The afternoon breeze blows over my face, cool and warm all at the same time with the late spring air. I breathe it in, trapping it in my lungs as my eyes bounce around the neighbourhood, landing on all the picture-perfect homes.

I've never lived in such a home. None of my foster families could afford it, especially my last ones. A couple I hope is presently roasting in misery for not protecting me from Alex. Instead, they continued to collect the hush money from his father.

No one protected me then either.

Willow has no one to help her.

She won't need help because she'll be dead soon. Like all the others.

The others who had no one to stand up for them.

Carmen. Mia. Anne. Gemma. Zoey. Rachel. Charlotte. Scarlett.

They had no one. What would they think about this? Would they want me to help save Willow or would they too want me to hide?

"The Teagan I met stood up to bullies to save others."

But you don't know that girl anymore. I don't know that girl anymore.

I can be her again.

The final thought slips in so effortlessly—so easily—and I can't suck it back in. *I can be.*

I've tried. I've failed. But I was alone in my fight. From over my shoulder, I take in the house again. The house where a small group of people are forming an army to get end one man's evil tactics simply because they know he's a vile human being . There's no other reason for their actions other than their own goodness.

And if they do succeed, I'm free. Willow's free. Countless future women are free.

I can help them. I can become me *again.*

No. My hair whips over my face with how fast my head shakes away its own insanity. I can't go there. I *won't* go there. Alex will win, like always, and I refuse to help them, all to be found an accomplice.

Not. Happening.

I take a step, managing to place a wider distance between myself and the house, but then a flash of bright blonde, blood red-tipped hair consumes my vision, making me pause.

Willow. Willow with dead eyes, who won't be making it much longer. Soon, her pain will end, and another will take her place. Whoever is currently working for him better be spending her final days of freedom in bliss.

Or you can save her. Save both of them—Willow and his current secretary.

No.

Yes.

I stop again, twisting to face the house once more.

Either way, one day, I'm dead. I've been surviving, but... surviving what? Ongoing hell, watching innocent women being dragged to their death while I keep quiet, when this entire time, I may have been able to help them in ways I never imagined.

Can help them.

I can help Willow. Maybe she won't be gone if we get to her in time.

We.

My hands fist in my hair. *Ugh, stop it, brain.*

But it's not my brain's fault. It's my own guilt finally beating out years of silence. Years of silence that can end if I only turn around and walk back inside.

No. Why am I fighting this? Jail is too little for what Alex deserves.

I release my hair slowly, wiping at my face instead. My fingers catch on the tear sliding down my cheek. I'm crying. Crying because my brain has already understood what the rest of me is fighting to keep up with.

Not only can I help Brent, Elena, and the others, but I *should* help them.

Before I fathom what's happening, I'm turning around, striding back up the path, and opening the door. No doubt everyone is down the hallway, as they were before I left.

I enter, shutting the door behind me in time for the soft steps to stop a couple feet away. I glance up from the hardwood flooring, meeting Brent's fiery gaze.

"I came back," I murmur, aware I'm speaking the obvious.

"I knew you would."

Twenty

TEAGAN

BRENT LEADS me into the kitchen, where everyone is seated around the table. Elena, on Ryker's lap, takes up a chair at one end while Tristan and Natalie, seated similarly, are across from them. Goth Guy has the chair farthest away from me. His strange blue eyes track me, watching as though I'm a rabid animal when I enter and lean against the far wall.

Everyone here I know, but this stranger is, well, a stranger.

"Who are you?"

Goth Guy smirks, glancing at Elena first. "Seems to be a common issue amongst you all. Hawke Blackwood. Lawyer. Long story short, I got Ryker released early, so we could work together on Alex."

His words stroke a slight interest in me. *So, Ryker had this plan before even being released?*

My eyes instead land on his tattoos and piercings, so unlike any other lawyer I've heard of or seen depicted on TV. "A lawyer?"

"It's unnecessary," Brent comments from the corner, misunderstanding my curiosity. "Alex won't be seeing a courtroom since I'll be killing him."

"After me." Ryker scoffs. "Should have done it years ago."

"Um, I think I'll need a piece of that," Tristan speaks up. "For everything the dick tried to do to Natalie."

My jaw sets, chin lifting while I scan the room, bitter disbelief building with every pass. While Alex made a crude comment about Elena and wants to sell Natalie off, *I* was the one at his mercy. Amongst all of us, *I* deserve the retribution for his actions.

I finally find my voice, only to speak at the same time Hawke also says, "No."

His denial has my own speech pausing in my throat, surprised he's not hopping on the revenge train with the rest of them.

"No," he repeats, pointing at Ryker. "You're a recent convict. If you kill him, I won't be able to save you this time." Next, he shifts his gaze to Tristan. "You're a goddamn cop. We're not even going there."

"We could say it was an accident," Tristan offers, a slick grin growing on his face. Natalie's hand lands overtop his, and I watch with fascination as her thumb strokes his palm, instantly calming him.

"No," Hawke repeats again before turning his attention toward Brent. "And you, no. Just no. We're not killing him because the only way we'll be winning the case is to make this as legal as possible with an arrest."

I laugh. Loud and boisterous. I can't hold it in. Or the scoff that follows. I shake my head, straightening from my slouch and pushing off the wall. "Your grand plan is to *arrest* him? Unbelievable. After all *this*," I gesture around the room, "I'd think you had a better plan. If you arrest him, every cop downtown will laugh in your face before releasing him."

"Which is why we're not bringing him downtown. The Royal Canadian Mounted Police are arresting him."

"The RCMP?" I repeat, a squeak to my voice. Federal police.

"I have a contact there," Hawke adds.

In the corner of my eye, I spot Elena turning on Ryker's lap. "You knew about this the entire time?"

He shrugs, obviously uncaring about the hurt in her tone. "I couldn't tell you everything, Dolly. Step one was the information Natalie and Teagan could provide. Step two was too ahead of where we were."

Elena narrows her eyes at his lack of admittance, but I've already moved my attention away from their drama. Obviously, it never ends with those two.

Hawke waves his hand. "Elena, there isn't much to tell. I have ties with the RCMP, but I won't say why or how. We'll leave it at that, but please, we need to focus on what's important right now: getting inside Alex's house."

"How?" I cross my arms, a cocky smirk covering my mouth. Getting inside his mansion won't be as simple as walking up to it and entering.

"With a bit of force," Hawke rumbles. "And with help from Natalie."

"Not a fucking chance," Tristan roars, standing up with such speed Natalie slides from his lap. Her arms shoot to the side, catching her balance, but it's a minor issue compared to Hawke's words. Worry ripples over her face and her eyes widen, darting between Tristan and Hawke.

Ryker adds, "Your plan is to send her into the damn lion's den unprotected? You never mentioned this part to us."

"We'll be there right there," Hawke mutters, rolling his eyes. He leans forward onto the table, bracing his fists on the smooth top as he scans each of us. "Look, Alex won't be up for a car pulling into his driveway, unless there's a reason for it. I figure, Natalie can go visit her brother." His brow lifts as he stares at Tristan, challenging expression in place.

"I think Natalie should get a say in this, no?" Elena chimes in from Ryker's lap.

As one, everyone spins toward Natalie and her eyes grow wider. Tristan steps in front of her and clasps her hand. The simple sight has the base of my stomach warming with desire—the effortlessness of their ability to touch one another like that. My eyes cut to Brent, and I notice his eyes are on me.

"We never spoke about how we're getting into Alex's house," Tristan says, the dip between his brows growing with his narrowing glare. "Why not send Teagan in? Considering she's been his pet for quite some time now, seems like the better option, in my opinion."

And this is where they turn on me. Didn't take them long.

Stop it. Logical Teagan slips through, and I catch Elena's eye—and her frown that she directs toward Tristan.

"Watch it," Brent rumbles, stepping closer to me. To make a point, I pace backwards, putting the same distance between us. *Now* he thinks I need a saviour when I've proven I've managed to remain alive thus far?

Either way, me arriving on Alex's front step will one hundred percent signal something being off.

"I can't," I speak up. "I only go over there on his orders. If I show up unexpectedly... well, I never have before, so I can guarantee his walls will be up and you will lose."

More than you already will.

Hawke nods, a small smirk tinging the corner of his mouth. "You see? It makes sense for Natalie to visit her brother. The moment Alex opens his door for Natalie, we'll fight our way in. Then, Teagan, you'll lead us to the basement."

"And then?" Ryker asks, his brows hiked. "I get the sense you have a backstory, Blackwood. If you won't share it, what is the exact plan to get the RCMP there?"

Hawke's gaze does a pass of the room before responding.

"They'll be on standby. You leave that to me. The rest of us will work on getting to that point. Understand?"

He speaks of this entire moment as if it's as simple as breathing—snapping fingers and making it happen. But what none of them realizes is what this plan—if it works—will mean.

I'll be free.

And Alex will be locked up.

If this works. But for a moment, I allow that dream to become a mental reality. It'll be a world in which Alex no longer controls me, in which Willow will be able to walk away free. Damaged, no doubt, but free.

And if the RCMP arrest Alex, with the basement as proof alone, he'll be found guilty. Alex revelled in telling me the local police forces ensured the DNA on the body wouldn't be traced back to him, but there's no fucking way he's also paid off the federal police.

I hope.

I'll believe for now anyway.

But that'll mean a trial, which means evidence and witnesses—Me. I'm a witness.

But more than that, it means the possibility of escape. If there's a trial, Alex has a chance to pay off the judge or jury. He has a chance to lord himself, forcing me to watch my villain go free.

"I'll have to testify, won't I?"

Hawke stares at me for a long second, his bright eyes shining past his dark hair. His lip curls, the ring disappearing into his mouth until he finally speaks, "Everyone, give me a moment alone with Teagan, please."

Instantly, everyone moves. Elena shoots me a small smile before following Natalie and Ryker out. Tristan takes up the rear until it's only Brent remaining, still by the wall, his arms crossed as his eyes remain on Hawke, a challenge in their depths.

"You too, Brent," Hawke says, without looking at him.

"No."

"Go, Brent."

He won't leave. I know because he's stubborn like that, so I nod my head toward the doorway. "Let me talk to him." My voice is low and pitiful, and ideally something he'll respond favourably to.

Brent's nostrils flare and his eyes bounce between us, hate filling their depths as we gang up on him, but until Brent works through his shit, I don't need more drama in my life. I feel his exit when he finally does walk—more like stalk—away, a huff left in the air behind him.

With his absence, Hawke falls into the nearest abandoned chair, his hand brushing over his face three times. "I never thought I'd ever have so many people in my house at one time. It's exhausting."

I align my gaze with his, leaning forward until the table presses into my stomach. "What's in this for you? Ryker and Alex always had bad blood between them. Tristan wants him for what he tried to do to Natalie. Brent..." I trail off, unwilling to piece together Brent's reasoning. "But you?"

Hawke's lips twitch, calling to attention his lip ring again. "I was simply a lawyer hired by a family. Their daughter was working for Alex, and they felt she pulled away from them. Then she disappeared and six months later, her body was found. They wanted me to sue Miller, but they had no grounds, other than a suspicion that he had something to do with it."

"Carmen," I murmur, heart hammering faster. His first victim. The only one of us with a family who cared enough. No doubt the chaos her family attempted to ensue guided his future choices.

His eyes flash. "It saddens me to hear you say her name. That you've seen her when—" He cuts himself off, swallowing hard and leaving me to fill in the gaps.

"Yeah," I whisper. "But you never answered my question, Hawke. Even after losing the first round, you continued to investigate?"

"Yep." His *P* pops and he leans back, crossing his arms. "We never made it to trial because the police claimed his DNA was not on Carmen's remains, so while his company headlined for a couple short weeks—a PR nightmare and nothing more—it's all that came of it."

"You knew, even then?"

"I felt it." His hand goes to his stomach. "In here. When meeting with Miller and his lawyers, I recognized something in the depths of his gaze. Cold, calculating evil. He knew what he was doing, and I couldn't let the feeling go. So I started to dig, and it led me to Ryker, when he was in prison."

"And then it went on from there," I finish. "You jumped on the bandwagon of insane plans."

His lips twitch, fighting a grin. "Basically."

"Again, though," my brows rise, hands spreading wide and open, "another lawyer would have given up by now. It's personal for you."

The room is devoid of any sound for a moment—even the sound of his breathing is gone. Then he chuckles, kicking back on the legs of his chair. "You ever look into a psychology degree because you sure as hell could add perspective to the field? You have the brain for it. Yes, you read me correctly. It is personal. Your situation... I get it."

Dark shadows dim the blue of his eyes and he looks away, obviously preferring not to go there. Instead, I dwell for a moment on his other statement.

"You speak of a future like I have one. The moment we miss our chance, Alex will kill us all, you know that, right?" And will save me for last to draw out the agony.

Hawke tips his head to the side. "I feel the need to warn you, as part of my education, psychology classes were mandatory. So, I know, you don't truly believe that or else you wouldn't be helping."

He's right, but still. "*If* your plan does work, and he's not paying off the RCMP, and with the evidence in his basement and Willow herself, we'll go to court, right?"

This time, his head tilts the other way, his question not going away. "You opened your past to us all down below. Would it be different inside a courtroom? Knowing if you manage to say your piece, he'll be gone."

Right. Like it's so easy. Things with Alex are *never* easy. Testifying with him staring me down won't be simple: to go against him so blatantly, aware if I slip up, he'll ensure I stop breathing.

"He'll be there."

Hawke leans forward, putting himself as much into my vision as possible. "Yes, he will be, but so will dozens of other people, including me. Officers. Elena. Brent." He glances at his hands and back up, emotion swimming in his eyes. "What you tell the court will ensure he never walks away. You're the only person who knows everything ever occurring in that basement. Your testimony *won't* be ignored, and I'll fucking make sure of it. Any images we present can be seen as being faked, but falsifying trauma isn't."

I flinch. *Trauma.* What an ugly word. Trauma occurs after watching someone die. After something so horrible happens, a person can no longer face reality and chooses to revert to the safety of their mind.

That's not me. I look upon myself in the mirror each day and stand straight when facing people. I don't cry myself to sleep, or stress about Alex every second of the day.

"I think you have it wrong. I'm not traumatized."

His mouth opens and shuts, eyes narrowing before he ultimately lets the topic go and instead says, "Either way, I think testifying against him will be important."

I imagine myself up on the stand, like you'd see in a show, looking out upon the crowd of spectators, the jury, the judge, and... Alex. Alex who will stare at me with hate and betrayal, knowing he was only caught because I opened my mouth. He'll be so mad and when he's found not guilty, there will be nowhere on this planet I can run to; no one who'd be able to protect me from his wrath.

The knowledge has my stomach knotting. But not the fact I'll be in constant danger. Rather, that he'll be deceived by me. It's... I don't know. Something feels off. Like betraying him is *wrong*, even after everything.

"And Willow?" *If we get to her in time.*

Hawke's face twists. "Let's see how much of her we save before thinking about that."

A staggering breath releases from my lungs as if they're catching up to the reality that this could be real. Willow and me, we can be *free*. As free as an accomplice can be anyway. I've seen enough TV to know when the courts listen to everything I have to say, they'll have a lot of questions of their own.

"What'll happen to me afterwards? For years, I've known what he's doing and kept it a secret."

Hawke lowers his face again, catching my gaze. His hand slips out and across the table, stopping a fraction away from mine. "Teagan, I *promise* you will be okay. I have ways to ensure all charges brought against you are cleared. You were a victim. Victims don't receive punishment."

Victim. Another ugly word.

Trauma.

Victim.

It's what the court will try to label me as. The media will steal the name. It'll be a term—a title—forever attached to me. The term implies weakness, but I'm not weak.

Hawke doesn't deserve to know what has my mind running, so I murmur, "Okay," if only to conclude this conversation.

He smiles gently, a strange look for someone appearing as scary as he does. "We should end this now, before Brent finds reasons to smash my house to pieces if I keep you too long."

Despite before, the thought has me smiling as I follow him out of the kitchen.

Someone is fighting for me because he cares.

It's as simple as that.

BRENT

THIS ENTIRE TIME I've been blaming Alex for every little injury done to Teagan, but then she announces *I'm* at fault for some of it. All because I was so damned determined to get the answers we needed, I wouldn't leave her alone, making her pay the ultimate price.

I'm a fucking moron.

I claimed I haven't changed since we were teenagers, but the truth is, I have. Back then, I would have done anything for her to see me as more than her overweight friend. Now, our souls are linked. I *am* her, and she is me. When I breathe, it's for her. When I kill Miller, it's for her. And when I bathe in his blood, it's so she'll be able to sleep the rest of her days away, protected from the world's monsters.

A hand rests heavy on my shoulder, pulling my body back to Earth.

"Dude, you practically have fumes escaping your ears." Tristan. "Breathe."

"I can't."

Elena cuts into my vision then, reaching across the room from where she's seated with Ryker, to take my hand. Her soft skin touches mine, yanking me back toward the past few years when I dated her. Now, it feels like a lifetime ago. It wasn't real for me at any time, and now, with the truth out, it's obvious it wasn't for her either.

"Brent, it's okay. We'll get him and this will all be over. We have her back."

But she doesn't know what Teagan told me. None of them do.

Despite her reassurance, my head drops low as my fingertips curl into the couch under me, wishing like hell it was Alex's skin my grip was digging into.

"When she was raped yesterday, it was my fault. He... Apparently, he was jealous of my visits to the club. It was the first time in a long time, and it was because I didn't back away when she told me to."

Elena gasps, the noise as loud as thunder in the otherwise silent room. "Brent, you can't blame yourself. It was Alex's doing."

"Because *I* enticed him."

She sighs, but I don't care how irrational I am. It's my fault. Teagan said so herself and now I'll spend the rest of my life begging for her forgiveness. For what he did to her, and for my earlier comments in the basement.

Yes, I'm fucking pissed she took off without a word. Hurt more than anything that she didn't confide in me, but I see now how wrong I was for feeling it when none of it was her fault, or even her choice. When Teagan ran from the basement, something in me died, but also, I was reminded of a story Tristan once recounted back when he was going through the Academy. It was about a trauma patient relapsing and committing suicide. He described her symptoms, the ones they saw, and they all came rushing back to me.

Confusion, numbness, thinking negatively.

I see them all in my Cherry-Girl.

She's haunted. Scared. Believes Miller will win this fight and he'll steal her away again, but what she doesn't realize is that now that I have her back, I'm not letting her go. I'll die before he captures her again.

She's numb. Through her story, a single tear dripped down her cheek. She recounted horrors like it was a mere walk in the park for her. Too much of her story was emotionless, as though she was reading a damn essay out loud.

She's traumatized and for all the right reasons. I don't see how anyone could endure what she has and not be.

Footsteps from the hallway yank my attention up in time to watch Hawke enter the living room, his expression flat and focused. I've seen it before. It means he's thinking hard. But as he moves to the side of the room, my attention returns to the doorway as Teagan enters behind him.

To me, she's always been the most beautiful woman. No one has ever shone brighter. Even the purple marks decorating her neck that have me wanting to tear something apart, don't take away from her beauty. It's more than her looks though. It's *her*, and I fear her time with Alex did something to snuff it out.

Anxiety tumbles through my limbs and I straighten my position, shooting an inquiring look toward Hawke. I'm dying to know what they've spoken about, and how I can assuage Teagan's worries.

Teagan stops by the couch, her nervous gaze bouncing around the room. She's purposely avoiding me though, giving most of her attention to Elena and Natalie.

For now, I'll allow it. I get it. She needs a moment. As long as she's aware it won't be forever, because contrary to her own personal fears, she's mine. My friend has returned, and I'll save her, fix her, and love her.

"What now?" Tristan asks.

As one, all our heads swivel toward Hawke.

The sooner we get the fucker, the sooner I can get the real Teagan back.

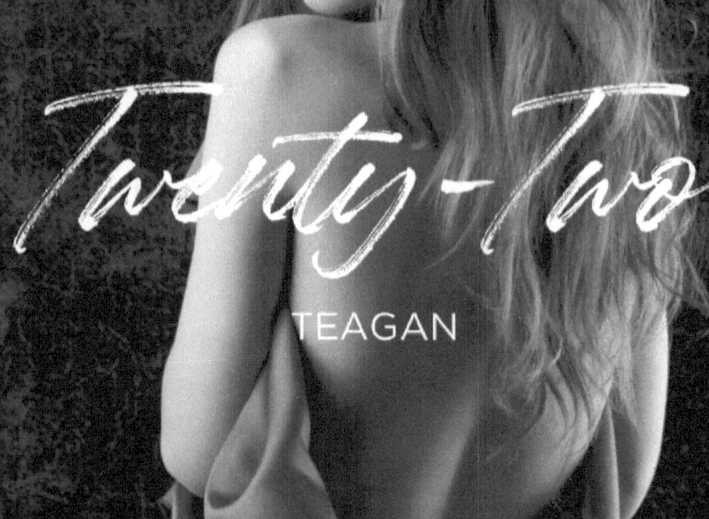

Twenty-Two

TEAGAN

"FIRST, NATALIE CALLS HER BROTHER." His attention finds her, still beside Tristan, appearing as a scared mouse in how her eyes flick around the room. "Say you want to visit, or anything that'll get us to the front door. We need a reason to show up."

After a long beat and another scan of the room, Natalie pulls out her phone. Even from across the room, I recognize the slight shiver coursing through her arm as she prepares for her phone call.

It's the fear Alex enjoys forcing upon people.

Natalie clicks a few times on the screen of her phone before resting it on her open palm. A dialling noise emits from it and then—

"Natalie."

He's worried. He knows what's happening. No doubt he has eyes on us now and—

Elena stands, coming closer to me. She's always had a relaxing personality, despite the drama Ryker brought into her life. Her presence eases my chest pains enough that I breathe a tad easier.

"Hey, Alex." Natalie's throat moves and I watch the hardened ball slide down the column. "What's up?"

Casual. *Smart.* Start with a simple conversation to ease Natalie's nerves.

Alex's staggered breath is so rough I hear it as though it was in my ear. "Honestly, Nat, not good. I'm a bit worried."

"Oh?" She scans the room, a furrow deepening between her eyes, showing us the question she also has. "What about?"

"My girlfriend, Teagan. She hasn't been answering my messages all morning. If I hear nothing by tonight, I'll send people to look at her house. I'm hoping she's simply busy."

My hands slap my sides in my speed to check my pockets. No phone. It must have fallen out when Brent and Ryker snatched me last night.

Which means Alex has been sending who knows how many messages. All going unanswered...

He's going to beat me. I won't sit for an entire week.

He's not going to be here next week.

Sure, he is.

Logic and my knowledge of Alex's tendencies battle with what Hawke and the others are insisting is a solid plan.

I gesture to myself and then the phone and back, mouthing words I hope she understands. *I'm here. Tell him I'm here.* If Alex believes I'm with Natalie, it may save his anger.

Natalie nods and says, "Oh, well, it's actually why I'm calling. She came here this morning, but realized she forgot her phone at her house and was worried if she didn't respond to any possible texts you send."

Alex blows out a relieved breath. Even through the wall technology gives, I feel it inside my stomach. It's a breath saying I'll be okay and unharmed for now.

But then his voice hardens. "You're together? Why would she— Thank you for the call, Natalie." He switches the path his words were heading in. "May I speak with her?"

Natalie lifts her eyes, colliding with mine, and they widen, unsure of her next action. I step toward her, only to be stopped by Brent's hand coming down on my arm.

The fuck is wrong with him? If I don't obey Alex now, I'll pay later.

Using as much muscle as I can muster, I jerk my arm, casting his hand from my body before deftly sliding around him, further ignoring his fury. He can be mad all he wants, but it won't be his skin paying the price for not speaking.

"I'm here, Alex," I say, learning close to Natalie's phone. "I'm sorry."

"Are you okay, babe? You usually respond so quickly, I wasn't certain. I got details about an event this weekend, so I messaged about it. Read it as soon as you get back to your phone."

"Of course," I reply right away, appeasing him in all the ways I know how. His texts never go unanswered for more than a moment. "I promise I won't lose my phone again. I'll message you as soon as I'm home later and get my cell. You have no need to be worried. I'm sorry."

I'm apologizing because it conveys awareness for my actions. It'll lessen the blows Alex will give later.

There won't be any blows.

If Hawke's conceptual plan works, but I know better than to wish too hard for something.

The room gets smaller as everyone steps toward me, varying emotions drawn out on their faces. Brent's arm reaches for me, as if he's aiming to yank me away. My hand slices the air, a universal *that's enough* sign.

"It's okay," Alex murmurs, halting everyone in the room. "Let me come get you from Natalie's and drive you back to the city."

He has no questions how I've made it an hour away without my phone? He knows Natalie doesn't have a car, causing me to wonder if he knows more than he's letting on.

"It's okay, Alex, I can take her," Natalie speaks up then. "I thought we could stop by and the three of us can have a chat. I ran out on you last time, but I want to continue our previous conversation about arranging a marriage."

I jolt, smirking. She's good, I'll give her that.

"You don't have a vehicle though." Alex's voice tinges on borderline suspicion, and based on Hawke's shuffle, he senses it too. He gestures toward himself.

Natalie quickly adds, "I've been borrowing a friend's car while he's out of town. It's how Teagan got here."

When I first was introduced to Natalie, she was a frightened bird, but it's obvious whatever's happened to her in the short week since I last saw her at Alex's, she's flown her coop and stretched her wings because the lie flows from her so easily.

There's a long moment of silence before he responds with, "All right, Nat. You win. I'll be seeing you both soon."

Is it just me, or were his words edged with a threat?

The phone goes silent as Alex hangs up.

"This is fucked," Elena's whisper fills the soundless room. "I can't wait to see the look on his face when we all show up."

"Oh, you're not coming with us." Ryker moves to stand in front of her, blocking her from even taking a step.

For the first time in a while, I smile. At least Ryker's protectiveness is good for one thing, because he's right in saying she doesn't need to come. If this goes south, there should be someone around to keep our memories alive.

"Ryker Ames, of all—"

"He's correct," I interject. "There's no purpose in you going and possibly endangering yourself."

"Then it's settled," Hawke says, his voice louder than earlier. "Us four," he gestures to himself, Brent, Ryker, and Tristan, "Natalie, and Teagan."

Elena *harrumphs* and crosses her arms. "You guys suck. I guess I'll stay home like a good little woman." Her nose scrunches with her true feelings regarding that statement.

Ryker taps her hand, more specifically the fourth finger on her left hand. It's bare, but for how long until he manages to solder a ring to it? "Consider it practice, Dolly. Now, if you'll excuse us, Elena needs to kiss her man goodbye before he goes off to war." Laughing, he pulls her down the hallway and out the front door, her squeal the only indication she's pleased.

My eyes land on the floor space they recently occupied, longing pushing my teeth into my lip. In high school, their romance—or lack thereof, I should say—consisted of Ryker being an asshole bully toward her. She's always oddly enjoyed it.

Elena is strong. She fought Ryker's ruthlessness with her entire heart, knowing one day, eventually, she'd win it. A girl like Elena might have withstood Alex better, but not me. Compared to her, I'm weak. Weak because I didn't fight back enough. I folded into Alex's little box and became the tool he required.

"So, we leave in ten minutes, I suppose?"

Hawke nods, his attention also locked on the doorway Ryker and Elena exited from. "When he's done fucking her, we'll go."

He backs out of the room, his phone in hand as he types manically away on it. His leave signals something for the others and Tristan yanks Natalie down to the couch, his lips immediately landing on the back of her neck. He murmurs something to her, but I don't hear what.

The love in this room is inspiring, showing that romance is still a possibility for people who haven't lost their souls to the devil.

Lucky them.

Brent's eyes study me, but I continue avoiding his gaze and walk toward the door. Like a damn lost puppy, he's right there behind me, so I throw my palm up.

"Don't, Brent."

"Teagan. Cherry-Girl."

My chest burns with his sad tone, but I head for the front door, hand still facing him. "I said don't, Brent."

These next couple hours will be it. After tonight, I'll be chained beside Willow to endure the worst pain in my entire life, or I'll be six feet under with the guys. Natalie, no doubt, will be traded off at the first chance because Alex won't kill her, betrayal or otherwise. Not when she can be useful in other ways.

My feet quicken until stopping on the first step of Hawke's front landing. The stone is numbingly cold through my jeans, but it's still more of a pleasant feeling than what will soon occur.

Twenty-Three

TEAGAN

"WE'RE HERE." Ryker's announcement is useless since no one can miss the giant mansion Hawke pulls up in front of.

Hawke unlocks the doors and Brent immediately exits the car, reaching back inside for me. I ignore his hand and climb out on my own, before placing myself beside Natalie, who has also exited the car from the other side. Tristan and Ryker bring up the rear.

Alex's home never ceases to amaze me. It's typical of a rich person's mansion, but spectacular, nonetheless. This time, the sight seems heavier on my heart. Every time I'm dragged here, I pray it'll be my final time, while I stupidly wish for Alex to release me or end my life, but this time, I *feel* it. Actually *feel* it's the final time.

Carmen. Mia. Anne. Gemma. Zoey. Rachel. Charlotte. Scarlett.
This is for them.

I inhale the early evening air, trapping it in my lungs before Natalie and I stride up the dozen steps toward his massive front doors. The guys follow a step behind.

Natalie lifts her hand to the bell. I'm watching, but my mind wanders, as though I'm no longer there. Nothing seems real—like this is a figment of my imagination and Brent never found me.

Perhaps Alex choked me out so badly, these past couple days are an illusion.

I'm expecting one of Alex's staff members to answer the door, but instead, it's Alex himself. His eyes settle on his sister and me, and that's all he has the chance to see, for the second Alex is revealed, Ryker pushes between us, lunging for Alex. In a flash, Alex is pinned to the nearest wall, Ryker's hand shoved tightly against his throat. Alex kicks out, his hands immediately yanking at Ryker's unyielding ones.

Yes, my mind hisses.

My stomach knots.

What the fuck? The sight of Alex being choked out should be the greatest thing I've ever seen. Payback's a bitch, and it's time for Alex to pay up.

Hawke also throws himself inside the house, yanking on Ryker's arm. "Remember what I said."

Ryker doesn't even blink. "Too bad for you, I don't fucking care. Miller and I have unfinished history." His teeth bare and his next words are spoken to Alex directly. "Hey, Miller. Been a long time. I'd say it's a pleasure but, well, it's not."

Between little breaths and pants, Alex manages, "R-Ryker Ames?" His face is blotching red; his wheezes are a sound I've dreamed of for so long.

"Hey there, fucker."

"You should be in prison."

"No, *you* should be in prison. But for now…" Ryker releases him, dropping him back to his feet, but before Alex can regain his footing, Ryker jerks his fist back and throws it straight into Alex's face. Blood spurts at the same time Alex curses and fumbles, the impact from Ryker's punch wreaking havoc on his balance. He stumbles back against the wall, his hands barely catching him.

Blood drips from his face onto his pristine white button-down shirt. It's a lovely sight; the image of *his* blood staining his clothing and not mine, or Willow's. *Or Carmen's, or Mia's, or any of the others.* This is right. This is everything Alex deserves.

Fire scorches down my throat, and I dry-swallow past the sudden discomfort. I shift my feet, aligning my face away from the sight of Alex getting beat on.

Why can't I watch and revel in this?

With Ryker off him for now, Alex wipes at his face, further staining his sleeve red. He straightens against the wall, sliding back into a complete stance as his gaze focuses on the space behind Ryker —and onto me.

They widen before finding Natalie, who also isn't looking at the scene. His examination continues, spotting Tristan and Brent beside us, and his eyes ice over.

"What the fuck is this—some sort of revenge thing for years ago? Let them go." He jerks his chin toward Natalie and me, clearly believing we're here unwillingly.

Instead of answering, Tristan captures Natalie's hand in his own. "Wanna try it again, Miller?"

Alex's eyes bulge wider than ever and my spine heats—with pleasure or something else, I'm unsure.

"W-what is happening? Natalie. Teagan. Babe."

His voice, so gentle and caring, sweeps its way into my heart, making it crack. It's that word. It does something to me. Makes me care about the pain he's in.

He deserves this, my mind screams. He does. He deserves this and more.

But that tone yanks me back to before he first raped me. Back to when Alex Miller was a hot, popular jock in school, before he was discovered to be a wolf in sheep's clothing.

His eyes narrow and the warmth falls away, bringing back the man I've known for years. "You fucking whore. What did you tell them?"

It's not the first time he's called me such names. Besides, they're more justified now than ever.

Brent shoves past me, moving right between Ryker and Alex. "Don't fucking look at her, you monster."

Alex's eyes glint with mischief as he scans the newcomer in front of him. "My my, Brent Thorne. I see you finally found a treadmill." His eyes stop on Brent's face and the smile slowly slides from his mouth with his next realization. "You were the one visiting Teagan in the club."

"I was," Brent growls.

Alex's grin returns, this time more vicious than earlier. "Then you should know, the very next day, it was my cock she was riding. She has quite the warm, wet pussy—always wanting more. Nothing's ever enough for her. But I suppose you wouldn't know that, so you'll simply have to take my word for—"

Alex's words are cut off with a guttural roar followed by a loud crunching sound as Brent tackles Alex to the ground and throws fist after fist into Alex's face. Yelling, crunching, sputtering, and blood squirting—all sounds of pain. Sounds I'm familiar with, having heard them myself during Alex's rampages, but still, I look away.

Natalie moves closer, her nose scrunched over a twisted mouth and distraught eyes. It's obvious, despite all Alex has done, she doesn't want this to be the ending of a possible family.

"Brent!" Hawke throws himself toward the duo on the floor and begins yanking at Brent's arms, attempting to grab hold, even taking a few elbows to the chest himself. "Guys, you could help," he shouts over his shoulder.

Finally, someone in the tumble gives, and they fall apart from one another, clearing my sight to take in Alex's mangled face. What Ryker did was simply an appetizer to Brent's hits.

Hawke positions himself between Brent and Alex. "It's as if no one listened to me at all. No violence. No matter how tempting it is."

Tristan merely shrugs. "I still need to get a punch in for what he tried to do to Natalie."

Alex coughs, struggling to push himself into a sitting position. The blood dripping from his nose and onto the marble floor beneath looks all so wrong. From the corner of my eye, I see Tristan's hand go to his waistband where I know he tucked his gun before leaving.

"What the fuck is wrong with all of you?"

"I think you know, you bastard," Brent spits. "You're fucking done. Take us down below where you're keeping her and maybe, just *maybe*, I won't allow Tristan to have his turn."

"Try to stop me, bro."

But no one pays attention to Tristan, instead focusing on Alex as his head lolls to the side. "I wish I knew what you were talking about. Teagan, babe, what's going on?"

His direct address has everyone turning to me. The need to respond is too strong to stop. My eyes lock on his blood-red shirt, staring without looking him in the eyes as I whisper my reply, "You're hurting too many people, Alex. It's not just me anymore."

He shakes his head slowly. "I should have fucking known you'd turn on me. Why I never killed you and saved myself the headaches is beyond me."

Brent's guttural roar echoes through the ornate hallway once more, but before he can move an inch, Hawke is right there, throwing his own body in the path.

"This will be over quickly. Take us down below," Hawke commands, his hands up and pushing against Brent's shoulders.

"No idea what you're talking about." Alex continues his firm lie.

Ryker shrugs before reaching down and yanking him up by his shirt. Hawke takes his other side, the two of them keeping a secure grasp on his form.

"Fine, Teagan, lead us."

Unable to stop myself, I look toward Alex. Maybe seeking permission, or maybe attempting to prove to him I'm winning. That it's *me* who's tearing apart his empire.

"Sure, babe, take us. Take us below so I can show your new friends exactly how you and I play together."

His words spark a flinch to my nerves, but still managing to swallow my fears, I confidently stride through the house, the multiple hallways, until reaching the basement door near the back of the house. It's a well-practiced journey I've sadly completed too many times. I open the door, flick on the light, and immediately start down them, listening as everyone follows behind.

"Wait." There's a click and Tristan is pushing past me on the stairs, angling his gun into the basement as he takes the lead.

"No one's down here," I tell him.

"We don't know that."

"I do. Alex never lets any of the staff down here."

Tristan doesn't move aside and makes it to the bottom. His gun swings in every direction before being satisfied no one is here and lowers the barrel a fraction.

While he's doing that, I continue past him, leading them through the short hallway where Hell is located. We stop at the large metal door, and I stare at the number pad, recalling the familiar numbers Alex once had it coded for.

"Go ahead. Type it in. It's the same code," Alex states.

He never changed it. My fingers dance over the buttons. 1-1-1-4.

November 14th.

The day Alex asked me out.

He claims it's his favourite day.

After a second, the door's unlocking system sounds. Various clinks, clanks, and groans before I'm able to push the large metal door open. Once again, Tristan nudges me out of the way, his gun poised in the air for any possible threats.

"There's no point," I murmur.

The only soul down here is too weak to even stand, let alone fight. Again, Tristan doesn't listen to me and angles his gun, but I remain quiet. Brent moves up beside me and his hand brushes mine, warm compared to the chill working its way through my bones. We follow behind Tristan, with Hawke and Ryker clutching Alex behind us and Natalie taking up the rear.

The sight isn't new to me. The large glass box, nor the figure curled up in the corner of it, shivering. The blood all over her body has dried and caked into her hair.

A collective gasp fills the area, followed by Alex's dark chuckle.

From beside me, Brent whispers, "Holy fuck."

Twenty-Four

BRENT

IT'S A DEN OF DEPRAVITY. Teagan's description left out a fuck ton.

All sorts of paraphernalia hang on the wall. Knives, rope, tape, hooks, things I can't even identify. Most of them are stained red, *that* I can tell from this distance. But the most horrifying thing is the glass cage in the centre of the room.

And the woman curled up inside it.

She looks up at the sound of our entrance, her fuzzy green eyes bouncing amongst all of us. A normal girl would fear the sight of more people, but it's as if she couldn't care less. Her head lowers back to the glass floor.

"Shit." The curse slips out easily, alongside the realization she's not fearing us because Miller's obviously destroyed any sense of self-preservation.

"Hold him," I hear Hawke mutter to Ryker. From his pocket, he pulls his cell and begins snapping photos of the entire room, zooming in on the girl specifically. "This is fucked."

"One person's perspective," Alex comments while in Ryker's unyielding grip.

I glance over, noting the tight expression on Alex's face. He's planning, calculating, with eyes that skim us all. I know him well enough to see he's close to snapping. Hawke is a moron for leaving Ryker alone with him. Behind them, Natalie's basically staring at her hands or anywhere that isn't this room.

"How do we get inside?" I ask, directing my question at Teagan.

She glances at Alex instead.

I share the fourth *what the fuck* look with Ryker. This isn't the first time since arriving she's looked to Alex for approval, and I'm now waiting for something bad to happen. Something Teagan hasn't told us yet. I inch myself closer to her side, so I can react quicker if necessary.

"Go ahead and show them. Unlock it, babe."

And why does she know all these codes?

Because she's been here for years, idiot.

My body vibrates with overwhelming rage as she approaches the cage, her hand going to a keypad.

"It's coded," she says before touching the corner of the panel. It lights up the number pad, and she clicks the same 1-1-1-4 as before. A number clearly meaning something to Alex.

After a second, the door falls open and Teagan takes a hesitant step forward. I let her, remaining outside the cage as she slowly approaches the girl, her hand held out.

"Willow."

Willow. It's exactly what the girl looks like too. She's thin as hell, likely from starvation, with the palest blonde hair I've ever seen falling on either side of her naked body in a curtain, as if to hide herself from the world.

She doesn't move. Not when the door opens or when Teagan approaches her. I shoot a quick look toward Hawke, coming up beside me, ready to intervene. In his gaze, I see my own thoughts reflected. Teagan needs to be the one to save Willow.

"Teagan," Alex purrs, whipping everyone's attention toward him. "Babe, look at me."

He continues to refer to her by that disgusting pet name and I wish I could rip his tongue out for using it. It's familiar. Miller shouldn't have *ever* been familiar with her.

She stops by the girl before looking through the glass at him. Something shifts in her gaze, and I wish I could spot it in that instance, rather than when it's a moment too late. Gone is the strong-minded Teagan from Hawke's basement. Gone is my broken and sad Cherry-Girl. In her place is whatever twisted version of her Alex generated over the years.

His next words change everything.

"Kill her."

I freeze. As does Tristan, who pivots his gun back and forth between the cage and Alex.

The only person who doesn't is Teagan.

She lunges forward, a battle cry flying from her mouth. She's barely moved an inch before Hawke shoves me into the cage behind her.

"Brent, stop her! She's fucking conditioned!"

Conditioned. Conditioned. Conditioned. No matter how many times I repeat the word, it means nothing to me. Wait—like psychological conditioning?

I throw myself at Teagan in time for her to wrap her hands around the girl's throat. I have no training whatsoever, and it's Tristan who should be in here, but instinct drives me to break Teagan's grasp. I push my own hands down, using force on the insides of her elbows. Her hands jerk away and in the same flurry of movement, I circle her wrists before yanking them behind her back. With the hold I have her in, I back us both away from the panting girl on the floor.

Hawke slides past us, crouching by the girl. Her eyes are dance around, a confused dip between her brows, but finally, she pinpoints her attention onto Hawke.

I'm not sure what happens next, but suddenly, her arms loop Hawke's neck. He mutters something in her ear before standing, keeping the girl cradled to his chest.

"No!"

Natalie's piercing screech flies from beyond the glass cage and Hawke and I spin to see the next chapter of this horror story.

Ryker is on the ground, groaning, while his hands clutch at a wound in his thigh. Blood is seeping from between his fingers. Behind him, Alex has his arm tight to Natalie's neck, a knife poised in front.

Where the fuck did he get a knife?

"Drop the gun," he demands to Tristan.

I glance at Teagan in my arms, her eyes staring blankly at my shirt. I need to release her to help, but I can't let her go.

Hawke spots the indecision in my gaze and shakes his head. "Don't. We can't leave them alone now that we have them."

Alex nudges his chin at us. "Out here where I can watch you both."

Right now, he has all the power and control. If we don't listen, it'll be Natalie who pays, and we'll lose Tristan when he goes insane.

I start toward the cage's entrance, my eyes landing on Tristan. The poor fucker's shaking. His arms quiver and I spot his internal conflict. It's taking everything he has not to lunge for Alex, but to do so would be risking Natalie's life, and Tristan would kill himself before allowing that to happen. He's forcing years of training aside for love.

Hawke keeps close to my back, pulling some of my attention away. He murmurs, "Reach into my back pocket. Click send."

Then he cuts in front of me, exiting the glass cage first, giving me easier access to the phone peeking out from his jeans pocket.

Knowing Alex is still intently watching us, I angle Teagan's body in a way that my arm can slip between us, and I pull out Hawke's phone, spotting the text message pre-typed out but unable to read it.

I tap *send*.

Natalie's gasp distracts the room for a moment, and I slip his phone back into its place.

"Alex." True fear rings as her nails scratch at her brother's arms.

Miller ignores her and nods toward Tristan. "I said, gun down. Kick it over here. You have five seconds before my blade is coated in her blood."

"Alex," Natalie tries again.

Tristan's gaze cuts to me as I leave the cage before shifting to Ryker, who's still kneeling on the ground, watching the scene from his frozen state. He repositions his legs, and I spot the strain on his face as he attempts to stand again. If he was strong enough to attack, this wouldn't be a concern.

Ryker's movement pulls Alex's attention to him. "Stay down, dog. Don't move." To enforce his words, the blade digs into Natalie's skin and red beads on the tip.

Tristan growls, instinct driving him forward a step, his gun cocked and locked on Alex's forehead.

Do it. One click, and the fucker's gone.

Acceptance passes through his gaze. He won't risk Natalie's life. He stops moving, only to begin crouching, the gun slowly lowering until the barrel is aimed at the ground.

Looking at Teagan, slumped against my chest, seemingly not present any longer, I get it. I'm not sure if I would take such a gamble either.

"Brother..." Natalie weakly appeals.

"It's too late for that, Nat. You chose your side.

The gun dropping against the cement flooring makes a painfully loud clang. It echoes through the room, a noise breaking through the discomforting stuffiness of the room.

"There. Now let her go."

Instead, Alex's arm tightens around her shoulders, and he nudges his chin at the gun. "Kick it over here first."

Tristan huffs, keeping his eyes on Natalie when he positions his foot to kick it.

Everything next happens in a flash. If I blinked at all, I'd miss it.

At the last second, his foot reangles itself so that it won't put the gun near Alex. I follow the trajectory through the corner of my eye, watching as his foot slides it forward and away from the group—

—and right into Ryker's waiting hand. Ryker grasps it, pivoting it at Alex, and pulls the trigger. The bullet whizzes and hits its mark in Alex's shin.

Alex cries out, his body jerking with the impact. The knife drops from his hand, and Natalie falls forward, lunging from her brother's arms straight into Tristan's, who grasps her tightly to his chest.

Alex's yell signals what happens next. A herd of men push through the doorway, dozens of guns positioned in the air as they circle the area, taking inventory of everyone before landing on Alex, now on the ground, blood seeping from his leg wound.

My arms tighten around Teagan, and I whisper in her ear, "It's over. You're free."

Twenty-Five

BRENT

PEOPLE ARE EVERYWHERE. The RCMP arrived on account of Hawke's perfectly-timed text message. They've taken control of the entire situation, quarantined the basement as a crime scene, and arrested Alex without question, exactly as Hawke said they would.

I don't know how the fucker did it, or what he's hiding from us, but I also don't care.

This is over.

Above the crowd, I spot Alex in the ambulance, handcuffed, while he gets his leg wrapped. Personally, I don't think the fucker should be getting medical assistance, and if he bleeds out, well, who really cares? It's not the way, apparently—something about human rights and all that. Officers line the ambulance, so I suppose it's all that matters.

Not too far from where Miller is, Ryker is also seated inside another ambulance, also getting his leg wrapped from where Alex stabbed him. His attention is locked on Miller, his eyes narrowed and lip curling, and I know he feels as I do about Alex getting treatment.

The paramedic attending Ryker mentioned it being a clean stab and it'll be a quick and easy healing process. I'm positive he's antici-pating the sympathy he'll receive from Elena.

"Where'd you learn to shoot like that?" I had asked him earlier, when they loaded him onto a stretcher.

He merely shrugged. "I didn't. Before today, I've never even held a gun."

Thank fuck he's a natural.

Beside his own ambulance, Tristan is fussing over Natalie. The nick on her neck stopped bleeding almost instantly, given its size, and by tomorrow, it'll be a minor scab. But Tristan doesn't care about any of that.

Over the crowd, I find the ambulance Willow is locked inside. It took her a while before she agreed to let go of Hawke. No doubt after the trauma she's survived, she latched onto the first sign of safety she's had in a long time.

"Sir, we need to get her checked out." A paramedic approaches, his kind, greying eyes settling on Teagan, who is still in my arms.

I haven't let her go and I refuse to. She doesn't want me to either, as her face hasn't left my chest. For a while, the only way I knew she was still alive is by the speedy pulse pressing against my skin.

I've whispered to her over and over, but there's no sign of recog-nition. Hawke believes her mind has gone to a different place. Once experiencing what Alex put her through—nearly murdering a person —her brain shut down.

All I know, the second we're home, I'm Googling the fuck out of conditioning.

Miller can rot in the depths of Hell. For everything he's ever done to her, to Willow, to anyone else, but somehow, hearing Hawke's words downstairs worsens the situation.

Conditioned. He's been fucking playing her for years. Training and designing her to be his little machine, ready for when he flips her switch.

In hindsight, her constant reactions and seeking his approval makes a ton of sense now. He made it so. Yet again, I hadn't seen what was right in front of me. I'm blind where she's concerned.

But now, she's safe. Safe and with me, and fuck if I ever let her go.

"Sir, we need to get her to the hospital."

"She's fine," I bark defensively and turn us, so she's away from his sight.

"Sir—"

"I got this." Hawke approaches, stepping between the paramedic and me, his hand landing on my shoulder.

"She's fine," I tell him, continuing to angle Teagan away.

"Brent," he starts, in a tone one would use to speak to a child, "she's gone through a lot and I'm sure she's never seen a doctor in all that time."

I shudder, the realization his words have weighing on my soul. I breathe in the scent of her bright red hair one final time before nodding. He's right. She needs this.

"I'll carry her," I tell the paramedic.

The man shrugs and leads me to the nearest empty ambulance, where I rest her on the gurney. Her eyes track me, almost unseeing as I lower myself out of the vehicle and to the ground. I'll tell Ryker where he can find me and then I'll head to the hospital with her.

Hawke, the annoyance he's been becoming, is right there, blocking my path. "She needs to go alone, man. Let the process take place."

My jaw tightens. If he gives me one more fucking order...

The threat I'm building in my head fades off as an RCMP officer immediately takes my place in the ambulance, pulling a set of cuffs from his pocket. In a blink, one is strapped to her wrist, the other to the bed. Still, she doesn't move.

"Wait, what the—"

Doors slam shut in my face at the same time Hawke yanks on my arm, tugging me a few feet away.

"Hawke, what is happening?" My vision works to catch up in time for the ambulance's lights to flash and the wheels spin, pulling away from the area.

She's leaving me. Again.

No.

Without looking at him, I demand, "Hawke, why is she in handcuffs?"

From the corner of my eye, I spot his attention falling to his feet, guilt shadowing his face and I piece together the rest.

She's being arrested.

"No!" It might be stupid because I won't catch the ambulance, but still, my feet push into the dirt and I take off in a run, in the same direction the ambulance's lights are fading from.

Tristan, the fast fucker, due to his police training, catches me quickly, hopping in front of me to block my path as Hawke catches up, panting and coming to a stop. Assumingly, Tristan was observing from Natalie's ambulance.

"*Move*, Tristan. If this was Natalie, you'd do the same."

"This is *not* the same, Brent, and you know it," he growls. "Teagan is *sick*."

"She's not."

Hawke pushes between us. "Tristan's right. She's been conditioned. She needs a hospital, and then a therapist. Dude, we really have *no* idea what she's been through over the years and I'm starting to think she doesn't either. She needs therapy and deconditioning."

I hear the words he speaks, but I don't fucking want them. My mind denies them, unwilling to fathom the truths behind them. My Cherry-Girl is strong. Of course she's aware of what he's been doing to her; she's of sound mind and that's all there is to it.

"The cuffs..." My weak murmur fades, the same second the ambulance's lights finally do too, making her totally unreachable.

Hawke's next words slice down my spine. "She will be charged."

Blood roars in my ears, and I shove at his chest, forcing him backward. "You fucker, you told me she'd be viewed as a victim. I thought you have weight with the RCMP." Useless fucker.

Hawke straightens, deleting the space between us, his expression not angry but rather determined. "Listen to me. She will be. But right now, she's an accomplice, and for Alex to be rightly sentenced, we need to follow the rules." He lowers his arms, the fight also going away. "Alex will claim they've been together for years, and the hospital is about to find evidence of it. She won't deny it either. They will place a court order for his camera footage. She knows about the other women, so she'll have to admit it all. As of now, she'll be charged for not stepping forward but before you freak out, you need to let this happen. Going in guns blazing won't do you, her, or this case any favours." His hands land on my shoulders as his eyes stop on mine, showing me his seriousness. "You need to go home, shower, and sleep. Any doctor, psychologist, or otherwise will see she's in need of help. Let them give her that help. Therapy and deconditioning, and then the court will drop the charges because she'll be found she wasn't of sound mind." He sighs, glancing over his shoulder where the ambulance disappeared and then at the mansion beyond. "I know it sucks, but you'll need to wait a bit longer for her. Let the process happen."

The process. She's a process.

"Kill her."

I freeze. As does Tristan, who pivots his gun back and forth between the cage and Alex.

The only person who doesn't is Teagan.

She lunges forward, a battle cry flying from her mouth. She's barely moved an inch before Hawke shoves me into the cage behind her.

"Brent, stop her! She's fucking conditioned!"

Conditioned.

Hawke jerks his head back toward the crowds surrounding the mansion. Between officers, on the edge of the lot, Natalie stands, peering through the dim evening, watching us.

"Come on. It'll be a long night. I'm sorry."

"Don't be," I murmur, falling in line behind him as Tristan brings up the rear. "You saved us all with your brilliance."

As we make it back to Natalie and Ryker's sides, and Hawke disappears to go with Willow, I glance at the darkness beyond the crowd again.

Come home to me, Cherry-Girl.

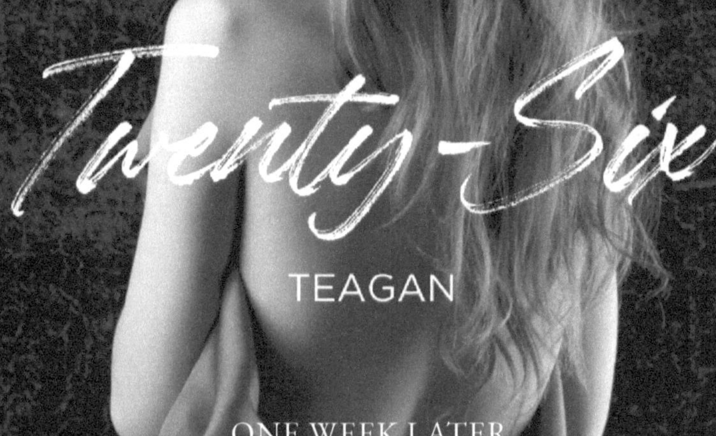

Twenty-Six

TEAGAN

ONE WEEK LATER

Cortville General Hospital, Mental Health Department

Week One

"NOT SURE WHY I'M HERE," I grumble, dropping onto the couch across from the phycologist. A damn psychologist. What a waste of an hour that would be better spent on someone who actually needs help.

"Don't you?" She raises a perfectly arched brow. In fact, everything about this woman is perfect, right down to her pink pantsuit and caramel, curled hair. It's obvious she's never been held captive. "Do you remember the events of the other day?"

"They're impossible to forget." They plague my mind every hour of the day. The surrealness in it all, that Alex got carted away. Temporarily, of course, because he'll return. Men with his money are never bogged down by the system for long.

"I don't normally jump right into the heavy, Teagan. I do prefer we get to know one another first, but I get the sense you're not a

165

person who enjoys dragging things on, so why don't you tell me about your past couple weeks."

"What's there to talk about?" My gaze lands on my interwoven hands on my lap, watching as the fingers clench around one another. "Everything was fine, and then an old friend found me again and insisted on knowing the entire truth. He broke the walls I've managed to keep erected for years, and by doing so, freed me."

"You don't sound very thankful."

"Again, everything was fine."

"Was it?"

Her pen pauses on the paper, awaiting my response, and for some reason, it sends a flush of anger down my spine. *Enough.* I lean forward so she can identify how serious I am with my next words.

"I know why I'm in here. Doctors are labelling me as a case you need to fix, but I'll warn you now... I. Am. Fine. I am wholly aware of what Alex did, and I hate him for it. I realize the courts will see me as guilty for hiding his secrets. So many times I wished I could fix it. But I'm also aware talking about the past won't solve anything. Alex Miller wins—always has and always will, so there's no point in you attempting to *fix* me."

When I lean back against the couch again, her pen begins writing again, but she says nothing.

I stand up and exit the room.

Week Two

"YOU'RE BACK."

I glare at the psychologist. She titles herself as a doctor, but I call her my nuisance because, apparently, according to the medical doctors, this *journey*, as they referred to it, is mandatory.

"Obviously. Seems no one will let me out of this place until I'm fixed."

"Hm." Her lips purse. "Which parts of you require fixing?"

I level my stare. She's seriously asking me this? "I already told you how I feel about myself. I'm fine."

Her attention leaves me for a moment to write something on her pad. I shift an inch, body tingling with the discomforting need to move. Coming here is one thing, but I'm starting to realize I hate the staring. The silent judging, but worse—the fake knowledge of what I've been living with. She believes she can sympathize, empathize, and counsel me, but there's no way for her to completely grasp my case.

"Your friend. The one who found you, to use your own words, what is his name?"

My stomach twists with her question. Of-fucking-course she's going here. "Brent."

"Tell me about him."

"Why?"

"Because based on reports and the way your face flushed red, it's clear you care for this friend. I want to discuss him because I feel he's a huge key to your healing."

"Whatever." I roll my eyes at yet another assumption she's making. "He's a friend from high school. Or, I suppose a few grades before that is when we first met. He was my safe space back then."

"In what ways?"

"I don't know..." My voice lowers with the weight of the past boring down on my throat. "I guess, in all the ways a person can be for one another. He knew everything about me, knew how to make me smile. I-I was a foster kid. Grew up in a few different homes and it was my final placement when I met Brent."

Her eyes flash with sympathy, and I look away, detesting it. Instead, I focus on a spot on the floor, picturing Brent's face.

"They never abused me or anything like that. Not enough for the system to place me elsewhere, but it was the discomfort of being there. I was a nuisance, and they treated me as such. I mostly remained in my room when I was there. Meeting Brent..." I bite down on my lip, testing my next words with a whisper. "He made it all worth it, I suppose. As much as I hated going home, I knew it'd be okay because the very next morning, I would see him again. He'd walk me home, and often pick me up in the morning to go to school together. He constantly texted me, ensuring I was never completely alone. Despite everything, he made me not want to run away."

I stop talking, and the silence in the room is stuffy, but I'm thankful for it too. As if knowing my needs, she's providing a processing moment.

And another moment.

And another.

Until finally, it's I who breaks it. "When I dated Alex, and the relationship got bad, I didn't tell Brent. At first, Alex wanted to keep our relationship on the down-low and I didn't risk it, even to tell Brent. It sucked, but it was what it was, you know?" I glance toward her again.

"Brent seems to be your safety net. It must have been hard to keep your relationship hidden from him."

"Yeah."

"Do you love him?"

"He's my best friend, so of course I do."

She shakes her head. "That's not what I'm asking. Do you love him?"

Always.

Week Three

"DR. LAZ," I greet, claiming my spot on the couch across from her. In the past week, I've taken care to learn her name and use it.

This thing we do weekly is still annoyingly stupid and pointless, since it won't change the past, but after last week and admitting my true feelings regarding Brent, and even accepting the benefits of his re-emergence in my life, I suppose there's something to this entire thing.

"You look at peace," she states. "On a scale of zero, being the lowest, and ten, being the highest, how do you feel overall?"

Good question. I mean, I want to leave, but the doctors are insisting I stay for my "mental well-being" but it's less horrible now. I suppose, the hospital is quiet and even a bit comfortable. For now, I'm safe.

Safety only lasts so long, of course. Once I'm freed, though, it's only a matter of time before Alex also gets himself out of the system —if he hasn't already—and returns for me.

"A five," I whisper.

"So we're halfway there. But Teagan, none of this goes away until we speak about Alex Miller and what he put you through."

My walls rebuild. I feel them, feel the stiff barrier shouldering its way through any of the peace I may have found thus far. Feel how the stone is cold and unwelcoming, and I cross my arms and lean further away, hiding behind that very wall.

"Tell me about your high school experience with Alex and why you remained with him through it."

Easy. "Fear. He paid off my foster family, so who else would have believed me?"

"Your friends."

"Sure, but who could have done something about it? Case-workers turn a blind eye once the child is in a home, and at that point, I was at the bottom of their priority list, since I was nearly of age and wouldn't be the system's problem for much longer. I was alone, so I kept it all inside. Is there something wrong with that?"

She tilts her head, gazing with those usual knowing eyes. "It was a defence mechanism. And yes, recalling the past won't change anything, so whether I believe it was a wrong method or not is irrelevant, but I wonder, in your opinion, do *you* feel there was something wrong with how you handled it?"

Um. I stare at her, mouth parting as no words come out. "I mean... I understand it might not have been the best method, but it got me through the past."

"Until you ran. Tell me about that."

I blow out a breath, recalling the night of the party. "Not much to tell. When the ambulance arrived and news travelled that it was Alex who was beat up, I saw a chance and took it. Before that, I felt trapped. Alex wouldn't have ever let me go, but for a while, I knew he couldn't stop me, so I used the chance to get as far away from him as possible."

"Last session you stated you didn't run from your family because you didn't wish to leave Brent behind."

The unspoken question is obvious. "I guess rape is different." I shrug. "Before Alex, I was a kid still. But being raped ages you. Now, it wasn't the fact that I wasn't getting warm hugs and kind words from the family who took me in. It was my safety." *My life.*

"You knew you were in danger."

"I'd be an idiot not to know that." My eyes roll. "So, I ran."

"Away," she finishes. "And still not toward your friends."

I groan, sensing how she's circled back around. "Because they couldn't do anything. Brent couldn't help me."

"But you didn't try." Dr. Laz glances at the notepad on her lap. "Also, it was a classmate of yours who put Mr. Miller in the hospital, no?"

"Well, sure. But punching and protecting are two different things."

"Are they?" This time, her head tilts the other way. "Or do you perceive them as two different items and it's that perception urging you to constantly run away?"

I scoff, shaking my head. "I don't know what you're talking about. I ran once."

"You ran from your family by using Brent as a safety net. You ran from Alex when sensing danger. You ran from Brent when he returned and proved to be a threat to the fake sense of security you've built around yourself these past few years. You ran from your friends when they tried to help you. You're running from therapy because of the truth it'll dredge up." She pauses, rolling her lips. "Those examples may not all include the act of physically running away, but you're still escaping. Mentally and emotionally, you're running."

Damn.

Week Four

"HOW DO YOU FEEL THIS WEEK?"

I shrug.

"Hm," she murmurs softly. "I sense you're back to the place you were in our first session. Defensive, defiant, not wanting to speak. Is that because you're still running, Teagan? You're running from reality now. One day, you'll be tired of it."

"What do you know?"

"I know Alex somehow conditioned you to his side, and every-thing he's done to you has modified the girl who should be out living her life."

"Conditioned?" Such a strange word.

She tips her head to the side. "Do you know what it means?" When I shake my head, she lays down her pad and pen. "I'll phrase it like this, Teagan. Reports state that you tried to strangle a girl. The one he had in captivity. Correct?"

"N—" I shut off my own denial, pausing at her strange question. Of course I didn't try to strangle Willow. That's not me; that evilness was all Alex. I wouldn't do that. "I..." My words trail off as I refocus on her previous words.

They're too exact. Too... *true.* I've never been close enough to Willow to—

In my mind, there's flashes of blonde hair covering a body lying on the cage's floor. Her body isn't moving and yet she's aware of her surroundings. With Brent by my side, I approach her.

"Kill her."

No... That's not real. It's not real. It can't be.

"I..." I stop because my mind is lying to me.

I lunge, hands aimed right for Willow's throat.

"No." The word is whispered, barely there, and yet so heavy in the room. "No. I-I didn't... Oh, my God."

I did.

"Wh-what—How?"

"What's in your head, Teagan?" Dr. Laz asks instead.

"What isn't in my head? I don't... How do I not remember doing that?"

Dr. Laz looks down, and for the first time since meeting her, she appears uncomfortable. "Mr. Miller conditioned you, warping your mind to view him as your master and you the subject, so that you'd obey any command he gives you. The order to kill was likely too much for your mind, and you blocked it out. Unfortunately, this is the outcome of trauma counselling. The realizations are difficult."

Difficult. That's an understatement.

I tried to kill Willow.

I choke. The suffocating air leaves me breathless, unable to breathe through the comprehension.

And then I cry. Hot, angry tears.

For me.

For Willow.

Week Five

"BABE, LOOK AT ME."

Babe.

Babe.

"Babe. That's the word."

I blink, returning from the memory trip Dr. Laz suggested I take. The trip in which I relive every single positive moment between Alex and me. She believes something is buried there.

"Babe," I repeat. "I hated the name, but every time he used it, I felt... *off*. For example, when Ryker hit him a few weeks ago, he referred to me by name and I felt this random hatred for the pain they were bringing him. As though I wanted to help him."

Dr. Laz scribbles furiously across her paper, nodding. "Good, Teagan. This is good. That word is a trigger for you then, so next, we need to unlink the meaning he's spent years creating."

"Undoing years of work doesn't sound easy."

She glances up, seriousness within her gaze. "It won't be."

THREE WEEKS LATER

CONDITIONED.

Trauma therapy.

Deconditioning.

All terms I hadn't known existed before eight weeks ago, but now they've become an integral part of my life. They *changed* my life. Returned a sense of identity back to me; a sense I haven't had since the moment I met Alex.

Alex knew what he was doing because he's a fucking mastermind. A mastermind who tried to make me *murder* an innocent woman. Before the realization in Dr. Laz's office, I never would have believed it'd be possible for me to do that to another, but now, I see it still is. It is, because if there's ever a person I'd willingly kill, it would be him.

He took my life from me. Dr. Laz forced me to realize so much. All the facts, all his preferences I've long locked away as being typical or even as a way to deal with them in order to remain alive. All of it, he twisted my mind to cause it all to seem normal.

None of this was normal. Not since the moment I fell into his trap. The moment I hid so much from the world, from myself, hiding away from the truth, allowing it to continue as if it was normal.

I should have continued to fight. He should have never won.

The worst part: I believed I knew everything going on, but was unaware of so much.

I've already heard how therapy can be transformative, but being a patient in Cortville's General Hospital's mental health department was more than that. Transformative is a small description for what it's done for me, and now they've deemed me "healed," I'm free to return home. Healed, as in, trauma is an ongoing battle I'll be dealing with for a long time still to come.

"Ready?"

The voice yanks me from my reflections, and I meet the observing eyes of a member of the hospital staff in the vehicle's rearview mirror. Upon being released, he's driven me downtown to the local police station. With me cleared to go home, I need to deal with what comes after.

It's time to face my past, present, and future.

"Thanks," I say, instead of replying to his question and slide from the vehicle, soaking in the warm breezy air. The hospital allowed me outside almost whenever I wanted, but the air by the hospital was still stagnant and sickly.

Here, it smells like freedom. Familiarity. City smog and the noises that accompany it—honking, yelling, cars speeding to and from.

It all goes away the moment I yank open the police department's front doors and step into the foyer. Behind the front desk, typing away furiously at a computer, is a uniformed woman. The bell chimes, announcing my entrance, and she barely glances from her screen to heed me any attention—just enough to say she looked—but quickly does a double take. Her eyes widen in recognition, and I wish I could shrivel into myself. I may have been hidden away from the world, but it's clear the world continued to spin.

In the past few weeks, no one has come to visit me. If they've tried, I was never told. I'd like to say the hospital banned visitors, but honestly, for all I know, they got what they needed from me—used me exactly as everyone else has ever done in my life—and abandoned me.

I shouldn't care, but the simple thought burns at the edges of my chest. Luckily, I have bigger issues to deal with than to worry about no visitors.

"Hi," I approach, swallowing down my discomfort, "I'm here for—"

She leaps to her feet, the keyboard banging against the desk with the force she uses to stand and rush to the other side of the desk—toward me. "Miss Faber, please come with me. I have your lawyer waiting in an interview room."

My lawyer?

Who do I know that is a—Hawke?

The woman leads me down the white hallway and around the corner. Thankfully, it must be the back halls or something since we pass no other officers on our way. At the end of her short path, she gestures to a door, one in a line of three, and I step by her, opening it. My hand, cold on the metal knob, quivers with curiosity of what's inside.

I don't shut the door, but she must have, since the soft click echoes through the room, loud against the silence as my eyes lock on the newcomer.

Hawke sits upright in his chair, his suit-covered arms resting lightly on the metal table between him and me. His fingers interlock overtop a brown folder. The suit is prim, matched by a dark tie, giving him a perfectly respectable look. His hair is pushed back, bangs tucked behind his ears, giving way to his piercing-free face.

"You're a sight for sore eyes. How are you, Teagan?"

I don't respond until I'm seated comfortably in the chair across from him. Or, as comfortable as I can manage with a stiff spine and chilling fears working their way through my body. Fear for the next steps. The big steps. The ones that will change everything.

"Alive." My eyes bounce around the basic room. Plain walls, and a single table with two chairs occupied by him and me. "What is this?"

"This," his hand shifts to the side until the folder is bared to our sight, "is good news. A pardon." He opens the cover of the file folder and pushes the first paper across the metal table toward me.

My eyes scan the document, not picking up on any familiar words. Once, then twice, I read it, mind still as blank as the first time as to what I'm reading.

"Provided you testify against Miller, the court will drop the charges against you. You'll be a free woman."

I wasn't even in the hospital for a day before RCMP officers bombarded me with questions and charges, even placing an officer at my door, before the doctors forced them out, claiming nothing they got from me would count, given the mental state they deemed me in.

But also, I'm not stupid. I know how the world turns. Since I've been keeping Alex's treachery a secret for years, I'm valuable.

"Seriously?"

"Seriously," he affirms. "The psychologist's reports wiped away the proof. Between fearing for your life, and his conditioning, you couldn't turn on him. Therefore, not your fault."

My brows lift, eyes moving from the document. "But I did. To you guys."

He shrugs, leaning back in his chair and becoming the man I met months ago. "A fact I kept amongst the group." Hawke's attention falls to the paper in my grip. "But, Teagan, do you understand what the terms are? If you sign this, you must testify against him or else the pardon is voided. And you can't leave the area until after the trial."

"I always planned on testifying."

"Think about what it means. I know how you felt previously."

Previously, before I knew everything Alex truly did; the way he played with my mind.

"I *have* been. For eight weeks." It'll mean seeing Alex again, sitting in a courtroom while I spill his dirty secrets. The thing I look forward to most is staring into Alex's cold, dead eyes as I lay out the gritty details of what he did to me, to every woman he's dragged down there, all the way back to the beginning of us in high school and watch him be condemned for his heinous acts.

I sure as fucking hope he gets ass raped over and over in prison because the bastard deserves nothing less.

That compassion—the bit of fear I felt when I led Hawke and the others down to the basement, all while knowing what it would mean for Alex—is *long* gone. Vanished, buried, to never ever be resurrected. I see now, thanks to Dr. Lax, why I felt it in the first place.

Babe. It was all in a single word. A simple word he made hold so much power.

"Well then," his fingers disappear into the front pocket of his blazer, and he pulls out a metal pen, "sign on the line."

I take the pen, noting the rich weight of it in my hand. It's a physical reminder of the weight of my decision. I grasp it, tightening my grip before pushing the smooth ballpoint onto the document, on the line he indicated.

Alex, you deserve this signature.

My pen scratches on the paper, and before long, I pull away, leaving my name in permanent black ink, something that not even Alex will be able to get away from. I've tattooed the document, and now the only thing remaining is to watch him burn.

"Where is he?"

"In holding until his hearing."

"Which is when?"

"Soon."

I glance away, locking my attention on the wall behind his head. It's all over, and yet only just beginning too.

"Thank you," I whisper after a long second. Emotion clogs my throat, and my eyes begin to burn. "Thank you for helping me."

"*You* helped *us*." He shuts the folder once more, sliding it from the table and into a bag at his feet. "Willow would still be there if it wasn't for your help."

Instantly, tears prick at my eyes and I look away. No matter how many times my actions to protect her have been validated, it's never been enough. I reassured Dr. Laz I'm over it, but the truth it, I'm not. The rapes, the kidnapping, the secrets are all one thing, but forcing me to kill another human is unspeakable. An act I'll *never* pretend to forgive him for, or to forget. I certainly won't forgive myself. But I do force my next question through my lips.

"H-how is she?"

"She's... coming along." His eyes skirt to the door, and he shifts. "She's at my house."

"And everyone else?" I can't help but ask.

Faces bombard my vision. So many people who pushed their way into my life, only to discard me when it mattered—when I gave them Alex. No one came to visit me. Not even—

Not that I blame him.

"Thanks," I say instead, having nothing else to ask.

He peers at me, his bright blues alarmingly alert. "What's next for you, Teagan?"

What's next? It's a question doctors have been asking me on the daily for a week. Because I lived through such a time in my life, there must be an after. Dr. Laz consistently reminded me how my life was orchestrated by one man, but with me gaining control again, it's mine to do with as I see fit.

I tell Hawke what I've been telling all of them—the lie I feed anyone who asks.

"I'm not sure."

I am sure though. I know what's next.

I'm leaving after the trial.

Perhaps it's dramatic. I certainly never admitted it to Dr. Laz because I know how she'd react based on her previous conclusions.

"Those examples may not all include the act of physically running away, but you're still escaping. Mentally and emotionally, you're running."

I certainly am. Because this entire area of the world is a problem. Deconditioned or not; having my trauma "managed" or otherwise doesn't change the memories this horrible region holds for me. Cortville is where I lived my lie. Newton is where it began. And Bridgetown, where Elena and everyone else lives, is entirely too close to this place—to the past. So my response is to leave.

Dr. Laz recommended starting fresh and creating a new identity for myself. Of course, she didn't mean a literal new identity, but I'm only using her words. I'll move, start over, and become someone other than Teagan Faber, babe, and Cherry—names and identities I've been masking myself in for longer than I care to admit.

But if I tell Hawke this, I have no doubt in my mind that he'll rush to Elena and inform her. And if he tells Elena, then he'll also tell *him* and they'll insist I stay, because it's the thing they believe I should be doing.

Everyone thinks they know what's best for me.

Maybe I'll go north, and find myself camping in winter woods, living in a log cabin. Or south, into another country, until I reach sunny temperatures. Or I'll hop on a plane and explore European countries. I can do anything now. Go anywhere and be anyone, and pretend these last few years were a nightmare and nothing more.

"Well," Hawke starts, "I suppose you have time to figure it out.

For now," he stands, pulling up his briefcase with him, "want a ride home? Your apartment was searched in your absence but you still have access to it for the time being."

Seeing as I have no way other than walking, since my wallet never made its way to the hospital with me, I say, "Please."

Hawke maneuvers us through the halls, the same way I came earlier—through the back hallway away from the rest of the force. We enter the front foyer again, where the female officer from earlier smiles and waves goodbye.

He then leads me a short ways away from the station and to the shiny black car. I pause as he opens the door, staring at the back seat through the window and recalling how, only a few weeks ago, I sat in the middle section of the bench and pretended I wasn't betraying the only life I knew.

I step inside the vehicle, encasing myself in the scent of expensive leather. A moment later, Hawke joins me and promptly starts the car, pulling away from the station. I watch out the window as we pass the building, thinking everything it represents.

Both the bad and the good.

After a long silent moment, he speaks. "You haven't asked me about a certain person."

I haven't because mentioning him—Brent—will mean I need to face what I'm ignoring.

The uncertainty of Brent's involvement.

Before Alex's arrest, he claimed to be angry about how my life was stolen from me, and that he wasn't there for me, but that could have been a scheme to encourage my words. If anything he said or did was real, then he'll fight me to stay, and I refuse to deal with that drama.

Dr. Laz believes I need to face my past, including Brent. She made me dredge up running away as a teenager and how that made me feel. What abandoning my best friend—friends, actually—did. It doesn't matter how leaving Brent behind made me feel back then, because the person I was then isn't who I am now. Therefore, only the present matters. And presently, my feelings toward him will not change.

Do I care about Brent? Obviously. But I'm not acting upon it. Brent's always had the whole knight-in-shining-armour thing going for him, and he'll continue with that trait until the day he dies.

He won't view me as Teagan. He'll view me as a trauma patient and handle me with rubber gloves constantly. I can't deal with it; I refuse to do so because it'll drag him down.

Brent's been successful in these past few years without me. He's close to graduation, and once finishing school, no doubt he'll jump onto a lovely, paved path. It's who he is. Unlike me, Brent lived in the picture-perfect house. The one with two loving parents and a white picket fence surrounding a house that always had baked goods wafting from the window.

"Teagan?"

I shrug. "Doesn't matter. Won't change anything."

Hawke grimaces, glancing at me. "You don't believe that."

Another person telling me what to do. I've had enough of that to last me a lifetime.

"I do." I cross my arms and angle my body away from him.

"He tried multiple times to visit you, you know," he comments. "The hospital staff finally banned him from the property since he was bothering them. He went nuts being unable to get to you."

My reflection in the window shows a desolate expression. So he tried.

"Then he left."

"Left?" I squeak. "He's gone? Gone-gone?"

"Gone-gone," Hawke affirms, his eyes cutting to me. "Once the hospital banned him, he took off. Said he needed to go. No matter how many times any of us have messaged him, he hasn't responded."

Somehow, I don't know what to feel. Pleased he's not around so when I leave post-trial, he won't be here, but maybe also a bit sad he's not. Like some part of me wanted to see him one final time. Electricity courses through my nerves, sparking them with this strange feeling.

"Huh," is what my mouth manages to form. It's enough for Hawke to focus on the road as he finishes the route to my house.

He parks and I stare at the familiar white door. A door Alex paid for. Inside is an apartment he paid for. Everything in my life was from him. The only money I wrangled from stripping were my tips. Alex allowed me to keep those for myself.

Hawke leans against the console after I stand from his car. "I'll be in touch with the court date. We're hoping to get it all wrapped up soon. Until then," he reaches into his pocket and pulls out a small card, tossing it on the passenger seat I vacated, "my number is on this. If you need anything, please reach out."

I take it, slipping it into the pocket of the sweatpants the hospital gave me. "Thanks, Hawke. For everything."

"Good luck, Teagan."

This time, I won't need luck because I'll be forging my own path.

Twenty-Eight

BRENT

SIX WEEKS AGO

"I'M HERE TO SEE A PATIENT."

The elderly white-haired man peers up behind spectacles as he examines my frazzled appearance. Frazzled because I haven't changed my clothes in the day it's been since Teagan was taken from me.

"Name of the patient?"

"Teagan Faber."

He remains silent as he twists toward his screen and types something into the computer. The longest moment passes in which he only hums and *ahhs*. My skin itches, body bouncing on the balls of my feet until finally—

"I'm sorry, she's not cleared for visitors."

Frustration burns a fiery path through my nerves, but I understand, so I back away from the desk, barely throwing a muttered, "Thanks," over my shoulder before stalking from the hospital.

She was admitted yesterday, and Hawke said she'll be treated as a criminal for a while, which means guarded. I'll give it a few days and try again.

DAYS PASS and I'm turned away every single time. No one seems to have a date for when she'll be allowed visitors. Better yet, they fucking *ban* me from the premises. Apparently I'm annoying too many of the staff.

So when I stomp back outside, I know I look exactly as I feel when Tristan pushes himself off the hood of his cruiser.

"No luck?" His lips fold down in a frown.

A fucking *frown* is his sign of sympathy. If it was Natalie in there, he'd be throwing every curse word invented until someone let him inside.

"No," I growl. "They banned me."

"Well, dude," his arms spread wide and his tone drops, telling me what he's doing before he even does it, "cop perspective here, and I realize it's not what you want, but if she's actually doing that bad, they need to ensure her brain is working again before they release her. Add on the criminal charges... Brent, she's not a typical patient."

My hands form into fists, the closest I'll manage to actually taking a swing at him as my nerves crave to do. I *know* he speaks the truth. I *know* he's trying to be straight with me and give me all the facts, but it doesn't stop me from hating him for it.

I turn back to face the looming building, scanning the windows all the way to the top. Behind one of those thin panes of glass is my girl. *My* girl, who's being kept from me.

I can't go home. I won't handle it. Sitting in my apartment, attending classes as though everything is normal again—like we didn't take down a psychopath who returned Cherry-Girl to where she belongs—it's too much. Too much routine for my sanity to accept.

I need out of here.

The thought is sudden, but the simple consideration instantly eases my tightened muscles.

I focus on the car Tristan leans against, and then the hospital before demanding, "Take me to a car rental place. I'm leaving."

One Week Later

ELENA

Where are you?

RYKER

Come home. Stop running away, drama queen.

TRISTAN

Dude, I regret dropping you off at all. Didn't realize you'd be ignoring us.

HAWKE

Running away isn't helping anything. Come home and wait it out with the rest of us. Brent, I'm working on getting her charges dropped and so far it's looking good.

NATALIE

We miss you.

Two Weeks Later

ELENA

I swear, Brent, you drive me nuts. I'm worried about you. I do care about you, you know.

Hawke doesn't want us to say anything, but the charges will be dropped. He got confirmation. Come home. Maybe you can visit.

Tristan and I tried to visit. No go.

I have news. I refuse to text it to you. Come home and we can talk like normal people. It's news you'll want.

ON AND ON IT GOES, for nearly eight weeks. I ignore every one of them and drive without a destination in mind. Emails from professors go unanswered, calls and texts from the group ignored; I shut the world off in favour of the open road.

Is this how Teagan felt running from Alex? It's quite freeing, to have no destination in mind, other than simply getting away.

Of course she didn't feel like this. She was terrified, looking over her shoulder at every turn. She's never mentioned *how* she made it to the other side of the country, and I consider all the sketchy situations she may have put herself in.

My hands tighten around the wheel until my knuckles bloom white.

Hey. I know you haven't answered any of us, but I hope you're reading them. You'll want this news. She's being released in three days.

Twenty-Nine

TEAGAN

THE MOMENT my feet pass my apartment's doorway, I feel it. The prickling air sending tingles down my spine. Must be the feel of freedom. It's strange, having never had it before.

I flick on the hallway light and toe off the cheap Crocs the hospital gave me to get home in before continuing down the hall and into my darkened living room. The last time I was here, I was still under Alex's ownership. So much has changed in a short time. So much, my brain still is working to keep up. Any moment now, my phone would normally be ringing with a message from him, demanding I be some place or the other, available for him to prance around and appear as the nice guy, before he goes home and rapes a helpless woman.

The simple thought—the simple *fact*—the *truth*—has my blood roaring until it fills my ears. I stop short of the room, halting by a bare wall. I'm not a violent person, but suddenly, I want to be one.

I want to *kill* Alex for what he's taken from me.

My life. Brent. Elena. My high school graduation. Any chance of a normal future.

My mind, which was the playground for his mental fuckery.

My body, which learned to react to his calls, his wants, his demands.

I became *his* and lost Teagan Faber. That girl died the moment I met Alex Miller and the girl who's been parading around using my name, hiding away in my body, isn't me. I don't even know who Teagan is anymore.

Teagan was a foster kid, unloved by the family who claimed to care for her, all to collect the government-appointed cheques. She was Brent Thorne's long time best friend with a connection so deep, she swore they were the same person. She was Elena Sparks's high school friend, back when trivial things such as boys and makeup were important.

My fisted hand hits the wall so fast; the punch occurs before my mind processes what I did. It doesn't matter though. Neither does the stinging pain shooting up my arm while the wall remains as though I merely brushed against it.

I don't know who to *be*. Where to start. Away from here, but to do what? Attend university? What job would I apply for with a resume citing stripping as my most recent job? Yet again, Alex wins, because when no normal retail or fast-food job hires me, I'll revert back to what I'm good at—dancing and removing my clothing for strange men.

My inner battle isn't counting Willow's, or even all the women before her. Women who had lives until meeting Alex, who had goals, hopes, and dreams. So many futures stripped away. Numerous women who lost their chance at a normal life. Willow, whose future now consists of wading through an ocean of traumatic memories.

For her, I hit the wall again. One punch for Willow, and a single punch for every woman he stole from their lives. For Carmen, Mia, Anne, Gemma, Zoey, Rachel, Charlotte, and Scarlett.

And while my heavy breaths, gritted teeth, and corded muscles may indicate my anguish, it's not what I feel for the women.

Rather, sweat accompanies my heavy breathing; my jaw fights to loosen, and the tightness in my chest stings.

Guilt.

Blame.

I'm to blame. If only I spoke up sooner—if only I saw through Alex's psychological torture and called his bluff and *somehow* found someone to believe me, I could have saved them all. I would have let him kill me if it saved them.

So many what-ifs. A guilt so heavy it'll bury me.

I don't know how many hits I've given the wall by now, but my hand is a cut-up, bloody mess. I flex my fingers, noting nothing is broken. No doubt there'll be a bruise later.

I *deserve* prison.

If not prison, loneliness. I deserve to go away, to leave everything I once knew behind, untainted by my horribleness.

As my back meets the wall, my energy dissipates at once and my body drops, until it's sliding down the wall and I'm crouching against it. I tighten my arms around my legs, and I wish it was as easy as this to hold the rest of me together.

How can I think about leaving when I can't even imagine standing and moving to another room? If I'm lucky, people will forget about me and let me die in peace.

"Teagan."

Brent. I'm hearing his voice now. I must be. My psyche has taken a dive to the past—to a moment in time when I was safe. Before Alex, when I was content to spend time with Brent. To take our walks and stop by the local ice-cream shop, where he'd always buy me a cone, and I'd tell him I'll pay him back. My IOUs probably totalled a few thousand dollars over the years, but he never complained.

"Teagan."

Go away.

And then a hand rests on my shoulder, his warmth radiating

from his palm and into my skin, waking me enough to lift my head and regard the figure in front of me.

He's here. Not a figment of my imagination, unless my brain is playing tricks on me.

He doesn't look the same. His hair is messy, strands falling every which way, as if they've been tugged on over and over. A shadow covers the bottom half of his face, indicating it's been a while since Brent has shaved.

"Brent?" My voice, thick with emotion, barely makes it up to him. "You're here."

"I am." He crouches down beside me, his attention dropping to my hand. "You looked like you needed a moment."

"What are you doing here? Hawke said no one's seen you in weeks."

"Because they haven't. I returned for you."

I scoff, looking away again. Seeing Brent reminds me of everything Alex took. He reminds me of everything I used to be, and everything I want to be. But how does one even begin to speak to an old friend after surviving what I have, and after the eight-week absence I've had? Normalcy isn't for us, and it'll be better for Brent if he leaves me alone.

"That doesn't answer what you're doing here. Go away."

Go away. Frustration burns inside my chest because the words hurt to say. Some part of me craves to have him remain by side, while the other half wants him to run far away.

Silence stretches between us, and for a second, I believe he'll listen to me, until he says, "Talk to me, Teagan. How are you feeling?"

I peer at him, the skin between my eyes dropping. He's seriously asking me *how I am*?

I scoff again, shaking my head. "Damn, Brent. You've gotten dumb in the past two months. How the fuck do you think I'm doing?"

He flinches but doesn't look away. Because he's a knight in shining armour, exactly as I stated earlier. This is who Brent is. Which is why he needs to leave. He'll attempt to rebuild us and fix our friendship, but all I'll do is drag him down.

"I'm not apologizing." Despite what Dr. Laz encouraged me to do. "I survived and that's all there is to it."

"You did," he murmurs. "I don't want your apology."

"How should I know that?" I level my gaze on him. "Because you're not telling me what you want."

"I want you."

Desire seeps into the edges of my sanity, encouraging me to take his offer. Instead, I blink, forcing any emotion from my face, so he can't determine my true feelings.

The conversation with Dr. Laz said it perfectly.

"Do you love him?"

"He's my best friend, so of course I do."

She shakes her head. "That's not what I'm asking. Do you love him?"

Romance can't be on my mind. Not when, even after therapy, I'm still so fucked up. Even if it's with *Brent...* it's too much for me to consider.

"Cherry-Girl, I've fucking wanted you every day during high school, and every day since you left. Weeks ago, when I kissed you, you believed it a ploy to get information, but that's the furthest from the truth. I kissed you because I wanted to." He shifts, lifting himself to his knees bringing himself closer to me. "I wanted you. I *want* you. So badly it's eating me up inside because I don't know how to process it because I'd be selfish to request anything from you."

My lips part, taking in much-needed air as my mind fights to remain in the present with him and not toss itself back into the past.

"When I couldn't get to you—when the hospital banned me

from seeing you—I had to leave. I couldn't handle staying, where you were so close yet so far. I rented a car and took off, driving everywhere and nowhere. I've missed classes and due dates. At this rate, I'll probably fail, but I don't care because the only thing on my mind was *you*."

Classes and due dates... He's fucking his future up because he couldn't *see* me. I shut my eyes against the swelling of tears. He's outlined the exact purpose why I need to get the fuck out of his life before I ruin it any further. He's going to need to redo his classes now, all because I was in the hospital. He tried to be by my side and paid the price—a price only *I* should have paid because it was for me.

"Teagan, as a child, you were my best friend. When we were teenagers, I stopped ignoring what I was feeling. You were everything to me, and I wanted so much more. Even when you turned me down, I accepted friendship over a relationship because I love you." He bends closer, his wide, honest eyes lining up with mine. "Don't you get it? You've always been it. Even when I spent the past few years believing you left willingly and hated you for it, I loved you."

"I'm—"

"It's okay," he cuts me off. And good thing too because I'm not entirely certain what I was planning on saying. "I'm not asking you for anything, Teagan. I'm here for you though."

"Because you still love me," I fill in, lips barely moving.

"Yes." Brent shifts, and his face comes closer to mine. His eyes flick to my lips, and I spot the desire filling them. I'm reminded of weeks ago when he kissed me, and how good it felt. How, even though it was dumb of me to kiss him back, I enjoyed it and didn't want it to end.

It's with those thoughts, my mind blanks, and I lean forward, pressing a barely-there kiss to his mouth, testing how much resolve he truly has—and how long my brain and body will allow me to do this for.

Dr. Laz taught me to view everything Alex had done to my body as torture only. Every rape, every forced interaction, is in the past. To move on with another person, I need to *feel*. Feel the moment, feel the differences, feel how my focus, my energy, my mind, and my body react to this different person.

Which is why, instead of shoving him away, my hands fist in his shirt, keeping a tight hold as my lips part, allowing him inside. He groans, leaning forward until his body weight rests lightly atop me. I feel the shake in his arms as he fights to keep steady.

The differences between him and Alex are here in every aspect of this encounter. In the way his heart thumps against mine, creating a union between us rather than a power struggle, and how his tongue hesitantly tangles with mine.

"Fucking beautiful," he murmurs.

I kiss him harder, hating how his words take me from the moment and remind me of every reason I need to be pushing him away. This is too good to stop. Too natural.

For now.

So, I don't.

His hand sweeps under my body, subtly moving me from the wall. With nothing to rest my back against, I lower myself to the floor and he follows me down—like he always has. Down to the floor first, but soon, down to the depths my sanity is lost in.

"Teagan..."

That's when the spell breaks. Shatters. Pops. And the outcome rains down on me.

I'm lying on the floor with Brent half on top of me. The very man I need to remove from my life, not to encourage further. I shouldn't have kissed him. I'm an idiot. He needs to go now.

I jerk my head to the side, removing access to my mouth, and push at his chest. I don't stop until he gives up and his weight redistributes to his knees.

"Leave." I sit up.

"Teagan—"

"Leave," I repeat. "Now. Please. Just go."

"No." Brent stands, lifting to his feet until he towers over me. "No, you're not fucking doing this, Teagan."

My hands weave around my legs as I readopt the position he earlier broke me from. He'll leave because I'll hurt him with my next words. Words that become poison in my mouth, but the concoction is necessary.

"I'm serious, Brent. Go. Now. This isn't what I asked for. I don't want you."

"Mentally and emotionally, you're running." Again, I am. I'm running from him and what we can be. This is too much. Too scary. I'm not who he needs.

Another man would appear hurt, but not Brent. Brent merely nods, his expression blank as he faces the door, only pausing to say, "Fine. You win, Cherry-Girl. I won't push you because you'll come to me. I know you will. Our souls—we've been intertwined since our very first meeting and neither time nor Alex took that away."

He steps back, and I lock my gaze on his shoes, remaining to stare at the spot his feet were until he backs away, walking down the short hallway. I hear my front door open and close once, and with his departure, he steals my oxygen too.

Thirty

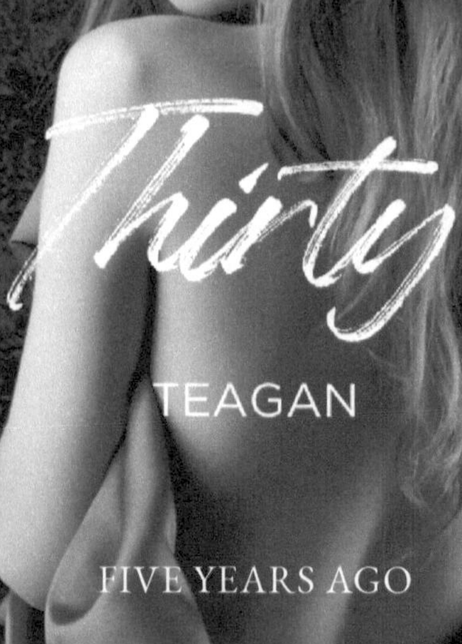

TEAGAN

FIVE YEARS AGO

I TRUDGE toward my locker at the end of the school, hating this part. The part where I grab what I need and go home, where I'm ignored or sent away until morning returns.

My eyes scan for Alex, even though he didn't indicate wanting to see me today. Dating him hasn't been the best. Not how I dreamed of it anyway.

Thankfully, Brent's already by my locker. Earlier, he mentioned wanting to talk, which is strange because we always do when he walks me home, so I don't see what makes today so important.

I wave to Elena as I pass her locker. She waves back, smiling, but shifts her attention to the guy approaching her. No doubt Ryker Ames will be on them soon enough.

Weird girl. His attention is so toxic, in my opinion, but she loves it. I guess she's waiting on him to one day wake up and realize he's always liked her. She's a smart girl but has stupid ideas, because life isn't some romance movie; it doesn't work like that.

This is the real world, and in the real world, the hot guys are the villains. Ryker is too similar to Alex to make me comfortable, but she won't listen to me.

Elena and I met when we shared a class freshman year, and it was an easy friendship. Brent fell in with Ryker Ames—who he claims is *fine,* but eh—and Ryker's best friend, Tristan Pence, who is less scary than Ryker, though still a dick.

"Hey," I say as I approach my locker. I twirl the lock, inputting the combination. "Damn, end of days suck. What did you want to talk to me about?" I yank my bag from my locker and roughly shove in everything I need.

Brent's mouth opens but is cut off by a screech, pulling everyone's attention toward the end of the hall. Sure enough, Ryker noticed the guy speaking to Elena. I look back toward Brent, anticipating his next words.

"Outside. Where it's quiet."

Makes sense. Knowing Elena, this will go on for a while. I toss the strap of my bag over my shoulder and walk the opposite way with Brent following me out.

We make it a dozen steps, each one filled with an anxious energy. I continuously throw glances to the side, my own anxiety increasing with every step. Between the two of us, Brent's always more relaxed. And why shouldn't he be? He goes home to loving parents.

Finally, he speaks, and his words throw a wedge into our friendship. "Teagan, I... I—Um." He pauses, and I note the bump in his throat as he swallows. "Teagan, I know we're only friends, but would you consider going out with me? Like, on a date? Like, romantically?"

Oh.

I stop breathing. My heart ceases beating. The only part of my body currently working are my feet as they continue padding over the cement sidewalk, but even they sound muted as my brain works to catch up.

He wants to date me.

Brent. My best friend. My confidant—in everything except Alex, because I can't. I can't admit what a moron I was for not spreading my legs when Alex asked me to. I mean, he's Alex Miller. Of course, he'd take what he wants.

But Brent. I've loved him for as long as I've known him. What began as a platonic friendship, I realized, right around the time high school began, is more. He may not be pretty like Alex, but Brent's goodness is within him. His kindness, his friendship. It's all there in every look he gives me.

That quote, *love is friendship on fire*, is completely true, and I soon understood its meaning.

Which is why this is so hard. Why, even though I stare into the bright afternoon sun, a tear forms and slides silently down my cheek.

I don't glance at him—I can't—but I hear the heartbreak and regret in his tone and know the exact broken expression he'll be wearing. "Sorry. I shouldn't have asked."

He'll hate himself for asking. It'll change things between us.

Yet, I can't hate that he asked me. It's given me the sweet confirmation about his feelings. That I haven't been the only one crushing. That if I took the leap, he'd catch me.

But I can't. Not with Alex in the picture.

"No," I finally whisper, voice clogged with tears, "it's fine you did, but I can't."

"Okay."

The rest of our walk is silent, and when my familiar front door is in sight, home suddenly becomes my solace. At least for tonight, it can be the place where I cry out old regrets and attempt to send the text message I'd been dying to.

ME

Alex, I don't think this is working. We'll both be happier with other people. You know I'm not giving you what you want. We should end this now before it's too late.

YEARS LATER, that day has always haunted me.
I should have sent that text.
I didn't because I was stupid.

THE NEXT MORNING is the first time I wake up and see the world differently.

Freer.

I shove the blanket off me—a blanket Alex paid for—and embrace the morning with an easy smile, unlike any I've had before.

I. Am. Free. And freedom is the beginning of something new.

Change. As soon as the trial is over, I'm out of here. I *must* move past the bad memories seeping through this entire apartment, city, and nearby towns. Brent will fight me, but with any luck, my words last night shoved him away for good.

My phone chimes from the bedside. I'm unsure how it even managed to get there; clearly, someone had been here to charge it. Either way, discovering it last night was both relieving and annoying due to the amount of waiting text messages on it.

Hey girl, let us know you're okay. Mason isn't saying shit.

Holy fuck! I just saw the news. WTF Cherry! Are you ALIVE?

I hope you're okay. Please contact me when
you can.

Various texts left by the girls I worked alongside. Each one of them brought a small smile to my face, knowing they cared enough to reach out, even when Mason likely told them to forget me.

The largest smile of all was saved for his.

MASON

Based on the news, I assume you are done
working here. I know this wasn't something you
chose, and every day I wished I could report it,
but Alex Miller held a lot of power, and I
couldn't, Teagan. Seeing what the news is
reporting… I'm so fucking sorry. I kick myself
every day, hating I never spoke up. If it's any
consolation, you were a damned good
employee and played the role well. If I never see
or even hear from you again, I do hope you have
a happy life. Be well, Teagan. Cherry. No other
woman will ever be allowed to use that stage
name since it'd be an insult to your memory. I
will miss you.

That message only arrived a week after my admittance into the hospital. I know why though, and I can't hate him for the delayed contact. Rightly so, Alex scared Mason, so no doubt, if I ever stopped coming in, Mason had to put his head down and never ask questions. Other girls would have been contacted after missing a shift, but not me. He knew Alex controlled my schedule.

I should be angry he let all this slip by. A normal person would be pissed, but Mason was too good. He was protecting himself and his business, the same way I remained silent about the other women to protect them. Mason and me, we made an identical decision. And while I'm allowed to hate myself, I refuse to be mad at him.

My phone chimes and it's no one from the club.

ELENA

If you never want to hear from me again, I understand. I'm happy you're free and I can't wait to watch the jury make the decision I firmly believe they will. I love and miss you. Hawke mentioned your release, and I would love to see you, but if you don't want that—if things are too different now, I understand.

In a moment of irrational emotion, I once toyed with the idea of leaving post-trial without a goodbye, but Elena doesn't deserve that *again*. I think about her—about our pasts and how excited she was to see me a couple months ago, and... I can't. I won't do that to her, especially when I feel she'll respect my decision.

I click the message and respond.

ME

I'll get a taxi to Bridgetown. Can we meet?

ELENA

Holy fuck. Yes. I'm living with Ryker. I'll send you the address.

In another message, it comes in.

ME

Be there in an hour or so.

ELENA

Can't wait.

ANY OF THE tip money I was allowed to keep, I pooled in case of emergencies. It's there I pull the money to pay a taxi driver to get me to Elena and Ryker's house.

Finally, the car stops in suburbia, in front of a picture-perfect house. *This* is where Ryker lives? Ryker Ames, a foster kid like I was. He went to jail for fuck's sake, and *still* ended up with a house like this.

Why is life not fair?

The moment my feet reach the front step, the door flings open, and Elena fills the doorway. Her blonde strands are tied in a messy bun on top of her head and she's wearing a shirt way too large for her —likely Ryker's—overtop black leggings.

She's never appeared happier. The glow emitting from her is blinding, and I blink a few times as I approach. My chest cracks open deeply and expands until my breath is gone.

"Oh my God, Teagan."

"Elena."

She waves her hand, urging me inside as she steps back. "Come in. Ryker left a bit ago."

I enter the pretty entranceway, noting the small table by the door, home to a decorative bowl, where a set of keys wait to be grabbed when the owner is rushing out. A freaking bowl for your keys.

Elena came from money. Her mother's a lawyer, so she never wanted for anything. She never went home scared, and half the time, my lunches were bought by her.

"It's..." She shuts the door behind me.

"Yeah," I tell her, agreeing with her unspoken words.

Surreal. Weird.

Elena steps by me, gesturing to the hallway. "Come on. We can talk in the living room, like old times."

When I would go over to her house, we'd camp out on her couch and watch movies while her mother delivered treats for us to gorge on. She's aiming to dredge up the past when I'm only here to bury it. Still, I smile, because her pleasant words spark better memories.

Despite my body sinking in a few inches in the comfy couch, my spine goes rigid and I sit stiffly, unwilling to get comfortable in her attractive life.

Elena lowers herself to the opposite end of the couch, her leg going beneath her other one as she leans back against the couch's arm, appearing entirely at ease.

"How have you been?" she asks right away.

"Alive. Which is more than I can say for some of the other women who've encountered Alex."

She flinches, though I'm not entirely sure why. She's not at fault.

"And the past few weeks...?"

I shrug, realizing then how bad of an idea this is. Like Brent, Elena's had a very sunny life. It's obvious once Ryker was released from prison, they had the reunion they've likely both dreamed off. She's going to school, no doubt maintaining a high GPA too. She always spoke about being a lawyer, like her mother, and I wonder if it's the career she's chasing.

"It was fine."

A ghost of a smile floats over her mouth. "You've always been strong, Teagan. I'm just..." She trails off, her attention moving to the other side of the room.

"You're what?" I prod, leaning slightly forward.

"So sorry I never tried to look for you. When you took off... I mean, I know your life wasn't the best, and when you never responded to my messages, I assumed you were done and I wanted to respect it." She pauses, shifting, before adding, "You should have told me, Teagan. Mom could—"

"Your mom sent Ryker to jail when all he was doing was protecting you from the Millers. Money works well, and Mr. Miller paid off the family fostering me." I'm so pleased Alex's father is dead. "So, no offence, but I think your mother would have done fuck all."

Elena flinches again, but this time, it's for a better reason.

"Sorry," I murmur, lowering my defences again and leaning back. After all, it's not Elena's fault my life sucks.

"Hawke said you'll be testifying." Her change in topic is welcoming, and I breathe deeply.

"Yeah. It was a condition of my freedom. Not that they needed to offer me anything. I'm not holding back when I'm on the stand. He deserves everything he'll get."

Ev-er-y-thing. I can't wait to watch him burn. To watch the courts strip him of his freedom and rape him as he's done to me so many times.

Once the thoughts bombard my mind, pushing them down is impossible, and all my hate spews out from my tense body, my teeth bared while I fist my hands by my sides, away from her sight. She doesn't need to hear this, but—

"Teagan—"

I cut her off. "Did you know when I asked him not to fuck me, he raped me? Or when I ran away, he dragged me home and tortured me for trying to escape?" Of course she knows all this. I told her alongside everyone else weeks ago. "I thought I died that day, but it turns out, he could do worse. Do you know how many times I wished it was only me and no one else? It's not their fault they got hired to work for a villain, but me... I *chose* my villain. I deserved what I got."

"Teagan—"

"No," I interrupt. "You don't get it, Elena. You've lived a good fucking life, able to attend college. Do you know what I've been doing in that time? *Stripping.* My foster mother always said I would end up whoring myself out, and damn, was she ever correct. Because Alex didn't *allow* me to go to school, or even work at a fucking fast-food job."

My thoughts fly out faster, and I move to the edge of the couch, nerves practically pushing me off the cushion.

"Instead, he *chose* my future for me. Put me in a place where I was forced to let strangers stare at me while I took off my clothes. While I was forced to hide what he was doing to me, to other women, from the people who could take him away. Elena, there were so many times I wanted to march myself down to a shelter, to the police—even if he's paying most of them off—to the damn FBI—and yes, I realize we're not even in the correct country to contact them—but fuck, *so* many times. You know why I didn't?"

"You were conditioned," she whispered, emotion deepening the darkness in her eyes.

"I was conditioned," I repeat, the words coming out slower as I roll them around in my mouth. "Conditioned, and I hadn't even realized I was. I feared what he'd do when I tattled on him, but not to me—no, I wanted to die—but to the girls.

"I saw more death and torture than your brain could ever imagine. Half-starved girls. Bodies strung up while he played with them. Carvings in their skin before he raped them, letting them bleed out and die while he was still inside them."

I shake my head, but it does nothing to rid myself of the faces in my mind. Of Carmen, Mia, Anne, Gemma, Zoey, Rachel, Charlotte, and Scarlett.

Of Mia when I tried to help her. She was the second one I tried to free.

She was the first death I witnessed.

He drew out the torture longer than usual, all to punish *me*.

Once I saw him ripping pieces of her body, I stopped eating for a solid week.

Dr. Laz dredged up all these memories, made me face them, to "process" them, to ensure I wouldn't snap when I saw Alex or had flashbacks. But can someone completely forget something like that?

"So, fuck yes, I am testifying. I want it to be *my* words that send the scum to prison. If the death penalty was a thing in our country,

I'd be begging Hawke to petition for it because Alex deserves nothing less. He warrants knowing what it feels like to be weak and helpless and unable to save yourself. Alex deserves…" I trail off, the fight slowly leaving my tone as well as my muscles. "He deserves *everything*, because that's what he's done to me."

When my vision blurs, I lift my hand to wipe at my eyes, and that's when I realize my face is wet with tears. I'm crying. Anger, sadness, or trauma, I don't even know what my body is feeling at this point.

"He did everything evil a person could do to another, and it's left me with nothing. *As* nothing. Elena, I can't stay here. I need to be far away from him."

Tears burst, and I become a blubbery mess. My vision goes away, and I don't notice Elena moving closer to me until her hand's holding mine.

"You get to decide that now, Teagan. I'm so sorr—"

"Don't." My hand flies up, throwing hers from mine. "Just don't. I didn't come here for your sympathy. I came to say goodbye."

"Goodbye? You're leaving?"

"I can't stay, Elena. I've been thinking about it. Cortville is full of bad memories, and here isn't much better. If I remain, I'll be constantly battling memories and history, when I can leave and be someone new. New job, new name. When I was at the police station, the cop manning the front desk wouldn't stop staring. My taxi driver kept giving me worried looks from the front seat. People know who I am here."

Ever the loyal person Elena is, all she asks is, "When?"

"After the trial. Once I see Alex go away." And he *better* go to prison.

Elena studies my face, but she must see the decision because her shoulders lower, her expression flattening into acceptance. "I'll miss you, Teag. I feel like I've barely gotten you back and you're leaving again."

While she studies me, I do the same to her, noting her same blonde hair, her same kind eyes—all her features I've always known, except older. "Maybe we can keep in contact?" I offer, halfway considering a simple phone friendship.

Her mouth breaks into a bright smile. "I'd like that." But then her confused expression returns. "Brent's allowing that?"

Allowing.

And there's the biggest difference between Elena and me. Elena craves the permission, the submission, and the control Ryker has over her. It's a playful control though. But I've been trapped with someone who demands true submission, who's had ultimate control, and who very rarely gave me permission for anything I wanted.

I hated it. Every second of it.

No man will ever *allow* me to do something again. From here on out, everything happening in my life is because I *choose* it.

As if she reads what I'm thinking, she rushes to add, "I mean, because he's been a mess for the past two months. He took off, not even telling Ryker or Tristan where he went. The guys mentioned telling him you'd be released from the hospital this week, so I'd imagine he'll be back soon. But, like, he *really* cares for you, Teag. I see it now, and I'm silly for ever thinking he loved me at all when—" She breaks off, her hands flying to her mouth, eyes bulging from between her fingers.

I turn my head slowly, imagining I look like something out of a horror movie.

"When did he ever love you, Elena? What did he conveniently leave out when he showed up at my apartment yesterday?"

Thirty-Two

TEAGAN

I'M NOT mad at Elena. She was a victim as much as I was when Ryker and Brent played their cruel game. She doesn't blame Brent, but I do. Because a man who was able to deceive someone like that is a man I don't want in my life.

Yet, I stalk downtown, toward the address Elena reluctantly gave me. He may not be there, but I'll park myself outside his door until he returns.

I take the elevator up four floors to his downtown apartment and stop outside the door she instructed, before banging my fist into it with enough force I'm sure the building next door could hear me.

It swings open instantly, and Brent's surprised, elated face is what greets me for the briefest second before I wipe off that smug joy as I barrel into him, shoving him away from the door, so I can slam it shut. My hand grasps the first thing it feels when shooting to the right, which happens to be an umbrella. It flies through the air, narrowly missing his head as he ducks out of the way.

Shame.

Once upon a time, I wasn't a violent person. But it's become the norm when one's life is obscured in it.

"Teagan! What—"

"You're a damned liar, Brent Thorne." My hand whips up, finger pointing at him, ready to stab it through his body. "You say you're the better man, but at least Alex never hid his nature."

Brent steps back, his hands blocking mine. "Teagan, what the fuck are you going on about?"

"Elena."

Before adding more, I allow him the opportunity to tell me the truth. He does, but not with words. His expression shifts, his mouth dropping open as his eyes bulge and his mouth shapes into one distinct word: *Fuck*.

"I went to visit her. She let it slip about your past."

Hearing the story, I forced from Elena, *hurt*. As in, my heart physically felt as though it was cracking, the edges filling with a prickly mixture of hate and anguish. Sure, I get Brent wasn't a monk these past few years, but with my *best friend*. With *Elena*, of all people. For such a shitty reason too, making him a shitty person.

"You went on about loving me since we were children, and how when I left, you broke inside." I cross my arms over my chest and hiding my broken heart from sight. "You didn't miss me for long."

Brent steps closer, his face reddening. "Did she tell you *why* I was with her?"

"Because you were following Ryker's request. Oh, trust me, she tried to make you seem like the good guy, but you're not. I see who you truly are—a liar, who'll tell me whatever you think I want to hear. I'm *so* fucking done, Brent."

I turn away, giving him my back, but Brent's quick grip stops me, as his large hand wraps around my bicep and spins me back around.

"What I find interesting, Cherry-Girl," he steps closer until our chests align with one another, our hearts beating roughly against one another, "is how you kicked me out of your house yesterday, claiming to feel nothing toward me. Yet today, you show up at my door, yelling at how I betrayed you by *pretending* to date your friend." His mouth scrunches into a cocky grin. "Sorry to tell you, but those are actions of a person who cares."

His realization is a jolt to my heart because he's right, even I can't let him know that. "It's the principle of the matter, Brent. You told me one thing, but your actions proved another."

"It is," he agrees, his arms snaking around my hips. I back up, but he clamps down on his hold and I'm pinned to his chest, my arms stuck between us. I should be freaking out, but instead, I'm focusing on *not* feeling his body. "Except, a person who doesn't care would not be as hurt as you are."

His hand brushes my shirt as he moves it upwards to my neck, which clenches in response. His fingers continue their sweeping motion as he gathers a chunk of my hair in his fist and yanks gently, angling my face in such a way to stare at him without the ability to pull away.

"I never loved her, Teagan," he murmurs softly, eyes locking on mine. "I told her I did because it was necessary at the time. If I knew there was ever a chance of you returning, I would have told Ryker no. Even when I was with her, I never stopped thinking about you."

"But—"

He moves, at a speed quicker than I've ever seen him make and suddenly his mouth is fused with mine. His tongue dances along my lips, begging me to open, and when I do, his tongue meets mine at the same time realization hits.

While not our first kiss, this one feels like more.

Our first one was masked by hate. Our second, relief and misery.

This one is pure lust. Craving. This kiss is real.

Because as much as I hate to admit it, he's correct. I'm fucking jealous, knowing my two best friends "dated" when I was in Hell. When Alex was raping me, they were having date nights, living their best lives, while I was a ghost from their pasts.

But this kiss right now is a goodbye. I've made my peace with Elena, and now it's time for Brent. We need this—for both of us—and then I'll be able to walk away without regrets or what-ifs.

Maybe it's stupid to kiss him back, or for my arms to find purchase around his neck. Or to lean into him, pressing my hips into his, my breasts into his chest, and kiss him in ways I didn't think I'd ever be able to kiss a man again.

When he pulls away, he snatches my hand and lays it upon his chest, overtop the chiseled muscle.

"You feel that? It beats for you—only you. Anything before this moment—Alex and Elena—they don't matter."

His lips capture mine again, this time harder. My back meets a nearby wall, and he crowds my body, the same way Alex has time and time again. With the familiar feeling, my blood boils beneath my skin and my hands come up to his shoulders to push him off me.

But the warmth from his own grip stops me—brings me back to the present, reminding me that the hands holding me, tenderly cupping my face, aren't the same ones that caused me pain over and over.

That Brent would never cause me pain.

My hands fist in his shirt and I pull it up his chest. I've seen him topless before, when we'd swim at the public pool as kids, but he did not look like *this*. Smooth skin, muscles rippling beneath my hand, and so mouth-watering delicious I'd be happy to simply stare at him for hours on end.

Brent rips his mouth from mine, panting in the space left between our bodies. "Teagan, we should stop. You're still upset."

I shake my head, disliking he's choosing to try to end this. "No. Help me rid my mind of him. You said so yourself, I want you, and this is me agreeing to that."

"You came here to yell at me."

"And I did exactly that." I lift on my toes and kiss him again—a brush of my lips against his—while my hands dance along his chest and toward the button on his jeans. Electricity follows my path, encouraging me to do something I never willingly have before. Even while kissing me, I feel his jagged breath as I take charge. My hands find the snap and the sides fall away.

"Teagan," he murmurs against my lips. "Are you sure? I don't want to hurt you."

"You won't," I whisper. "Replace his touch with your own. It's what I've dreamed about for years."

My words awaken him. He growls his agreement—it's the sexiest thing ever—and finally stops resisting this. His hands drop to my legs, and suddenly, I'm hoisted in the air. My legs wind around his waist and he walks us down the hall.

Then my back is resting on his bed, and all my previous worries remain at the doorway. For now, the only thing that matters is Brent and me and this moment. His hands slide around my body as he releases me, and my arms unwind from his neck.

"Teagan, you're a dream come true."

"Then let's allow the dream to finish." I tug off my shirt and toss it to the side of the bed, shivering when the air hits my body. Being naked is no longer embarrassing. Strangers have seen more of me than they should have ever been allowed, and Alex happily made me sit without clothes for hours in his cold basement.

Brent hisses, his eyes landing on my breasts. "You're fucking beautiful."

"You're so busy talking," I smirk, "I'll be finishing myself if you don't hurry." My hands find the button of my jeans and unsnap them before stripping them from my legs and reclining back.

Keeping eye contact, Brent does the same, leaving his boxers on. He climbs overtop me, his arms balanced on either side of my head. "I'll take it from here."

His easygoing grin has my heart skipping a beat. It's the Brent from high school. My friend. Easygoing, humorous… and *mine*. The one I fell in love with.

Brent kisses me again, this time slower and gentler than before, but not for long. His kisses travel down the length of my neck, pulling a low moan from me. His path continues over the curve of my breasts, and he stops at the edge of my bra to whisper, his warm breath coasting against my skin.

"I won't be rough with you, I promise. It's not really my thing, but still, if I'm too rough, please tell me to stop." His head lifts, so he can make eye contact. "I'm serious, Teagan. Tell me if I need to stop —if you're feeling overwhelmed at any point. Say the word and it all goes away."

I nod. I won't because I don't believe he'll ever be that rough.

And then his mouth slips underneath my bra, his teeth tugging it away from my skin until he's able to latch his lips around my nipple. His tongue dances around the bud, warming it, before releasing me with a pop and doing the same with the other one.

Alex never touched my nipples, at least not in any way to be nice. "That feels really good," I whisper.

His hands slip beneath my body, and I arch my back, giving him an inch of space, so he can unclasp my bra. He tugs the material away, throwing it in the pile with my other clothes. His warm hands cup me, weighing both breasts while his eyes find mine again.

"This is better than a dream."

I smile. Simple, but truthful. An easy smile to tell him how content I am.

He grabs the sides of my panties and strips those from my skin too, and it's then my insides clench with the very real reminder of what's about to happen. About who's been here, and *only* ever touched me here.

Focus on the differences, I remind myself. The way Brent's touch is pleasingly gentle, and his lips soft and warm.

As if he senses my nerves, he makes a humming noise in the back of his throat as his finger lightly traces a pattern over my stomach. "Do you trust me?"

I nod. Even after his past with Elena, I do. Maybe I'm not as smart as I believe myself to be because, here I am, still falling for liars. Like I didn't learn my lesson.

"Good."

Thirty-Three

TEAGAN

HE BENDS his head until his light hair tickles my stomach. He presses his lips softly there, to the skin right above my belly button. My breath shudders, and I arch into his gentle touch.

"You okay?" he checks.

"I'm better than okay."

He kisses downward unhurriedly, over the curve of my stomach, across my hipbone until his breath blows over my core.

"If you want me to stop, tap twice against my shoulder."

I don't respond. I'm unsure if I can—if my nerves will unlock for the new experience.

When his tongue lightly flicks against my core, I fly. Not actually, but it certainly feels like it. And when he finds my clit, I die. He sucks on it briefly before finding my pussy again, where he pushes his tongue lightly inside me.

Alex never put his mouth on me. Not like this. Not here.

Anytime Alex touched me was only to shove something inside me—his fingers, cock, or something else. He never licked me, savoured me like I was a meal.

And when Brent groans and increases his speed, it becomes

another thing on the ever-growing list of things Alex has never done. Brent groaned for me, like he couldn't help but consume more of me —because he wants *me*. *Me*—not to simply dominate me.

"Brent," I whisper because I have nothing else to say.

How does one tell someone that they're fulfilling every forbidden dream they've ever had?

His hands capture the inside of my legs, gripping them possessively rather than painfully. His hold ensures I'm ready for his mouth, but I know if I want to be freed, he'd release me. Because that's who he is.

But why would I want this explosion of the cosmos to stop? After all, I believe it's what's happening inside me. It's the only possibility because, when his tongue takes another trip around my centre, I fall into bliss, hips jerking off the bed and into his mouth. I cry out into the room, yelling his name.

"Brent!"

He growls, and the simple sound nearly has me coming again. His possession isn't cruel. It isn't a noise that says he'll lock me inside a box. Rather, it's freeing.

When my body comes down, I push into a sitting position, placing a hand to his face to cup his cheek, so I can draw his attention toward me.

"Thank you for that."

His brow furrows. He doesn't understand the gift he's given me.

"You were the first to ever do that."

"To give you an orgasm from oral?"

I shake my head, strands of my red hair fanning around my shoulders. "To give me oral."

His pupils narrow to such small dots and his nostrils flare. But before he goes down whatever road he's about to take, I propel him forward, using the back of his neck, until he's braced above me.

My hands find his hips and I push at his shorts, needing more.

Needing what I've imagined when Alex raped me in front of Willow. An act from so few weeks ago, yet it feels like a lifetime, with how much things have changed since then.

When Elena told me what had happened between them, I believed him a liar exactly like Alex. But as his fingers trace the edges of my body, it's difficult to imagine Brent—my Brent—anything remotely like the disguised devil.

Brent breaks our kiss and helps me shuffle his shorts from his body, all while his eyes remain locked on me. They glint with adoration, rather than the evil I'm so used to. When he's freed from the confines of his shorts and his cock bounces against my hip, I freeze.

It feels the same. So similar. It's the same.

"Teagan."

But the voice is different. So distinctive. It's not the same.

Rather than the dark eyes of Hell's depths, I'm staring into sky blue ones. Blue eyes that are honest, wide, and only hold love.

"Breathe, Cherry-Girl. Come back to me."

A voice and eyes attached to the man who knows me better than I know myself. Who won't hurt me. Who's *never* hurt me, even when he believed me to be on Alex's side.

"I'm okay," I breathe finally, returning to the present.

"Are you?" His brow quirks, his mouth a ripple of nerves. "We can end this right now. Please, say the word, and we will."

If I do that, I won't have this chance again. This is goodbye—the beginning and end of us.

"I'm okay," I repeat.

From the space between our bodies, his cock is erect and ready, and I reach for it, thumb lightly stroking over its soft head. He groans, but it's low and pained—in the back of his throat, like he's holding back.

My hand wraps around his length, feeling him twitch in excitement. His face pinches, but not in pain. I stroke him once, twice, waiting for the break in his tough exterior, and when he finally does —when he finally lets himself *feel* this and gets rid of the guilt he's obviously holding onto—it's beautiful.

"You feel really good," I tell him, a barely-there whisper he can hear.

He feels *right*. Touching Alex was always forced and masked with the discomforting knowledge that if I didn't do it correctly, I'd pay for it. Even as my hand drifts up and down Brent softly, testing the limits and speed of what it'll take before his expression shatters into pleasure, I know nothing would cause him to hurt me. I could hurt *him* and he'd merely pull away rather than beating me.

"Goddamn it, Teagan. I won't be able to hold back for long if you keep doing that."

"So don't."

My blasé attitude masks the sensations coursing through me. The ones making tears prick behind my eyes, threatening to break. His statement is significant. He returns power I've long lost—control I hadn't realized I ever had. *I* am making Brent feel like this out of choice and touches willingly given, rather than taken.

Brent's sudden kiss breaks my concentration, and my hand goes limp between us. It no longer matters though, because he shifts onto his knees, his cock brushing my core.

"Let me take care of you this time."

Despite the words, my body goes still, muscles clenching. The head of his cock brushes my opening, at the same time my mind drifts toward a few weeks ago.

He thrusts his cock into me, driving it through the barrier of dryness. As he moves inside me, like a knife stabbing my insides over and over, my eyes clamp shut and my mind readies for its journey back to the first time again.

And then the first time.

I feel as the worst pain I've ever felt, and ever will, rips—breaks—

me as he shoves into my body, rupturing through the blockade my dryness created, uncaring in how my insides burn in response. I gasp, eyes clenched tightly as I work through the pain his invasion brings.

"Cherry-Girl, come back to me. *Stay* with me. Don't go there."

My eyes shoot open—*when did I close them?* —and land on blue pools. Concern fills them to the brim, agony causing his hips pull back.

No! This isn't what I want. I don't want him to stop.

"Come back, Teagan."

I'm trying, Brent. I want to.

His hand lifts, hovering over my face as though he means to touch me, but doesn't. He's uncertain, I realize. Unsure of whether touching me is a bad idea or not.

I reach for it, bringing it to my face and with his soft palm, I shut my eyes. Again, my mind goes to the past, but this time, not to Alex. Rather to Brent.

To how everyday he'd greet me with a smile. To every time he walked me home. To every text and call, ensuring I was never alone in that house of misery. To every time he bought me ice cream because I couldn't afford it, or his mother ensured I ate a meal before heading back home, knowing I wouldn't be fed as well as I should be. To every weekend I spent at his house, watching movies and binging on popcorn. To every tear I shed, and every hug he gave to remove my misery.

"Teagan."

My eyes fly open. My hand goes to his neck, and I pull him in for a gentle kiss, his lips molding to mine. And when the kiss ends, so does my painful memories.

Alex won't ruin this. I refuse to allow him to steal this moment. After everything, it's what we deserve. After all I've lived through, it's what *I* deserve.

"I'm okay," I whisper, and then repeat, "I'm okay now. Please, Brent. I want you."

Doubt clouds his eyes, but he still gets back into position. His cock brushes my opening again, but with my eyes on his, I know who it is—and who it *isn't*.

"Teagan, are you—"

My hand slaps over his mouth, shutting him up.

"Brent, please," I beg, my words no louder than a pained whisper. "This is our time."

Our only time.

Brent studies my face and the acceptance he finds has him saying, "Okay."

His hand slides up my body until he finds mine, and our fingers interlock. His arm continues its journey until our fused hands are resting on the pillow above my head. His other hand angles his cock, so all he needs to do is push inside.

"Eyes on me, Cherry-Girl."

As if they could be anywhere else.

With his hand melded to mine, and his eyes trapping my soul, he pushes inside.

I tense.

I wait for flashbacks to bombard me. For Alex to weasel his way back into this moment.

But he never does.

Brent continues until he's seated fully, his cock stretching me to new, wonderful widths.

"Teagan. Cherry-Girl." The marvel in his tone refuses to be ignored.

"Brent," I murmur back.

"Is this okay? Do you..."

"I'm fine." And when a tear builds at the base of my eye, I realize how true my statement is. "I'm better than fine, Brent. You're perfect. Thank you."

Thank you for being you.

Thank you for loving me.

Thank you for this moment.

Thank you for being my friend.

Thank you for being my everything.

His hips roll, moving his cock inside me in a beautiful way. He pulls out before gliding back inside me. And again, eliciting sparks in the base of my stomach. My hips arch, encouraging him further. Our beating hearts line up.

"This is why you can't leave me, Cherry-Girl. Stay with me."

He's speaking generally, I think. To stay in the moment, but I can't. Won't. We'll have our moment and then—

"I fucking love you, Teagan Faber. Always have, always will. I'm so sorry for not searching better." His hand tightens around mine, figuratively pushing his apology into my body. "For not searching longer. For giving up on you."

"It's okay," I whisper. Alex covered my tracks well, to ensure no one from my previous life would ever find me.

"It makes me sick knowing what he's done to you. It makes me murderous to know what he did to you because *I* chased you. I'll spend our entire lives apologizing for my idiocy."

This time, when he pushes inside my body, it's my heart he hits. My delicate, fragile heart. Because there is no "entire life" for us.

"Nothing will ever be good enough to fix what happened that day, but it won't stop me from trying."

"It's not your fault." Words contradicting previous ones I once told him; ones that accused him of Alex's actions. To condemn him would be no different than Alex constantly victim blaming me, when it's not his fault that Alex is a psychopath.

"It is," he counters. His free hand comes up beneath my knee, lifting my leg, adopting a new position, one that has me crying to the ceiling with how deep he's able to get. He kisses me softly before trailing his lips down my neck, toward my breasts.

"So many regrets," he murmurs. "But there's one I'll never have."

"What's that?"

"Meeting you."

With his words, I come, my orgasm building in a larger, more powerful way than Alex was ever able to drive me toward. My hand clenches around his, my head tipping into the pillow beneath me, and my hips continue rocking, chasing every bit of the high until it ends.

My orgasm drives his and he growls into the skin of my neck, his hand tightening painfully around mine, but it's a welcome pain. It's a display of his desire.

"Fuck, Teagan. Cherry-Girl, I love you so much. You've returned to me, and I'm never losing you again."

And then he tucks me into his side and falls asleep right away, his soft snore filling the room, despite it being only mid-afternoon. I study him, noting the dark marks beneath his eyes, but also the obvious peace settling over his form.

After a few more minutes, I gently tug myself from his arms and redress, hating every moment of this.

He claims to want me, but when he realizes all the agony loving me will bring his perfect life, he'll hate me.

I'm broken.

I can't—*won't*—do this to him.

At the doorway of his bedroom, I stop briefly to whisper four final words before escaping.

"I love you too."

Thirty-Four

BRENT

WHEN SOMETHING CHANGES, it's obvious. It's in how the air transforms, becoming electrified with energy.

When I received my acceptance to university, it was an excited energy.

When Elena learned the truth about our relationship, it was an angry energy.

As my eyes open, I feel the difference in the air. It's a gloomy energy.

Teagan isn't where I last saw her, curled in my arms. Rather, her spot is cold. I glance at the time on the clock by my bed, noting how many hours have passed since she barged her way in here.

Another man would assume she simply had places to be and couldn't stay, but I know her. And looking back, I *see* it now. It was all in how she kissed me, gentle but desperate. Why she was so determined to ensure we finished.

She's running again.

She won't respond, but it doesn't stop my fingers from flying over the screen of my phone.

ME

Come back, Teagan. If you don't, this time, I'll chase you.

In the past eight weeks, I've read everything on trauma and PTSD. Pulling away from loved ones is a common symptom, and maybe it'd be better if I let her do it. Allowed her the time to figure herself out, and then she can return to me on her own time.

But that's not me. I've spent too many years without her, and now that I've had her—that I've tasted her—she's inside me. She's a part of my soul and a soul won't survive without its other half.

She can run all she wants, but I'll chase her, hunt her down, and drag her back to my side.

Run, Cherry-Girl. Run. Because I'll be right there.

My phone chimes, and I nearly leap from my skin in eagerness, but disappointment has my heart slowing when the text isn't from Teagan.

HAWKE

With Willow agreeing to testify, and Teagan released from the hospital, they've decided to expedite the trial. It's tomorrow.

Before I took off, Hawke explained the process to us. How, while Teagan was in the hospital, the courts would be assembling a judge and completing jury selection, something he would be taking part in. Hawke is preparing for the court battle of his life since Alex, of course, has pled innocent.

This is over tomorrow, Teagan. And then you and I will begin.

Thirty-Five

HAWKE GAVE me a specific time to arrive at the courthouse, stating the trial would already be in session, and I would enter partway through to give my statement. Hawke claims it's better this way, despite wanting to witness the entire thing. He feels Alex's presence could have some effect on me and will modify what I end up saying on the stand.

Whatever. As long as this ends, it's all I care about.

When I approach the courthouse, everything becomes real. The giant stone cylinders lining the double front doors, where Hawke said he would meet me, represent my new future. One where I'm free and Alex is condemned.

Carmen. Mia. Anne. Gemma. Zoey. Rachel. Charlotte. Scarlett. Willow.

Me.

This is for us. When I speak those words, they'll be for us. Other than Carmen, none of the girls had families looking for them, therefore no one has been missing them. But *I* miss them. I'll live the rest of my life to the fullest *for them.*

"Teagan." Hawke approaches, his voice yanking me back to the present.

"Hey."

He looks the same as I saw him last. Very lawyer-y. His tattoos are covered again, his piercings removed. Only this time, rather than his hair combed back, it's messy and falling over his face, as if he's yanked on it a few times.

"You okay?" I nudge my chin toward his head.

"Yeah." But he's not. His eyes are distracted.

"What happened?"

"Willow recently finished on the stand. I stopped in to see her before coming out here."

Oh. I picture Willow—at least the version of her from my memories.

"How is she?"

"Fucking strong." His expression breaks, ease seeping through the cracks. But it's more than that, I realize, peering closer. Beneath his professional pleasure, there's relief, if not pride too.

"You care for her." A man in love is so obvious.

His pale skin flushes red. "I might. This day... It's hard. I had to put her on the stand and listen as she recounted everything, while fighting the urge not to lunge across the room and strangle Miller."

I envision it. Imagine Hawke's tattooed hands gripping Alex's neck, squeezing the life out of him, and smile at the notion.

Hawke glances at the phone in his hand. "Well, we should go in. Recess is nearly over."

We step inside the ornate courthouse. Marble floors gleam, despite all the metaphorical blood that's been dragged across them. I suck in deep breaths, holding them in as I follow him down the hallway, toward another set of double doors, these ones smaller.

Hawke pauses by the opening, glancing back. "Remember,

Teagan, Alex won't be able to hurt you. Nothing he says matters. Whatever he has you recalling, I want you to remember where you are, what you're doing, and why you are. You're not alone in this. Now," he grins, becoming the guy I met in the basement weeks ago, "let's burn this fucker."

Then he takes the lead and I enter behind him, eyes lowered, but not for long. Not as everyone's attention turns toward me, and the courtroom becomes deafening silent.

This is where I crack. Where it all becomes real—but what becomes real? Stopping Alex was a faint dream for years, if only so he could leave me alone. But this is *real*. This is about to happen. I'm in a courtroom, where people are all gathered because of what he's done. Years of silence, years of torture, hate, and depression has a precipice. And that is now.

I stop breathing, making my eyes blank and unseeing as I follow the black blob of Hawke's form toward the front, past everyone, and to a table with a dozen or so papers scattered over them.

Brent's eyes are on me, and though I order myself to resist, I can't avoid his siren call and glance back. Our gazes clash. Despite not responding to his most recent text message, he doesn't appear angry. In fact, he's fierce. Protective. A look I've seen when we were kids and someone bumped into me. He was angry they knocked me to the ground and spent hours ensuring I wasn't sore. The bright blue of his eyes blaze.

Beside him is Elena, who shoots me a small smile, and Ryker gripping her hand, looking as impassive as ever. Beside him is Tristan and Natalie. While Tristan looks as Ryker does, there's black smudges beneath Natalie's eyes from where she's been wiping at her makeup.

Natalie almost experienced Alex's villainy far worse than Willow and me. She received his love and gained a family member, all to lose it when the sheer covering fell from his empire. I add her to my list of women I'm doing this for.

Anger swirls in my gut, and my hands fist on my lap. Teeth grit, and I think about Dr. Laz and how proud she'd be right now. Memories plague me, but for all the right reasons, fuelling my anger and not my trauma.

Hawke gestures to one of the free chairs at his table. "Sit here. The judge will call you up soon."

"Okay."

The doors open again, and I can't help but glance over to watch a man enter. He's dressed like Hawke, only with the addition of cockiness; the sign of a lawyer who wins a lot of cases and feels good about this one. He flicks his finger at Hawke as he passes, a grin lining his mouth.

But it's not the lawyer who pisses me off. It's the man walking behind him.

Dressed in a flawless suit, easy grin, and beautiful face, Alex glances at me. The simple power of his gaze drops my shoulders, but my fight remains, enough to return his look with all the hate I can muster.

"Teagan," he greets, tilting his head.

His hand whips out, smacking against my cheek. The hit is sudden and hard enough that my body loses balance and stumbles to the side. Blood from earlier drips from a cut on my forehead, now reopened with his newest hit.

Tied to a chair, hands bound behind my back, I buck. A useless feat, but anything is worth it to attempt to get away from what he's forcing me to watch. How he stalks the small glass cage, toward the cowering Mia. Her arms are folded over her head, but still, she meets my eyes through the bit of space. Instead of the hate I deserve, there's only sorrow. Sorrow, followed by a goodbye.

I blink, shaking away the memories. Dr. Laz would disapprove that I allowed the memories to consume me again, after weeks of work to ensure this very thing wouldn't happen upon seeing him. Shame burns at the edges of my heart.

"Unfortunate how this turned out," Alex says, before taking his own seat beside his lawyer.

"Babe... Kill her."

Anger burns away the memories. He made me attempt to kill someone. I lift my jaw, turning my head away from him. Beneath the safety of the table, my hands weave together and I shut my eyes, taking those deep breaths Dr. Laz spoke to me about.

In. One. Two. Three. Out. One. Two. Three.

I do this twice, and when my jaw unclenches and I feel as though I won't lash out, I open my eyes, staring forward at nothing.

Carmen. Mia. Anne. Gemma. Zoey. Rachel. Charlotte. Scarlett.

Willow.

Natalie.

Me.

The recital of the names brings me enough strength to glance at Hawke, who's re-angled his body to block Alex from view.

"Focus, Teagan."

From behind me, I hear a whispered, "Cherry-Girl, reclaim your future."

Reclaim my future.

His simple words do something to my insides. They twist them up, consuming all previous fears, and I nod, though at no one in particular.

"I can do this," I tell Hawke, saying it to also remind myself.

"All rise," a new voice calls out, and the entire room shuffles as everyone stands. I scramble, straightening my blouse and brushing a crease from my dress pants as I go.

A man comes from a door in the far corner, and he takes his position in the judge's chair. Salt and pepper hair top inquiring eyes as he scans the room, briefly settling on me, before he sits. With him sitting, everyone else follows suit.

"Court is assembled again. Prosecutor, rise and call your next witness," he calls out.

Hawke does immediately. To the judge, he declares, "I call Teagan Faber to the stand."

"Go ahead." The judge gestures toward the stand beside him.

Carmen. Mia. Anne. Gemma. Zoey. Rachel. Charlotte. Scarlett. Willow.

Natalie.

Me.

I stand, straightening another crease in my shirt that isn't there, and stride around the table, with a ramrod spine, toward the stand. Jury members stalk my movements, but I pay none of them any attention in fear they'll undo my newfound sense of bravery.

Once I'm settled in the stand, Hawke also walks forward, and the entire courtroom falls in a hush. I glance past him, toward Brent, seeing his pinched expression. Then I peek at Alex as he stares me down, eyes narrowing with challenge. He sits forward and his arms rest on the table, reminding me of when they last held me—pinned me—as he took what he wanted.

My throat goes dry, my palms damp. Tingles shoot through my body, and suddenly, I need off this stand and away from—

"State your name."

In. One. Two. Three. Out. One. Two. Three.

Do this and Alex goes away. Don't let him bother you.

Once the feeling of running passes, I respond, "Teagan Faber."

Hawke nods once before his arm shoots out, gesturing toward Alex. "Do you know who this man is?"

I nod, wishing I didn't, because it could have prevented so much.

"Verbal answers only."

"Yes. Alex Miller."

"Can you tell me how you know Mr. Miller?"

"We went to high school together."

Hawke rolls his lips, an apology darkening his bright eyes. "And what was your relationship with Mr. Miller?"

"For a while, we didn't have one." I allow myself to peek at Alex again; he's relaxed into the backing of his wooden chair, his brows furrowed as though he's interested in my statements. "We were simply two people in the same grade. Eventually, he asked me out and we dated."

Hawke nods, lips pursing, and he rocks on his feet. "How did you feel about your relationship?"

I shrug lazily, giving the blatant truth. "I was a teenager. How does any teenage girl feel about her first boyfriend? I really liked him for a while."

Hawke's eyes widen, an act we both know to be fake, and he stops moving. "For a while? Can you elaborate on that?"

"I, um, I told him I wasn't ready for sex yet and..." My words die off, and I can't help but look at Alex. The corner of his lips curve in a way that won't seem obvious to anyone else, but I know him and his tells. He's thrilled. All it does is cause my teeth to grind together.

"And?" Hawke prods.

"He left the day I denied him, but returned the next and," I swallow, preparing for my next words, "forced me." A deep breath locks in my lungs, and then— "He raped me."

Powerful words.

Words that have me wanting to crawl from this stand, but one thing therapy was good for, was being able to say those words and not run away. It's what Dr. Laz insisted I be able to do. Accept and admit, without allowing it to crush me. Rape will *not* be my end.

Jury members' pens scratch furiously across their notepads.

Their actions are encouraging, and I straighten for Hawke's next question.

"Did you tell anyone?"

"No, but my foster mother found me in bed. She didn't do anything. I was scared, I guess. His father paid my foster family off, so I knew anyone I told would be paid off as well by the Millers."

Hawke nods again, and his arms go around his back. "Thank you. Miss Faber, did you willingly continue this relationship with Mr. Miller?"

"I guess." I shrug since I'm not entirely sure how to respond. "I mean, my head was in the stars for a lot of it, until I realized how bad he was."

"Did you continue this relationship after high school?"

The truth is sour in my mouth, and I wince. "Yes, but I didn't want to."

Hawke nods, and when I think he'll make me delve deeper into the reason I remained by Alex's side, he instead asks, "Can you tell me what your life with Mr. Miller was like for the last few years?"

This time, I look to Brent. To Elena. And to Natalie.

"I was owned by him. Fear kept me quiet. I worked the job he demanded me to, was by his side when he ordered me to be, and did everything he asked. For the first little while, it was only me. He... he would rape me often."

Hands crowd me, ripping my clothing off me, as he throws me against the nearest wall before he slams himself deeply into me, cleaving a cry from my throat.

"If I acted in a way he didn't approve of, he would beat me. Or torture me."

"Fucking whore." His slap rings across my cheek as he nudges me through the doorway of his office. "Thinking you can run from me like that."

"Did you ever consent to any of Mr. Miller's actions?"

"Never," I whisper, keeping my eyes on Brent, pulling the strength I need from him to delve into the memories I've buried. His scorching gaze provides exactly that. "I begged him to stop so many times."

Hawke nods once and steps toward his table for a moment. With the break in questioning, I refill my lungs because I suspect the worst is yet to come.

Thirty-Six

TEAGAN

HAWKE LIFTS a small metal device and points it toward the TV in the corner of the room. "Miss Faber, I will be showing you images. Will you identify the women in these pictures for the court, please?"

Pictures. Women. *Fuck.* My strength crumbles, and I lower my eyes to my hands. I'll have to see them all again and... I can't.

Carmen. Mia. Anne. Gemma. Zoey. Rachel. Charlotte. Scarlett.

I know what he's going to show me, but it doesn't stop the bile from filling my throat as the screen flashes with Carmen's mangled body. It was both his worst and most generous act to any of them. Worst, because Alex was learning psycho techniques, but most generous, because he didn't do half the stuff he later did to his other victims.

I've seen a similar image before, when Alex taunted me with his newfound hobby and "success." When he fucked me in pure elation because he was so riled up.

I can't do this. Nothing prepared me for this. Dr. Laz wasn't showing me images of the previous victims to prepare me. For a second, I hate Hawke for putting me through this.

"Miss Faber," he prompts.

In the silence, from the crowd, another sound rises. An older couple gasps, the woman throwing her head into the man's neck. Her family, presumably. The only one of us to have a family. One of Alex's errors he soon resolved.

A family... What's it like to have one to love and care for you, to miss you when you're gone?

In. One. Two. Three. Out. One. Two. Three.

For them, I look up again. For the victim, I respond, "Carmen."

The screen flashes to another. This one, her dark hair has been ripped from her scalp due to the number of times he dragged her around the basement. Bile rises up, and again, my eyes drop, but only for a second. I breathe deeply, stalling the breath in my lungs.

It's over after this.

"Mia."

I tried to save her. We both paid a horrid price for that attempt.

On and on it goes, and each time, it gets a bit easier, though not much. Every image brings with it a heavy amount of self-hatred; the thought that if only I said something sooner, she might still be alive and well. But every picture also reminds me that once I give the name, we're one step closer to winning.

Hawke switches off the TV, giving me back my breath. With the TV off, even the jury blinks. I spot a woman staring at her notepad, her eyes red-rimmed.

"Can you please tell the court who you believe hurt these women?"

Believe? Rather, I know. But I understand the careful game Hawke must navigate.

I don't answer, not right away. Instead, my gaze travels down the length of the jury, meeting each one's eyes as they stare, waiting for me to speak. Then I look toward Brent, Elena, and Natalie, each one of their fierce expressions warming my insides. Finally, I focus on Alex. Alex, whose eyes are narrowed again, a contrast to his relaxed form. I study his fisted hands, one resting on the table, a promise of how he's hoping he'll be able to hit me later for my incoming words.

"Alex Miller."

The jury scratches on their papers while the aged man by Alex's side leaps to his feet.

"Objection!"

"Grounds?" The judge sounds bored.

"Lack of proof."

Hawke's eyes cut sharply to the side. "I'm getting there." They soften as he takes in the judge once more. "Your Honour."

"Proceed."

Alex's lawyer sits down, obviously unwillingly, as Hawke continues his questions.

"Miss Faber, at any time, have you directly witnessed any act done to them?"

Too many times. "More than once. Or he'd show me images and videos afterwards. He revelled in power and enjoyed controlling me through fear. I tried to help Mia escape, so he made me watch when he tortured her. That was the first one I saw in person. The most recent being Willow."

I glance over toward Brent, unable to help myself. His expression is one of horror, since I never told him about Mia. Unlike Elena, who I had told, and she sits with pinched features as I recount it again.

Hawke's jaw clenches, but through gritted teeth, he asks, "When did you witness him injuring Willow Avery?"

"A few days before he was arrested," I respond. "I don't know the exact date. He took me down to meet her. He r-raped me," I swallow a staggering breath, "against the glass cage she was being held in. At the time, her injuries were fresh, and he said I made him so angry he hurt her first, and then me."

Two things happen then.

The jury's notes increase.

Alex smiles.

"In total, how many times has Alex Miller raped you?"

"I don't know. Too many times to count."

From the corner of my eye, I spot Elena laying her hand upon Brent's shoulder, but he shows no sign of feeling it.

"How many women do you believe he's killed?"

"Eight," I whisper, the number getting stuck inside my dry throat. "All the women you showed on the screen."

"How many women, are you aware of, have been taken by him?"

"Nine. Those eight and Willow."

Hawke glances toward the judge, then the jury who's listening raptly. After seemingly satisfied, he says, "Thank you, Miss Faber. Those are all the questions I have for you, unless there is something you would like to add."

I look toward the judge, who's staring down at me, his kind eyes waiting patiently.

I look toward the back of the room, to Carmen's parents, whose attention is locked on me.

I look toward Brent, to Elena, Ryker, Tristan, and Natalie, a mix of old and new friends.

I look toward the door, knowing somewhere beyond them is Willow, who's fighting the past.

I look toward Hawke, whose lips are tilted in a small, reassuring smile.

I look toward the jury, who watches, curious of what more I'd say.

I look toward Alex, whose cockiness has now shifted into something darker—something rare. Fear.

And finally, I look toward my fisted hands. I don't know when they ended up like this, but they did, and I relax them, smoothing them on my pants before I raise my voice to the waiting crowd to speak words I've been subconsciously practicing for years.

"Alex Miller will make you believe what you want to hear. It's what he did to me, and what he's done to all the women he's encountered. In high school, I judged him to be a hot guy but had no idea of the monster hiding within.

"When Ryker Ames hit him," I glance to Ryker and Elena, "I escaped. I managed to get a few provinces away before he found me and dragged me home. That was the first time he hurt me in ways beyond rape. He tortured me. Threatened my friends. Ryker Ames went to prison because no one believed his claims, but they're completely true. I'm not the first girl in high school he forced, though I don't know who the others were.

"His business, from what I know, is clear, but—"

"Objection!" Alex's lawyer jumps to his feet again. "Slander. Relevance."

The judge peers beyond his stand, kindness fading from his eyes as he stares at Alex's lawyer. "Overruled. I'm curious what Miss Faber has to say. Continue please."

I nod, but I'm barely listening, while my mind is solely focused on my speech. "His business is clean, but his associates are not. There's a network of people who keep women as slaves. Each year, Alex hosts a party where they can trade women."

Alex whispers something in his lawyer's ear, but my words continue rolling, while my gaze settles on Natalie.

"He wanted to sell his sister in a business deal. Normally, he doesn't participate, since his interests are a bit darker, but with his new family member, he saw an opportunity."

Natalie flinches, turning into Tristan. His eyes dart to the other side of the room, to Alex, and darkness grows a mask over his expression.

"Alex Miller is not a good man, and I urge you all to understand that. He took my past, present, and future. He controlled what I did, who I saw, and what job I held. He gave me a lifetime of horrors. He took innocent lives by luring them in to work for him, and brought them to his house where he never released them. I owe so many people an apology. Every one of those women, myself, and my own damn soul for not speaking up sooner. For so many years, I hoped Alex would tire of me and strangle me hard enough that my life would fade away. I say these words," I move my attention to the jury, "in hopes you don't see what everyone else does—a pretty face with wealth, charisma, and prestige. Look past that and hear what I say to you, remember what Willow told you, and believe what Mr. Blackwood is showing you. Alex Miller needs to pay for his countless crimes. If not for me, then for the women who are not here today to tell their stories."

My back falls against the chair, energy exiting my body. Saying that... was a lot. A lot that had to be said, so the jury understands the power behind the name Miller. But with it all out, a new sense of contentment takes over. Like, for now, I did what I could and Dr. Laz would be pleased.

With my final word, Alex cries out, but I don't hear him. Don't pay him any heed as his lawyer shushes him and stands, replacing the spot Hawke backs away from.

A strong air of emotion clouds the room, and I hope it's overtaking any disbelief the jury may have had before my speech. Hawke is working to help me, while Alex's lawyer will try to break me down.

I can't allow that.

"Miss Faber, have you ever told my client no?"

Already said I did, you moron. He's aiming to victim-blame, but I've had enough of that.

"Of course."

"But you never spoke against him to any member of the law?"

"No."

"Would you agree you were an accomplice then?"

"Objection!" Hawke shouts, jumping to his feet. "Unfair badgering. The matter of Miss Faber's involvement has already been dealt with by the courts. A fact everyone was made aware of *before* this trial began."

"Agreed," the judge says. "Next question, defence."

Alex's lawyer huffs before shooting a dark look toward Hawke. "Fine. You entered into a relationship willingly, back when you were both in high school, did you not?"

"Yes, but I already said, I didn't realize what kind of person he was. And when I finally did, I didn't think anyone would believe me." This time, I level my stare at the lawyer, even leaning forward to throw his own words back at him. "Tell me, if you were in my situation and never had anyone on your side, how would you react? You'd build your defences and remain silent, if only to survive."

The man flushes red—with embarrassment or anger, I'm not certain. Beyond him, Hawke smirks, tipping his chin up in a universal sign to continue.

"Besides the point, Miss Faber. You blame my client, when he so clearly was enticed by you."

Disbelief scrunches my brows. This is a new level of blame, but it's one I'm not falling for. Annoyance has me biting down on my tongue and glancing toward Hawke. He nods, encouraging me on, when I wish he'd end this.

"No woman *ever* asks to be raped, beaten, and tortured. So, no, I don't believe *I* had anything to do with how he," I throw a finger toward Alex, "lived his life."

The jury takes more notes, as Alex's layer walks back to his table. From it, he lifts a sheet of paper that he drops onto Hawke's table.

"This has already been submitted for evidence, if you recall. I have here, psychological testing ran on my client. He shows no tendencies of harming another, or even himself. The doctors have cleared him of any possible diagnoses."

Because he paid them off.

Hawke jumps to his feet, gesturing to the side. "That doesn't clear Mr. Miller of the accused charges. Mentally, he may be stable, but he could still harm another, as my client has clearly stated."

Alex's lawyer slowly turns toward him. "Your client can be lying, Mr. Blackwood, have you thought about that?"

Around me, this entire thing comes crumbling down. While I don't have the document in hand, I look toward the judge, who is still reading his copy, while my heart cracks. *Is this where we lose?*

A moment later, his gavel whacks, silencing all the talking. "Prosecutor, sit down. Defence, do you have anything more to ask Miss Faber?"

"No." The lawyer falls back, taking his seat once more.

"You may step down, Miss Faber. Thank you for your cooperation," the judge says, gesturing to the chair at Hawke's table I vacated earlier.

Once I retake my seat, the judge stands. "If all evidence has been presented and there are no more witnesses, I invite both the prosecution and defence to give their closing statements. Prosecutor, you go first."

Hawke stands, turning his body toward the jury stand.

"My client, Miss Faber, has lived through years of physical, sexual, mental, and emotional abuse at the hands of Mr. Miller. Miss Faber is a girl who, like so many others, wanted to finish high school and go to college and have new experiences. Instead, she was pulled into a treacherous scheme and coerced to keep Mr. Miller's secrets, if only to keep herself and those she cared about safe from further harm. I implore you to consider the evidence shown here today. The testimonies of Miss Teagan Faber and Miss Willow Avery, the images, the psychological reports. Miss Faber is seeking restitution in the form of freedom, and while the defence will want you to view the facts differently, I ask you do not allow them to sway you. The defence aims to cover Mr. Miller's abuse with their own reports of his mental stability, and testimonies that claim he is innocent, but all they are doing is the same manipulation tactics Mr. Miller has been doing for years—fabricating a lie and covering the truth. For the safety of Miss Faber and Miss Avery, of other innocent and unsuspecting women, but also the women who have lost their lives at the hands of Mr. Miller, I beg you to look past the name Miller and see the truth in what has been presented here today." Hawke pauses before ending with, "Thank you."

He sits down, not making eye contact with me. His hands go beneath the table and he wipes his palms up and down his lap twice, as Alex's lawyer stands up, also facing the jury.

"Jury members, you have been dragged in here for a lie, it is true, but it is not a lie my client, Mr. Miller, has concocted. Rather, it's a lie from women who would prefer to see my client's name disgraced. Look at Mr. Miller here," he gestures to Alex beside him, "and ask yourselves, does this look like a man who would murder, rape, and harm innocent women for sport? My client is a Miller—a name that garners a lot of responsibility and a legacy for decades to come. He does not wish to have it sullied more than it already has been. The plaintiff, Miss Faber," he gestures toward me, "is simply a woman scorned, seeking revenge for a relationship gone wrong. The images are fabricated, the reports faked; a scheme being planned for years by Miss Faber. Mr. Miller is innocent and I implore you to see the truth in what has occurred here; a smokescreen meant to distract and overwhelm you. Thank you."

Once he's seated again, the judge speaks directly to the jury. "The jury will convene now to deliberate the evidence. We will continue when they have a verdict for us." He whacks his gavel and everything feels okay.

This will soon be over.

Thirty-Seven

TEAGAN

HAWKE IMMEDIATELY STANDS and leads me out of the courtroom, nudging me past everyone, including Brent.

"Come with me," he mutters, as we break out into the hallway. The sound of his shiny shoes clack against the marble flooring with the speed he rushes me through the lingering crowd.

"Teagan!" Brent.

I continue walking, following Hawke until he leads me to a side room, equipped with a long table and a water jug on it. The door is slammed shut and locked behind us before Hawke pours me a glass. I take it as he slumps in a padded, velvet chair, his hand rubbing at his forehead.

"Fuck."

"That doesn't sound good." I sit too, despite the hardwired nerves begging me to pace.

"Just..." He trails off, dropping his hand away from his face to study me. "How are you? I know that wasn't easy, but damn, your final speech... If the jury had any doubts prior, they don't now."

My fingers tighten around the glass, anxiety clenching my stomach. "You think we'll win? You don't believe he paid them off?"

Hawke shakes his head once. "I think it would have been a stupid move on his part. With everything he's done, if the jury doesn't find him at fault, questions will be raised, and his lawyer will have more to answer for. They won't ignore multiple counts of first-degree murder."

Hope clogs my throat. "What's the sentence for that?"

"Life. Twenty-five years per murder. Plus, whatever they want to stack on for the torture, kidnapping, rapes, abuse... you see where this is going. He won't have that many years left on the planet. Teagan, you'll never see him again."

A breath whooshes out of me as relief replaces the anxiety. Never is a long time, and still, it won't be long enough.

Hawke's wrong about one thing though. I'll see Alex again, in my memories and my nightmares. He'll be a shadow upon my life, and on Willow's.

"If you don't mind," Hawke stands, "I'm going to see Willow. I'm sure there's a group of anxious friends on the other side of this door, and if you don't wish to see them, lock the door behind me."

"Just Brent," I murmur, staring at the glass of water in front of me. "Keep Brent away please. I can't."

Understanding crosses his expression. "I'll convince the guys to remove him if he's hanging around."

"Thanks." The door opens and shuts, but I don't watch him leave. Sure enough, there's a rise of voices, and one stands out.

"Dammit, Hawke. Why?"

Hawke must say something in response, thought I don't hear what, because it's the last Brent speaks.

He'll want answers for yesterday, or to console me about today. Right now, I need to do this alone. He has to deal with not being the superhero for once.

I drop into the chair, finger tracing the edging of my glass for a solid two minutes before the knock inevitably comes. I'm not surprised he's returned, but I hate myself for not locking the door when I had the chance.

I stand, hoping my voice will carry through the thick, rich wood. "Go away, Brent."

Rather than a gruff tone, a feminine and familiar one comes through. "It's not Brent. It's me. And Natalie."

I should tell them to leave me alone as well, but with her words, my heart flutters and some of the agony fades away, making me want to open it. So I do, a few inches, enough they can slip through it.

I stare at Natalie rather than Elena, recalling the first time I met her at Alex's party. He acted like I was the loving girlfriend. Countless times that night, I bit my tongue to prevent from saying what I wanted to—to tell her to escape and get out of here and never respond to Alex's calls again. But I didn't because Alex remained by my side.

When she disappeared, he was annoyed. To her, he pretended to be worried, but he wasn't in the slightest. Men like Alex don't get worried because they don't have concerns.

Which is why when she entered his office the following day, I had to say something. I couldn't help me or Willow, but I could help her. Could save her before she was tied into his web of lies.

"I'm sorry," I whisper.

Her mouth curls down. "I don't even know why I'm crying. I've accepted this, but I guess, watching him smirk at the evidence... He has no remorse. It's all a game to him, and *that's* what hurts. Knowing I share blood with a psychopath. For a while, I ignored the gut feeling and just wanted a family. He gave me that and I—I don't know."

Tears swell in her eyes again and I glance away, toward my feet, feeling like shit for drudging up the past. Elena wraps an arm around her shoulder, curving Natalie into her body and for the first time ever—in my life, I think—I'm jealous. Its red-hot amber flames lick down my spine and into my hands, which fist by my side.

When Alex was stealing my life, Elena moved on and found solace in a new friendship. I have no bad feelings toward that, but I should have been by her side too. I should never have *left*. We should have gone on, became roommates, and experienced all the firsts of our adult life together.

For so long, I've been fighting. Fighting and losing. Simply surviving. I refused to get close to any of the girls at work and couldn't exactly bond with any of the women Alex dragged into his basement. I lost out on "girl time," and became a recluse to hide amongst my own miserable shadow.

It isn't until now, as I observe them, I realize how much I've been truly missing.

Elena lifts her head from Natalie, sees me, and somehow reads me exactly like she used to. Her free arm stretches toward me in an invitation.

I take it.

One hug. Three women whose futures have been ripped from them by Alex.

Elena lost Ryker.

Natalie lost the chance of a family.

And I lost myself.

I don't realize I'm crying until Natalie and Elena loosen their hold. When I pull back, strands of their hair stick to my face and won't detach until I wipe them away.

"This is nearly over," Elena murmurs. "And after today, I think we could all use a very strong drink."

"Agreed," Natalie chimes, also wiping at her eyes.

I remain silent. After today, I won't be around for that drink.

Elena's heavy gaze lands on me, and with her frown, I know we're thinking the same thing.

The door opens again, and Hawke enters. He appears different than earlier—more frazzled. If possible, his hair is an even larger mess, his eyes skirting the room until they land on me.

"Court is being called back into session. The jury has made their verdict."

"ALL RISE." We do so, until the judge enters the courtroom and retakes his seat on his bench.

His attention diverts immediately toward the jury. "Have you elected a foreperson?" When an elderly man in the front row stands up, he continues, "Has the jury reached a verdict to each count presented?"

"We have, Your Honour," the man says.

The judge nods, gesturing to the bailiff off to the side. "Please give your paperwork to the bailiff."

The man hands over a small stack, which then gets passed to the judge. He scans the documents briefly before examining the room. Only the sounds of bated breaths and sharp inhalations, mine included, can be heard when the judge begins speaking.

I glance toward Hawke, noting his bouncing leg beneath the table. He's anxious, despite his reassurance that we'll win. Past him, Alex's lawyer is adopting an identical position, likely for the opposite reason. My eyes collide with Alex's. He smiles, and it's more natural and less malicious than I've gotten used to. I'm uncertain how to feel about that.

"The defendant will rise and face the jury."

Alex stands, giving me his back.

This is it. With Alex turned away, I risk glancing at Elena and Natalie behind me, but their attention is both on the front. A nervous energy hits my body, and my leg begins moving in tandem with Hawke's.

"As to the first count of the eight known instances of murder, we the jury find Alex Miller... guilty."

I cry. It's still so far from being over, but I allow the tears that instantly swell to remain.

For you, Carmen, Mia, Anne, Gemma, Zoey, Rachel, Charlotte, and Scarlett.

"As to the second count of the nine known instances of kidnapping, we the jury find Alex Miller... guilty."

Nine, because they're including Willow in their counts now.

Tears run rampant down my face, and I don't bother wiping them.

"As to the third count of the nine known instances of captivity, we the jury find Alex Miller... guilty."

Good. A simple thought, but it's all my emotions can muster at the moment.

"As to the fourth count of the ten known instances of ongoing torture, we the jury find Alex Miller... guilty."

I bite down on the cheer. This is for them. For all of them. For the women who aren't here today, and for Willow. For me.

The judge continues, "As to the fifth count of the psychological torture and conditioning of Teagan Faber, we the jury find Alex Miller... guilty."

I sob. I can't help it. It breaks from me, and my hand slams over my mouth, unwilling to allow my own happiness to block the sounds of Alex's verdicts.

They believed me. I spoke up and they believed me.

"As to the sixth count of the ongoing rape of ten women, we the jury find Alex Miller... guilty."

Your turn to be ass-raped in prison, asshole.

The judge lowers the papers, focusing on the jury. "Is there anyone who does not agree with the verdicts just read?"

A resounding, "No," echoes through the lines.

It's over.

It's over.

Guilty.

It's the only word that matters. Guilty. Alex Miller has finally been found guilty.

I'm free.

Before my elation gets the best of me, the judge stands up, his voice bellowing above the air of excitement. "Alex Miller, the jury has found you guilty of the listed crimes. You will be sentenced to nine consecutive life sentences in a maximum-security prison, without parole. You will be remanded into the custody of the province immediately. Bailiff, take him into processing please."

Then he whacks his gavel down and it's done.

Hawke hops to his feet before stepping away from the table, his hand held out toward Alex's lawyer, who begrudgingly takes it with a frown.

I stop watching them, in favour of twisting around and taking in the row of faces behind me. This was my fight, but they were all casualties in the war. Ryker appears smug as he kisses Elena with pure passion, and Natalie's eyes are still red from crying, but she's smiling as Tristan pulls her onto his lap, and Brent's fierce expression blasts into me.

My attention diverts back to the villain in this story in time to observe the bailiff slapping cuffs on Alex's wrists. A fresh wave of tears fall at the simple sight. A sight I've dreamed of, but a reality I never imagined.

The bailiff tugs him away, but I move too, wanting to be closer. Maybe it's stupid and silly, but it's the view my mind needs to comprehend.

Alex spots me, and rather than appear pissed at the outcome, he smiles. "It's been fun, Teagan. I'm sorry we couldn't have forever."

Hawke steps between us, partially blocking me from view. "Don't respond to him."

Hawke's disruption tears Alex's attention from me, and his lip curls. "Say goodbye to Willow for me. Can't wait to visit her dreams each night."

"Go to hell," I spit, despite Hawke's hand resting on my arm, holding me back.

Alex and the bailiff step around us, heading for the back door, but Alex's heels dig into the smooth ground, and he glances at the group who's crowded behind Hawke and me.

"Ames." He nudges his chin at Ryker. "Guess it's my turn to experience prison." Alex's attention shifts a fraction. "Elena, too bad you didn't take me up on my job offer."

Natalie pushes through then, getting closer, until the bailiff holds up a hand. "Why?" Her sorrow-laden voice is no higher than a whisper. "Why try to be a family to me at all?"

Alex's lawyer also comes up to his side. "Say nothing more, Alex."

But Alex doesn't listen, and he shrugs lazily, scanning his sister. "Women are good for one thing, Nat, and only one thing. Why would I not capitalize on that?"

Tristan growls, but Ryker shifts in his path, blocking Tristan from reacting in a way that'll force us to convene again, for an entirely new reason.

None of it matters any more though. Whatever Alex did in the past is over and the only way to go is up. It's one thing Dr. Laz mentioned to me a lot in those final couple weeks of therapy. The past is the past and there's only one way to live the future—in the present.

Alex is pushed away, his bound hands held by the officer, but as they approach the door, Alex manages to turn. He studies the group, his eyes landing on Brent, who has come up beside me, and then on me.

He smiles, and it's one I've seen countless times before.

His evil *I've won* grin before he pushed his cock inside me, or when his knife sliced at my skin, or when he gripped my neck so tightly, I was certain he'd kill me. It's a smile I'll feel for the rest of my days.

"Goodbye, Teagan. Just remember, your life will always be mine. No one you care for will be safe."

And then the bailiff shoves Alex through the open doorway, removing him from my life. From all our lives. Finally.

Thirty-Eight

TEAGAN

LIKE EARLIER, Hawke grasps my arm and practically drags me from the courtroom.

"I have a few more battles to fight with his lawyer," he says in hushed tone as he ushers me through the crowds beyond the door. "I need to get Willow home. I assume you're good to get yourself out of here?"

"Yeah." We stop by the front entranceway, my feet finally catching up while my eyes lock on the crowd exiting the courtroom behind us. "Thanks, Hawke. For everything. Seriously."

He winks. "My pleasure. Good luck, Teagan. I hope to see you around."

But the look in his eyes tells me he's aware of my plans. So, when he pushes back through the crowds to rescue Willow from wherever he's hidden her, I send a silent goodbye his way.

My hand rests on the metal handle. One push and I'll be exiting the courthouse and entering my new life.

One...

Two...

Three—

I step outside, and the normally warm spring air feels hotter. Its heat welcomes me into its fold, hugging me as it takes me away into a sunnier future. A future that'll only begin with—

"Teagan!"

Brent. He knows me; therefore, he knows why I'm out here, rather than celebrating. Even before turning, I envision his eyes filled with hurt and betrayal.

This time, I'm *choosing* to walk away from my best friend. He'll believe it's an easy decision, but it's not. My heart hurts—it's shattering as I spin on my heel, steeling myself for what's next. But it's called self-sacrifice. For Brent to be happy, he needs stability and purpose, which are things I can't give him.

Brent stops one step above me. Behind him, closer to the courthouse, is everyone else, minus Hawke.

"Where are you going, Cherry-Girl?"

But he knows. I know he knows. It's in the way his eyes drop to the cement steps then climb back up. It's in the way he glances toward Elena, who nods softly, already accepting what I told her yesterday.

"You can't. You're free to be who you want, Teagan. To be *with* who you want."

"I can't do that here, Brent. I-I'm sorry."

He steps—more like stumbles down, with how his feet slide over the steps—until he's standing on mine. "*Why?* Tell me why you insist on running away."

"I just—" I shake my head, biting down on my weak explanation. He won't understand it. He hasn't lived through what I have. "I don't know what I want, Brent. I'm sorry. Once, yes, it was you. It was going to college with you and Elena. It was living my best life, but now... I don't know what it is. I need to get away from here— from everything this place *is*."

Brent's face flashes red, and in the next instant, his hands bind my upper arms and he drags me against his chest. "Up. The only way is up."

I struggle against his hold, hands pushing at his chest. Brent, the ever-opposite of Alex, allows me the space, but he keeps holding on.

"No, I won't allow you."

Allow. He still doesn't get it, even after everything.

"Yesterday..." Brent trails off, his voice crumpling with every syllable. His grip loosens as the rest of his body's energy dissipates and I manage to step away.

"Was everything I dreamed of and needed."

"*Fuck*, Teagan, you make me angrier than I ever thought possible. After everything, you're honestly leaving?" Arms fly, but I back away, stepping down another step to put distance between us.

"That's not fighting fair," I say, hardening my tone, so he recognizes my seriousness, peering at him through slitted eyes. "You know why I did that."

"But I don't know why you are *now*. You're free, Teagan. Cherry-Girl." My nickname fills the thin air. *"Stay."*

I look away, unable to watch Brent's pitiful agony any longer.

After another moment, he asks in a quieter tone, "Remember what I said to you in Hawke's house?"

Words that branded themselves in my brain. "That you'd chase me."

"Have you ever known me to be a liar?"

"Not in the slightest." I meet his gaze, hoping he continues to see my seriousness. "But don't chase me. Not this time."

He stumbles back, landing on another step as he simply stares at me. I watch as his expression shifts from heartbreak to acceptance to wonder. Finally, he asks a question filled with so much hope, so much want, it nearly breaks me in a way Alex was never able to.

"Do you love me, Cherry-Girl?"

More than I can admit.

If I tell him the truth, he won't let me go. He'll fight for me, and this will never end.

If I lie, I'll break him. But a broken man won't fight for what he loves.

"No."

"Yesterday—"

"Was driven by physical want. I'm sorry."

He crumbles. Energy leaves his body, and everything falls. His shoulders lower, he wavers as if the light breeze will knock him over, and his expression drops deeper than I've ever seen.

When kids made fun of his weight, he was dejected. When I arrived at school with no food in my lunch, he was vicious. When I rejected his request to date me, he was wrecked.

But nothing he's felt in the past is remotely like what I watch cross his expression this time.

Broken. No—shattered.

Shattered and splintered. And I'm the glue to rebuild him.

But I won't fix him. Not this time.

And while the guilt is a heavy burden, I fight against it. At least while I'm here. Once I'm alone, I can break. I can cry and sob and scream for making this decision that feels so wrong, but it'll prove to be the best in time. Even he'll come to see it eventually.

As Dr. Laz put it, I'm running. This time, physically, emotionally, and mentally. I'm okay with it though.

I glance past Brent and scan the group. Brent will be fine. His friendship with Ryker and Tristan has always been strong. He and Elena obviously managed to find common interests. And with Natalie, Hawke, and perhaps Willow eventually, he'll be happy. He'll finish his degree, make something of his life, and I won't drag him down.

Which is why, without another word or glance at Brent, I turn and walk down the stone steps, leaving my heart behind to die.

Thirty-Nine

BRENT

IT'S NOT the first time she's rejected me, but somehow, I know it'll be the final time.

She doesn't want me. She's never wanted me. It's obvious now. Yesterday, I hoped I got through to her—opened her up and found that she does care for me.

The first time she left, she was running from Alex. She was surviving his cruelty, even before the worst came.

The second time she left, she was taken away in an ambulance and locked away for her protection. It was a time for healing and mental stability.

Which is why, this time—the final time—she's *choosing* to go. Of sound mind, free from the past, and yet—

Feet scrape on the steps. Without turning around, I know it's Elena. I recognize her scent. I *feel* her, because while our relationship may have only been a ploy, I genuinely came to care for her. It's hard not to. She's too good, too kind.

Which is why when her hand rests on my shoulder, pressing empathy and sympathy into my body, I turn and capture her in a hug, uncaring if Ryker will tear my head from my body. Through everything, friendship bloomed. She may not be the woman I want to be holding, but her tight grip secures my heart inside my chest.

"She'll come back."

She won't. I saw it in her face.

"She loves you."

"She doesn't," I counter.

Elena pulls from my arms, wiping away her own tears. "Girls know these things. She loves you, Brent, but she's freaked out. It's Teagan's way; you must know that. She's a runner."

She ran when Alex was in the hospital, instead of reporting him. She ran away from all of us at first, after we admitted our plans for Alex. She accepted everything—even his conditioning—because she was running from alternate actions she could be taking.

"She's running away from the possibility of a future," Elena continues. "Let her. Eventually, she'll tire herself out. She believes it's best for both of you because she fears dragging you down. She fears what you could be for her."

"You mean someone to love her?"

Elena lifts a perfectly manicured brow. "Think about what you said to her. You won't *allow* her to. Now, think about what her life's been like."

Oh. I stumble, her words threatening to knock me over entirely. I'm a damn moron. Of course, she's scared. I'm no better than Alex.

Elena's smirk widens. "There you go. She's only ever been kept and controlled, and she has no idea how to take your words. You need to prove you accept all of her; that you're not scared of what she might bring to your life—the memories, the trauma—and you won't control her."

"If I chase her, she'll see it as me trying to drag her home." Like *he* did.

"Maybe." Elena nonchalantly shrugs. "Or, for once in her adult life, someone will be fighting for her. She has a family here."

So, when Elena backs away and walks back to Ryker's side, I get to planning.

LOGIC and my heart still battle, even as I fly down the highway in the only direction out of the city. Having a cop as a friend is incredibly useful, especially when he was able to track where Teagan went after the courthouse, and where her bus is headed.

Logic tells me I should leave her be, as she requested, and let her do what she needs to, and then she'll return on her own time. Except my heart can't let her go. Elena claims Teagan loves me, and I suppose I blocked out the truth because I did feel her love yesterday.

Textbooks declare trauma victims will protect their own emotions in any way possible, and it's what Teagan's doing.

I'm coming, Cherry-Girl. This time, I'll find you. I promise.

The evening sun shines in my rearview mirror, so I don't notice the car approaching until he's practically tailgating me. I huff and flash my blinker to move into the right lane, to allow the car to pass.

That's when the pop comes, and my car—Hawke's car, actually—swerves before straightening, moving more sluggish now.

The fuck?

Still, I manage to drive the car into the next lane. My focus is on the empty highway; mind busy on what the noise could have been.

With my attention diverted, I don't see when the car comes closer, crowding my lane. Don't see how the driver specifically controls the vehicle to collide into mine. I slam on the brakes, aiming to get out of its path, but it's too late.

Metal meets metal. A screech sounds—my tires gliding across the cement.

Pressure slams the driver's side door into my arm at the same time my car rolls to the right.

And continues rolling.

Until the forest lining the highway blurs with the speed the car turns over.

Then everything goes black.

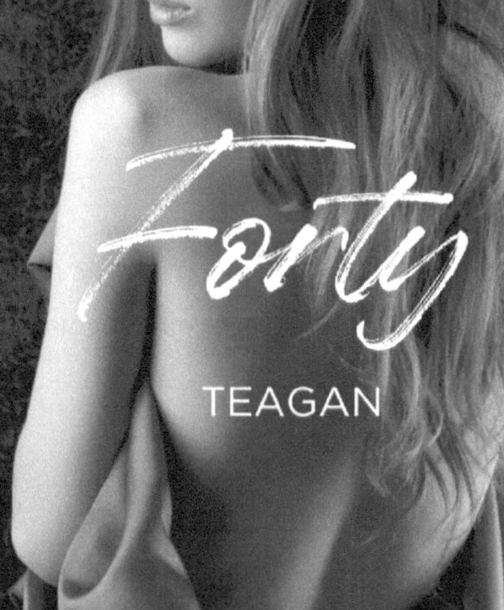

Forty

TEAGAN

AFTER LEAVING THE COURTHOUSE, I marched downtown to Cortville's bus station and bought a ticket that'll get me two provinces over, with tip money I was certain to bring with me to the trial. I didn't go home. Didn't bother deciding what and what not to take. It all remained; a memory of a previous life.

It's been hours, and we're finally pulling into a small town. So small, I'm shocked they found room for its name to fit on the map. The sun has long set, but we still have hours to go. The schedule has us slated to arrive late tomorrow.

The best thing about the drive has been the silence. The highway doesn't have the most up-to-date infrastructure, so since leaving Cortville, I've had no service. Which means not needing to stare at Brent's texts he'll no doubt be sending.

Brent doesn't give up.

And if he does show up? Then what? Do I have the strength to drive him away again?

I descend the bus's steps and head toward the fast-food restaurant they've dropped us off to use the restroom and replenish our food supply. On my way inside, I connect to the Wi-Fi, letting my phone receive service once more as I self-sabotage my own peace and accept whatever messages are about to bombard me.

None of them from Brent.

ELENA

Call me when you have a chance.

And then a missed call from her, not even five minutes later.

ELENA

Please pick up.

HAWKE

Answer your phone.

ELENA

I'm sorry to bother you, but my conscience won't allow you not to know.

And then two more missed calls from her, and one from Hawke. The most recent being an hour ago.

Elena and Hawke, and no Brent. A knot forms in my stomach, tightening, until shaky fingers manage to dial Elena. My call is answered right away.

"Teagan, thank fuck," she breathes. "We've been trying to get a hold of you for hours."

"Sorry, no service on the road. What's up?" I aim for casual words in hope they'll match the news she has for me.

Instead, her voice wavers as she delivers news that leaves my heart as broken as I left Brent's earlier today. Maybe it's penance for my actions. Maybe it's the universe telling me to stop ignoring what's so clearly in front of me.

"Brent. He was in an accident. He was on his way to you, and a car ran him off the road." She pauses, and her next words are barely a whisper. "He's not well, Teag. Doctors induced a coma. Just thought you'd want to know."

This is worse than I imagined. Something out there is punishing me.

"No one you care for will be safe."

Alex. Of course. Of-fucking-course.

He foreshadowed this.

I'll never be safe from him. I'll never *be* safe from his treachery. It won't end but—

"Where is he?" I demand urgently.

It won't end, but I can do one thing.

"Cortville General Hospital. It was the closest one when they found him."

"I'll be right there." I hang up, already seeking out the driver to determine when the next bus back will be.

IT'S two in the morning by the time I burst through the emergency room's doors, eyes seeking Elena, who I messaged when nearing the hospital. I find her across the room, by the elevator. She's dressed in the same outfit from the trial this morning, but her eyes are red, her makeup smudged across her face. She looks exhausted, but she's here. For Brent.

For *my* Brent.

And I wasn't.

I've held onto my emotions the entire trip back, but now, being at the hospital where he's somewhere close hits my heart differently.

I rush to her side, roughly grabbing at her hand and demand, "Is he okay?"

"He's alive." Elena presses her lips together in a flatline before sighing. "His body isn't holding up well though. Broken bones... cuts. A lot of swelling. Doctors say he wasn't awake when they brought him in. We've been trying to contact his parents, but none of my calls or texts have gone through."

His parents. Two loving people who were basically also my parents. More people from my past I've locked away when I realized Alex wouldn't release me.

She smacks the elevator button, enticing the metal doors to squeak open. The second we're in, Elena hits the 5 and the elevator begins ascending. The numbers climb too slowly for my sanity, and by the time it arrives on the fifth floor, I feel as though I'll die from agitation. When the ding finally comes and the doors slide open, I rush from it, scanning my immediate surroundings.

"This way." Elena nudges her head to a hallway at our left. It leads to a small sitting area, where I find everyone waiting. The most noticeable is Ryker, who's gripping the back of the chair nearest to the room's opening while his gaze burns into the seat's cushion. Across from him, on a small couch, is Tristan, who stares at the smooth-tiled floor with the same expression as Ryker's. Natalie is curled into his side, her eyes closed, but her breaths come too deeply for her to be sleeping. He grips her hand tightly, as though fearing what could happen if he releases her. Beside their couch is another, which Hawke occupies. Curled on his lap is Willow.

Willow is here. As in *here* and not hiding from the past. The way she is lying on Hawke is intimate, as he previously hinted at. They're together—as together as someone with her past can be.

Or they're truly together. Together and facing her past. Unlike me, who ran when things got—

"Come on," Elena whispers, "we'll check you in with the nurse. They don't want us in all at once, but we've been taking turns sitting with him."

We walk past the waiting room and toward the nearby nurses' desk at the same time Ryker's dark eyes snap to me. I look away from the hate—the blame. Not that it's misplaced; it *is* my fault. I couldn't face my own emotions and Brent paid the price.

After checking in with the nurse, who is all kind smiles and sympathy, Elena leads me to a nearby room.

"How are they okay with us camping here this late, past visiting hours?"

"Tristan flashed a badge. Ryker flashed money. Then they saw Hawke, and yeah, something happened there, though he won't say what." She rolls her eyes, but despite the action, I'm grateful. Her hand rests on the door's handle. "Go in."

She leaves then, and heads back to Ryker, claiming the chair he's still holding onto. Her movement awakens his daze, and he bends over the chair's backing to press his lips to her forehead.

My gaze slides from Ryker and Elena to Willow and Hawke.

In some ways, she had it worse than I did, and yet, she's somehow managing. She's not running from this area and all its bad memories. Hawke's helping her blaze her path.

I want that.

You could have had that.

Brent would have helped you.

My psyche might be right, but it'd be Brent who paid the price for my selfishness.

But it's a price he'd willingly pay. Be selfish.

As if wanting to dig the knife in deeper, Hawke shifts and his hand lands on her hair. His fingers comb through it. With the change, she opens her eyes, finding him watching her. Her responding smile is so happy, so bright, I have to look away.

Why isn't she broken, like I am? How can she be smiling only hours after the trial? I don't understand...

I gather my broken pieces and push the handle down, opening the door into the dim room, silently gasping at the sight.

A pale Brent, except for where cuts mar his face, lies unmoving in the hospital bed. Bruising has begun blooming across his skin, down his arms, and up his neck. His head is bandaged, and his arm is in a sling. His other arm has needles and cords connecting it to the beeping machine behind him.

I stare at the bumps on the screen—at the rhythm of his heart-beat and my knees buckle, relieved to see evidence that he's alive.

Fuck you, Alex. Fuck you to the depths of Hell. I hope you're raped over and over and over until you're bleeding and pray for death.

If only he hadn't gone to jail, then I could kill him myself. I thought I hated him already, but my hate was only a taste of what I truly feel now. He continues to find ways to hurt me; it never ends.

I'm not religious, but right now, I pray. I pray for Brent to wake up, to be healed, and to give me his typical bright smile. I pray for myself to stop being so fucked up. And I pray for Alex to die. I pray to undo these past two months, so I'd still be under Alex's control. I'd make the trade willingly, if it meant Brent wouldn't be lying in this bed.

The fact of what I'd sacrifice restarts my heart—makes my feet move to the chair by his bedside. Instead of using it though, I fall against the bed, my hands cupping around his own—the one not bound by a cast.

"I'm so sorry, Brent. More than I can ever say."

There's no answer, but the slow rise and fall of his chest is reassuring.

With him asleep, I let go. I release all the pent-up words my heart's been hiding; words unburied by this accident. Not a realiza-tion, but a willingness to admit the truth.

"I'm sorry for everything. I lied to you, Brent. I lied when I said I don't love you. I do. I'm just... I'm broken. I'm scared anything good in my life will be stolen by Alex. You were my friend, my saviour, my everything. I'll always regret not telling you about Alex back then and saving us years of agony. Hiding the truth began a domino effect that ended with you in this bed, and I'm so fucking sorry. If I could redo everything, I would because I fucking love you, Brent."

My forehead falls onto his hand, hating how he's unable to hear any of these truths.

"When you asked me out, I wanted to say yes. From the moment we met, you became my greatest friend. The guy who made me smile, even in the darkest of days. We had a connection, but I pushed it away for—"

Alex. Saying his name out loud in Brent's presence would be an insult.

With everything out, my ass falls onto the hard, plastic chair, but I don't let go of his hand. I won't until he wakes up.

After a few minutes of only the sounds of our breathing filling the quiet room, the door opens, and I stand, placing myself between Brent and whoever enters.

A large form with angry eyes enters first, followed by a slight woman with pale hair.

Ryker and Willow.

Instead of dropping my guard, I straighten, confused by the duo.

"Hey," Ryker whispers, a tone gentler than I've ever heard from him, "Elena and Natalie are both passed out, and Hawke's on his way too. He's had the busiest day out of all of us. We're going to head out now that you're here."

My head tilts slightly, both shocked and confused. "You're leaving me alone with him?"

Ryker shrugs, his eyes landing on his friend. "You're who he really wants by his side, and I'm not gonna stop that. Plus, Miller's at fault here. Not you. You did what you had to; we get it."

His words should off me some relief, the knowledge that they aren't blaming me, but instead, I jerk, focusing on who he is blaming.

"You know?"

Ryker jerks his thumb toward the door. "Tristan talked to the officers who arrived on the scene. Brent's tires were shot, and with how the metal was crushed, it's obvious the hit was forceful. The highway had tire marks skidding across one of the lanes, so yes, this wasn't an accident. Police don't know why or who's at fault, but, well," he smirks wryly, "we do."

"Is there any proof?"

Ryker's nose wrinkles and his arm drops back to his side. "No, and that's the annoying part. Tristan can't find record of him ordering the attack, so right now, we have nothing else to go at him with."

"Not that it really matters," I shrug, "he's gone, so how much *more* punishment can we stack on him?" I mean, revenge would be nice, but our efforts are better put on Brent's care. At this point, we can only hope someone in prison kills the bastard.

Ryker does this weird head nod thing that says he agrees with me. "Well, we're going to head out, but we'll be back tomorrow. Text Elena if you need anything."

Ryker backs away, but Willow stays. We've never been alone together. Hell, we've never even *spoken*. We're two people who dealt with similar fates, yet our paths never formally crossed. I owe her an apology for not getting help sooner. If it wasn't for Brent, she'd be like Carmen, Mia, and all the others by now.

When Ryker shuts the door behind him, Willow finally speaks. "Teagan—"

"Stop," I interrupt, taking a step forward. "Don't speak. Willow, I have so much to say—"

Her hand slashes the air, shutting me up. "No, we don't need to do this now. It's not why I'm here. I just... Hawke told me why you left. It's hard, and I know it's worse for you, but it's okay to love him." Her bright eyes soften when they land on the bed behind me. "Don't spend the rest of your freedom allowing Alex to still control your life. Because when you run away, when you hide from your memories and don't have your happy ending with the man who loves you, then *he* wins." She shrugs, her lips pursing into a frown. "And that's depressing. And not fair to either of you. You want Alex to go away forever—to never be a bother to you again? Don't leave."

Willow backs away, the weight of her words hovering long after she leaves. She speaks as though it's so simple, but it's not. She doesn't get it.

"Because when you run away, when you hide from your memories and don't have your happy ending with the man who loves you... then he wins."

He wins.

I don't want Alex to win. I want Brent safe, happy, and alive. I want to be with him. I don't want to do what Dr. Laz says I do.

"You're still escaping. Mentally and emotionally, you're running."

I'm tired.

My eyes eventually slide shut, but right before I sleep, Brent's fingers twitch.

Forty-One

BRENT

I LIED *when I said I don't love you. I do. I'm just... I'm broken.*

Even in complete darkness, my girl's voice is here, telling me what I've always coveted.

You were my friend, my saviour, my everything.

You were my everything too.

I'll always regret not telling you about Alex back then and saving us years of agony.

Me too.

I'm scared anything good in my life will be stolen by Alex.

I won't allow that. It's why I'm still holding on, waiting to return to you.

I'm sorry for everything since coming back into your life. If I could redo everything, I would because I fucking love you, Brent.

I love you too, Cherry-Girl.

I'm so sorry, Brent. More than I can ever say.

I'm sorry I forced your hand.

Hopefully one day I'll be able to tell her that.

Hopefully...

When this blackness is replaced with red.
Red, like my Cherry-Girl's hair.
But for now, my body is still enjoying the darkness too much.

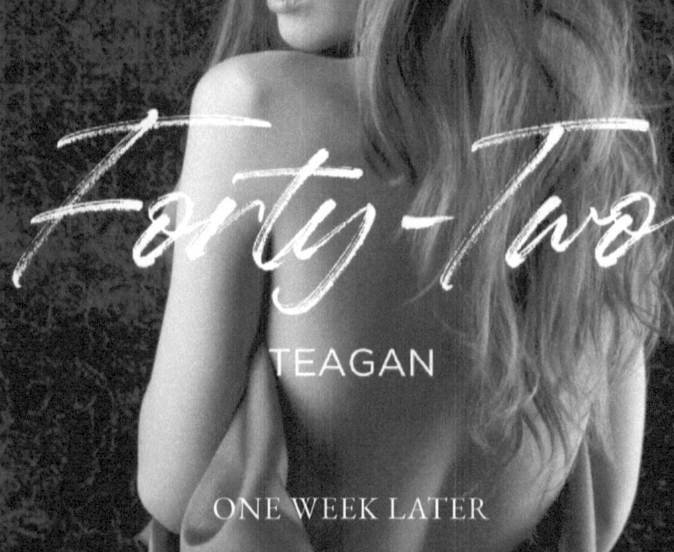

Forty-Two

TEAGAN

ONE WEEK LATER

AT THIS POINT, I'm sure I'll require my own hospital bed from the cramps in my poor body. For the entire week, I don't leave his bedside, even sleeping in the hard chair, until finally, the nurses realized I wasn't going anywhere and dragged in a more comfortable recliner from the maternity ward, along with a blanket and a pillow.

"Girl, I'm kicking you out of this room," Elena announces as she and Natalie push their way in. It's middle of the day, during visiting hours, so the hospital is more lenient on the number of people in Brent's room.

"She's right, Teagan." Natalie waves her hand through the air as Ryker and Tristan enter behind them. "You need a shower and a change of clothes."

I gesture toward the attached bathroom. "I've been showering in there."

Ryker turns skeptical eyes on me and grunts. "There's no shower in there, which means you've been sponge bathing."

"And?" I shrug, still not standing from the recliner I'm curled up on. "Better than nothing, right?"

Elena sighs and glances pleadingly toward Tristan, who holds up his car keys in response. "On it. Natalie and I will take her."

They think so. "I'm not leaving. He might wake when I'm not here."

"Then I'll punch him and knock him out until you return." Ryker holds up a fist, but Elena nudges his arm away, laughing and shaking her head.

"Funny," Tristan comments, right as Elena and Natalie each grasp one of my arms and force me to my feet.

At this point, I wouldn't put it past them to carry me out of the room, so I brush back my matted hair and mutter, "Fine. I'll go, but I won't like it."

THREE WEEKS **Later**

It's the one-month anniversary of Brent's accident and Alex's imprisonment.

Other than showering every few days when someone forces me to, I don't leave Brent's bedside. He hasn't moved since that first day when his fingers twitched, but I talk to him constantly, something the doctors approve of.

I recount every moment of our childhood and tell him how our lives should have gone if I'd said yes when he asked me out. I tell him what really went through my mind when he kissed me in Hawke's basement, and how sex with him was the best thing I'd ever experienced.

I tell him why I left after Alex's trial; why I felt the need to run, but also how I'm selfish enough now to not. I plan to drag him down into my darkness with me and he'll have to deal with it.

They say when you nearly lose someone, it changes everything, and those people are absolutely fucking right. What happens when

Alex tries something again and I'm halfway across the country because I don't want to admit my true feelings, and I lose Brent before I even really had him?

Why am I being *that* girl? The self-sabotaging one. The one Dr. Laz described me as.

I don't want to be her anymore. Alex won't take more of my life from me. I won't run again. I'll remain and I'll *live*.

My eyes drop to the magazines the nurses brought in at some point. Of course, being where I am, they're not celebrity gossip magazines, but rather medical journals.

I'm *really* enjoying the psychology articles.

Everything I experienced, everything Alex did to me—there's a name for it. I'm a damn *term*. Dr. Laz explained my trauma, but reading about it in blatant medical terms and meanings has been informative, interesting, and intriguing.

I think about Willow, and any other woman who's ever lived through something like she has and—

I glance toward Hawke, who's leaning against a wall across the room, chatting quietly with Tristan and Natalie. His work hasn't ended; he's been combing over Natalie and Alex's father's will to find any claim that some of the Miller fortune is hers.

"Hawke," I call, gaining his attention, "remember once when you said I'd be a good therapist?"

"I do." His attention falls to the magazines by my feet, and even from his distance and odd angle, I see the moment he reads the titles because his eyes light up. "Yeah?"

I shrug, remaining noncommittal for now. "Maybe. Step one." I nudge my chin toward the bed.

The door flies open then, a middle-aged man and woman bustling through, pulling suitcases along. Their clothing is rumpled, and the woman wears flip-flops and shorts, despite the weather still being too chilly for such attire. It's obvious they've just returned from a trip.

It doesn't matter. Not as I take in the familiar greying hair—though it wasn't grey when I last saw her—and the gentle face of the man at her side. I stand, approaching the people who were more like parents to me than any foster family I was ever placed with.

In all my concern for Brent, I can't *believe* I forgot about his parents.

Mrs. Thorne glances from her son to me. She blinks, her brows lowering, and I see the moment I become familiar. "Teagan Faber? As in... *Teagan*?"

This is a bad idea. No doubt they hate me for the past. "Um," my eyes dive to the floor, "yeah."

Gentle arms swarm me and I'm yanked into a hug I don't deserve but have been desperately craving. With her touch, my walls shatter. Tears explode from my heart, and I hug her back, unwilling to let go.

From over her shoulder, I meet the eyes of Brent's father. His hand brushes over his combed hair. "We were in Hawaii for the past couple months. Retirement is nice." His lips twitch into a semismirk. "We caught the news about the trial, well after it was done. Teagan, what you've lived through..."

Mrs. Thorne releases me, and I already miss her touch. "We dislike international calling charges, so our service was off. We only recently learned of what happened to him." Her eyes dart to Elena in the corner. "Thanks, hun, for the FaceTime. The whole concept of video calling is strange, but... well."

Of course they know Elena. They probably love her too because she'd make the ideal daughter-in-law.

Elena catches my eye and she subtly shakes her head, mouthing, *Don't go there.*

Either way, I'm not the reason they're here, so I step back, opening the path to their son. Mrs. Thorne falls into the chair I've been living in, while her husband steps up behind her, scanning Brent's broken body. It's healed in the month he's been here, but colourful bruising still decorates his skin.

"It's my fault. He was chasing after me when he got ran off the road. I-I'm sorry, Mrs. Thorne."

"Annie, dear. Remember?"

Of course I do. But being informal with her after all this time isn't something I deserve.

Mrs. Thorne—Annie—ever the sharp one of the duo, glances up, scanning the circle. "Why do I feel there's more to this? Explain what the hell is going on."

Forty-Three

BRENT

MOM'S VOICE.

I'm positive I'm dead, and my mother has come back to haunt me.

There's Dad's voice too.

And then my girl's voice. My Cherry-Girl. Maybe I *am* dead, and I'm in Heaven. It's the only explanation for why this blackness is still here, yet the three people I love more than anything are with me.

Blackness.

Blackn—

Fading.

The blackness is fading.

It's blurry, but there's a splash of colour against the black.

Of white. And of red.

I think I need to open my eyes now and get past the black, but I'm also uncertain if I can…

Forty-Four

ONE WEEK LATER

THE FOLLOWING THREE DAYS, his parents remain by Brent's side from sunup to sundown, along with everyone else, though Willow and Hawke less.

Most times, it's only me watching over him. Seeing his chest rise and fall, catching the hiccups on the monitor, and staring at his hands, waiting for them to twitch again as I continue to recount our past.

I'm so busy staring at his hand as I tell him over and over how much I love him, begging him to return, that I don't see his beautiful blue eyes open.

"Do you know how long I've waited for you to tell me that?"

For the first time in a month, I feel alive. I breathe. My heart beats. I look up at my future.

"Brent."

Brent is breathing. His heart is beating. We're both here.

And despite the elation causing me to scramble to my feet, I then fall back down into the chair. "Fuck."

"Not the hello I hoped for." His mouth lifts in a half-smile. "You love me, huh?"

Maybe it's the fact that he's awake and alive. Maybe it's the fact that he's making humorous comments while I've been living in my new form of hell for over a month, but I laugh and cry at the same time, and it comes out as a blubbery mess.

"I do, Brent. I'm so fucking sorry for everything. I'm sorry."

Brent lifts his free hand, the one not in a cast and pats the bed beside him. "Can you please come here?"

I climb in next to him, fully aware a nurse would murder me if she witnessed us in his bed together.

"Don't let me hurt you." I shuffle to the edge of the bed, the farthest away from his injuries.

"Cherry-Girl, you've hurt me in worse ways. A little physical pain is nothing so long as you're close to me."

He's joking, but his reminder sparks a whole other wave of fresh tears.

"Teagan, I'm kidding." His arm comes around my body and he tugs me on his chest.

I breathe in his scent. While not the freshest I've smelled him, he reminds me of home. My home.

"I'm sorry, Brent. I pushed you away. I-I... I really didn't know what to do after I was out of the hospital. And then you were trying to claim me, and it freaked me out. I didn't want you to be living with my trauma. Not when you had such a perfect life. Had I known Alex would pull one last trick and you would have been injured, I wouldn't have left."

His finger comes up beneath my chin and he angles my face toward his. "It's my fault. I was pushy. You needed slow and I wasn't giving it to you. I do owe Alex one thing."

My brow furrows. "What's that?"

"You wouldn't have come back otherwise."

The stark fact is, well, *stark*, but also possibly not a fact. I shake my head into his chest. "I think I would have returned. I'm stubborn like that."

"Don't I know it. Now that the apologies are out of the way, can you please kiss me?"

I do, pressing my lips to his in a gentle kiss, but he soon takes over and parts my lips, turning a chaste kiss into one that has my pulse pounding and my palms going sweaty, and I need to remember where we are.

I pull away, and even though he tries to latch on longer, I manage to separate us and tap his heart twice with my hand. "We have time for that later. For now, we should get the doctor in here to check you out."

Brent frowns, but the corners of his mouth lift too. "Sure sure. Before you go, can you let me know one thing?"

I pause from sliding off his hospital bed. "What's that?"

"Can you give me a head's up if you're planning on running again? I'm sure you've seen by now I'm willing to roll cars simply to get you back, but yeah, a head's up might not be a bad thing."

Instead of answering, I laugh and shake my head. I'm not going anywhere. Not without him anyway.

Before I find a doctor, I announce to the waiting group, "He's awake."

At once, they form a mini stampede, with Ryker taking the lead and Tristan hot on his heels. Elena and Natalie step through the doorway next. Natalie heads to Tristan's side, but Elena pauses and studies my face.

"I'm glad you're happy, Teag. Welcome back."

Welcome home. That's what I get from her words.

She moves to his bedside and Hawke and Willow enter next. I stop short at seeing her again, but Willow merely smiles gently and follows Hawke into the room.

Before attempting to leave and find that doctor, I pause again, turning to the group. Turning to my friends. Old ones, new ones, and some who were mere acquaintances once. In one form or another, Alex ruined all our lives, but he's also brought us back to one another.

We're a family now. I'm truly an idiot for trying to escape what's right here.

I'm so busy watching everyone else fawn over Brent, I miss how his eyes find mine, making me flush with possessive heat. But not a dangerous possessiveness; simply one that says *I love you* and *come back to me.*

The very words he's been saying to me for so long. Only, I was too deaf to hear them.

But no longer.

Forty-Five

TEAGAN

IT'S another three days before the hospital releases Brent. According to his doctor, he awoke from his coma naturally and his arm was wrapped in a sling to get him through another few days of healing.

During those days, he never stopped touching me, no matter who was in the room with us, as if still marvelling over the fact I'm here. So the moment we enter his apartment, Brent is on me, tearing at my clothing.

"You gave me a taste once, but it's not enough. It'll never be enough."

My hands pull at his shirt, helping him maneuver it from his chest and around his injured arm. "Let me know if anything hurts, and we'll find a new position."

"Stopping will be the only thing that hurts me."

He kisses down the column of my neck while his good hand works at my shirt. I help him pull it over my head, tossing it to the side. Rather than waiting for him, I also remove my pants before doing the same to his.

Last time we did this, I was saying goodbye. But not this time. This time, I'll be showing him how much I love him.

The second he's bare, my hand finds his length, stroking him until he's thick in my hand and his groans fill the silent room.

Then I drop to my knees and swallow him whole. The last time I did this for a man, it was with Alex's hand controlling the speed, the pressure, and when he came, using the strands of my hair to maintain that domination. If I didn't follow his commands, I paid for it.

I close my eyes, pushing Alex away from my memory in favour of Brent. In favour of someone who loves me. My tongue swirls his head before I take him deep.

"Fuck," he groans, "you have no idea how many times I've dreamed of this."

I moan around his length, knowing the vibrations will be pleasurable, and smile when he twitches in my throat. At the last second, he pulls away from my mouth, panting. My tongue captures a drop of pre-cum that escaped down the side of my mouth.

"Fuck," he curses. "That was... Wow. I want to come inside you."

I lift to my feet and lead him into the bedroom, ordering, "On the bed. I'll be on top, so we don't injure your arm."

Brent's brow quirks. "I love your commands, but I'm not obeying any of them until I get my taste. After all, craving it is what woke me from my coma, therefore you owe me." His fingers flick to the bed. "Lie down, panties off, and spread your legs."

I shiver. His domination is something else entirely. Something I *should* hate... but I don't. In fact, lust pools at the base of my stomach and I remove the rest of my clothing before following his order.

"Fuck," he curses again, eyes locking on my centre. That simple gaze has my insides flushing. "Cherry-Girl, you're perfect. So pink, ripe, and tasty, like a damned cherry." His eyes study the rest of my body, and when they reach my chest, my nipples harden. "I've changed my mind. Flip on your hands and knees."

I make a humming noise in the back of my throat and do just that.

"Are you okay? The position—"

"Never better," I interrupt his dark thoughts before they fully develop.

"Good." This time, his word is growled—hungry.

The room goes silent for a moment, and I wait, hands fisting in anticipation. The bed dips—

And then his mouth touches me, and I nearly leap off the bed.

His mouth *eats*. There's no other word for the way his mouth works at my pussy and ass, eating me out from behind. Days' old facial hair scrapes at my skin as his tongue finds purchase inside me. He continues to pump inside me until I'm rocking against his mouth.

"Come for me," he growls. "Only me."

"Only you," I agree, words panted out as another ripple rocks my insides. "Oh, God!"

"Cherry-Girl, give me your orgasm."

And when his tongue spears me, I do, crying out as I rock wantonly against him until long after the orgasm ripples from my body and leaves me entirely spent.

But instead of pulling back, he continues, enticing another orgasm to the top.

"I don't... think... I can."

"You can," he purrs. "And you fucking will."

And then I do.

Over and over. Three more times, until my legs are dead and give out.

Finally, and regrettably, he pulls back, lightly tapping his hand against my ass.

"Yum. You're delicious."

"Like cherries?" I tease.

"Like the ripest form of cherries."

I begin shifting, readying to flip around, but his hand on the small of my back pauses my movement. "No, stay."

Brent lines himself up behind me, and I'm thrown back to all the times it was a different body doing this. To when *he* pinned me against the cage, forced me to study what he had done to Willow while he took me roughly from behind.

The soft touch yanks me back to the present, to the man who's touching me. To Brent.

"Is this okay?" he checks. "We can change positions."

"I'm good now."

"Are you sure?"

"Yes."

His cock taps against my centre once before he slowly pushes inside, filling me at an angle I've never enjoyed until now.

In fact, I've never enjoyed sex until Brent. With him, it's more. It's right. It makes me *want* to have sex, to fuck, to make love—all the forms of intimacy. He makes me crave testing boundaries—to try things I'm uncertain I'd enjoy but want to still attempt.

When he's fully seated within me, our mixed moans fill the room. He shifts on his knees, creating a deeper angle and his free hand comes around to my front, finding my swollen clit.

He hums. "You're beautiful, Cherry-Girl."

His hips lightly rock into mine, and I meet him thrust for thrust, begging him to go deeper, harder, until I feel him and only him.

"I love you," I gasp in the last second before I orgasm again.

Before we orgasm together.

Before we fall into the abyss together.

He continues moving long after he's spent and gone limp, only pulling away when I fall back on the bed. But instead of joining me, he rolls me onto my back and lowers himself.

"What are you doing?" I ask lazily, eyes shutting as I fall into the blissful sleepiness taking me under.

He doesn't respond. Not verbally, anyway. His tongue enters me, yanking away impending sleep.

"Fucking delicious," he rumbles against my thigh. "I can taste myself inside you."

"Because I'm yours," I reassure him, enjoying the way my own words sound on my tongue. I'm his because I've allowed myself to be taken by him. Captivity with Brent will be sweet—freeing.

He tongues my clit as his finger sinks inside me, keeping his cum deep in my body. He pumps fast and then slow, speeding up and slowing down as I rock against his hand, my pants begging him for release.

"You own my soul, Cherry-Girl. Just remember, you're in absolute control."

He may claim that, but for the next hour, I let him control me. My body and my orgasms as I come more times than I ever believed possible, and by the time I pass out, my body unable to physically handle more, the sheets beneath us are a beautiful mess.

Just like me.

Forty-Six

TEAGAN

"IS it only me who finds this a bit odd after everything?"

Elena throws her head back, dropping popcorn in her open mouth. "Yep," she says around the crunching kernels. "Just you. Nat, what do you think?"

"I mean," Natalie leans forward, catching my eye from where she sits on the opposite end of the couch, "it's nice. I feel like our group continues to expand, but it's good, you know. It's right."

Right.

"If you say so."

Elena's eyes cut to me, sharp, but then she catches my smirk, and her own smile grows. She sets the popcorn bowl on the floor then throws her arms over the back of the couch and yanks us both into her side.

"You know what, though, I don't fucking care. Natalie said it best. This is right. You each represent my past and my present, but what I love most, is that you'll both be a part of my future."

"Damn right." But there's too much suffocation here so I wiggle from her arms, shoulders jerking side to side until Elena releases me.

"But there's so much lovey-dovey stuff happening here. Can we *please* start this movie?"

Elena rolls her eyes before taking her arms back and once more lifting the popcorn to her lap. My hand dives in, grabbing a handful as Natalie clicks play on the newest romcom.

When the title flashes, my eyes slide to the right, to Elena. It's like old times. Better than old times because we gained another. I look past Elena toward Natalie.

Elena whispers, "Like old times, eh," stating my thoughts. She turns her head slightly, enough that I catch the twinkle in her eyes. Her free hand finds mine and our fingers interlock. "I fucking missed you, Teag. You're not allowed to leave ever again."

"I don't plan on it," I whisper back.

And then I settle back against the couch in Ryker's living room, where Elena, Natalie, and I have commandeered it for a girls' night. A goddamn girls' night. Events the women from the club would speak about, but I've certainly not experienced in the past few years. Alex never allowed me to be close to anyone, and for their safety, it's something I never seeked out, even in secret.

Not a problem anymore.

And never will be again. I'll kill anyone who tries to take this from me.

Forty-Seven

TEAGAN

ONE MONTH LATER

WHILE ELENA and Natalie are graduating, Brent is marching me to Hawke's house. He believes that what I'm about to do is more important than attending our friends' graduation ceremony, and Natalie and Elena agreed.

It was three against one, and I lost.

In four years from now, when I graduate with a Bachelor's in Psychology, I'm banning them all from my graduation and we'll see how they like me then.

"I hate you all," I grumble, knocking on the front door. Not that I need to, since Hawke is in on this too. In fact, he's all for it, insisting it'll do both of us some good.

Suddenly, everyone is a friggin' doctor around here.

The door swings open, and Hawke breathes deeply, smiling. "Hey. She's upstairs in my room."

"Hiding again?" Brent steps in behind me.

"No. Resting after—just resting. She's dressed though." He winks, and—*Oh.*

Brent nudges me in the back, toward the staircase. "Go on. We'll be down here. Take your time."

The sight of the staircase makes my nerves ignite, my skin tingle as I ascend, leaving the guys below. It's not that I don't want to do this—I do. Hawke's right; we both need this. What I don't want is the strength this conversation will take from both of us. How many ghosts it'll dredge up—ones we'd both like to keep buried.

At the top of the stairs, I find the only bedroom and knock on the door lightly.

"Willow? I'm here. Can we talk?"

There's only silence for a long second, before the door slowly opens and Willow appears. She's staring down, avoiding my face, and I'm dying to know what's going through her mind.

We're two souls having shared the same horrors from the same man, so I'm not entirely sure where to go from here. I scan the room, noting the rumpled bedsheets, and then the glow Willow is basked in.

She's so happy and deserved to feel that way years ago. *Years*, if I only said something back then.

"Willow, I'm so sorry." My legs buckle, and I slide to the floor against the door. Willow crouches too, keeping a few inches between us. "I wanted to help you every single day you were in his cage. Trust me, I did."

Her mouth opens and shuts twice until she says, "You couldn't. I'm not mad."

Mentally, I scoff. "You should be. You should hate me." I deserve nothing less, and after a deep breath, I admit, "I did it once. I tried to save a girl. Got her nearly out of the basement when he found us. Her death was harsher, swifter, because *I* tried to help. She paid the price of my idiocy, and I was forced to watch every brutal moment of it. So I stopped and turned a blind eye to every one of them." I meet her eyes, but she's blurry behind the wall of tears I hadn't realized were there. "To you. Your life would have been worse and ended sooner had I tried."

"I understand," she murmurs. Arms tighten around her form, causing me to wonder how much she means what she said.

"I *hated* knowing what he did to you, Willow. Hated it with every fibre of my being, but I turned it off, you know? Pretended I was okay with it since there was no way out."

"And for you too. You lived through hell."

Sure, but it got better for me. I shake my head, staring at the wall past her. "Not like you. My cage was large, gilded and all that. He controlled me in other ways, but at least I didn't have to see him—endure him—every day."

Though I'm not looking at her, I feel her heavy, disapproving gaze. She might believe I'm irrational for these thoughts, but the truth remains, she was only there because I didn't say something years ago. She *must* know I didn't approve or want any of it.

There's a shuffle, and suddenly, she's right there, her arms tightening around my neck.

"You survived, Teagan. We both did what we had to do. Besides, Hawke told me what you did. How you led them all to Alex's basement. *You're* the reason I'm alive and having this conversation. I owe you my life. You gave me my freedom, Hawke, and a future. You've paid your dues, so please, Teagan, don't beat yourself up about this any longer."

She stands, taking my hands and pulling me up with her, and I don't fight it.

"Alex is gone and locked behind bars forever. We both need to move on with Hawke and Brent and live our best lives. He'll always be a part of our pasts, but one we shouldn't focus on any longer."

I glance at the bed again, before wiping my tears and smiling. "Hawke, huh? How'd you move on so easily and *want* a relationship with him?"

And exactly like that, we each say, *I understand and agree to move on*, switching topics abruptly.

Her cheeks bloom pink, and she shrugs. "He's good for me. I'd still be shivering in the corner if it wasn't for his help. I... It wasn't easy. Or instant. The thought of another person ever touching me," she visibly shivers, "and yet, there was something else—a connection. The moment he lifted me out of Alex's cage, I *felt* something." The red in her cheeks deepen. "I suppose it sounds stupid."

"No." I shake my head. "No, it's... inspiring."

Willow smiles gently. "Hawke basically forced me into counselling. I didn't think it was required until I went, and everything just came out. My therapist helped me process so much of the abuse and torture, but she also told me that healing from trauma looks differently for everyone." Her lips purse. "I know you had also gone to therapy around the same time, and yet, you're wondering how I got into a relationship with Hawke so quickly. Trauma affects us all differently, and it doesn't make you weaker in any way, Teagan. You lived it for longer, so wanting be with Brent is a change for you, which makes sense. Move on when *you're* ready to, not when you think you have to. That was probably the most important lesson I took from my sessions."

I drop my gaze to the floor, repeating her words in my mind. I could argue she's simply stronger than me, but deep down, I know it's not the truth. I *am* strong. I survived. Her trauma is being processed differently than mine, and that's okay.

Her voice cuts through my thoughts. "Tell me about you and Brent."

AN HOUR LATER, Willow and I exit the bedroom and head downstairs. She gives me a gentle smile before throwing herself into Hawke's lap. An unlikely duo, but from what she told me upstairs, he's good for her, and she for him.

I meander toward Brent and take up a similar position. His head disappears inside my hair and he kisses my neck, whispering, "How are you?"

"I'm good," I murmur. "That was necessary. Thank you for pushing me into it."

"You're strong, Cherry-Girl."

"And yours," I respond back fondly. My hands cover his from where they rest on my stomach.

"Only if you want to be."

"I do."

Always.

My phone chimes then and I glance at the screen, eyes reading the words once, twice, before exclaiming, "Oh my God! Elena and Ryker are engaged!"

Brent chuckles, his laugh vibrating against my back. "I'm sure he's been planning that since we were in high school."

Hawke laughs too. "Based on everything I've seen and heard, I'd imagine that's exactly the case."

Another text chimes in.

ELENA

We're aiming to have it in a month. You'll be a bridesmaid, right?

Maybe it's silly I cry, but I don't stop the tears from falling. I don't even wipe them away as I flash my screen toward Brent.

A freakin' bridesmaid to Elena Sparks. Something we talked about in high school, but once Alex bombarded his way into my life, it's not something I ever foresaw coming true.

ME

Of course! Congrats. We're all so happy for you!

I twist my head, catching Brent in my gaze. "You are happy for them, right? No buried jealousy I need to stress about?"

Brent merely gives me a look that says exactly what he's thinking. "The last time we got into this debate, you know how I had to show you otherwise."

"Maybe you need to again."

Brent's eyes blaze, and without looking toward Hawke, he stands, placing me on my feet and says, "We'll be seeing you guys later. Gotta go."

"Thank you for not defiling my bedroom like Tristan enjoyed doing!" are the final words we hear before Brent slams the front door of Hawke's house and we run away to his apartment.

To our future.

Together.

Where I'm his, but he's also mine... and I'm okay with that.

Forty-Eight

BRENT AND TEAGAN rush away and head toward their happily ever after. Their futures are no longer my worry, not when I have my own happy ending poised on my lap.

I rub her back, my fingers getting tangled in her long, pale blonde hair. "How was it?"

"It was good," Willow murmurs. "I told her I'm not angry. I know she did what she had to, to survive. She told me about the time she did try to help a girl, and, well," Willow's gaze dives to her lap, "it was better for me she didn't."

I continue to rub my hand through her hair for a moment, enjoying how the silky strands feel. "I'm glad, Willow. I'm glad she's another chapter you've closed. You know, once Brent told Teagan he thanked Alex for bringing her back to him, and I know what he means now."

If I wasn't fighting to take Alex down, I wouldn't have met Willow. Staring in her green eyes, I'm yanked back to the moment I first saw her in his cage, buried in his basement of horrors. When I bent down to ensure she was alive after Teagan's near-attack and found a damn angel staring back at me, I knew then I needed her to trust me. And then when she, without question, wrapped her arms around my neck, something changed.

I made fun of Ryker's fascination with Elena, and Tristan's obsession with Natalie, and even Brent's lifelong love for Teagan. Love and me? We never existed on the same plane. Not with who my family is; it's not how we function.

But the moment her skin met mine, something shifted inside me. For the first time in many years, my heart skipped a beat.

I felt something.

Warmth.

And I knew no matter what happened after that moment, I was claiming the broken girl as mine.

Forty-Nine

THEY THINK THEY WON. It's laughable at best because they truly have no idea the power I wield; the influence the Miller name holds.

My father—*rest his soul*—always taught me to have my hands in many different ventures, to ensure if something were to happen to me or the company, I'd have a Plan B. And then a backup of that plan, and so on and so forth.

Money is far reaching and when you're a Miller, you have a lot of it, which means there is nothing that can't be bought. Everything in the world has a price to it, even people, making cash an important commodity. Certain individuals in my employ have access to my off-shore bank accounts, with a list of instructions, should anything happen to me, such as my current situation.

The moment I was arrested and charged, my accounts were frozen, but that's only the company's money—the legal entities the courts are privy to. The rest of my money is buried elsewhere, in banks all over the world, all tied to various pseudonyms.

It's that very money that paid for a man to conveniently drive Brent Thorne off the road. I could have had him murdered, but I wanted my message to be more subtle. A message I know my pet will understand.

The threat that no one she cares for is safe, and when—*when*, because it's a step in the process—I escape from prison, they'll all be dead. I'll leave Willow and Teagan for last, so they can watch the people they love die for the tremendous mistakes they made in believing they can best a Miller.

When it's only Willow and Teagan remaining, I'll take care of Willow first. A broken doll, sure, but one I have less care for. Sexy, delicate, with the most perfect cries as I slice into her body, she'll soon understand how stupid it is to believe she'll ever be truly free. No one I hold in my gilded cage *ever* escapes, and she's no exception.

And finally, it'll be my Teagan. Killing her won't be simple or easy. After all, she and I have history. An understanding, an arrangement of sorts, but that was before she went and fucked it up. When I escape, I'll drag out her pain. A yacht I have waiting in the Caribbean Sea will be her new cage, one that there will be no escape from since we'll be in the middle of the ocean. She's not stupid enough to jump off, knowing exhaustion will get to her before she can find land.

In the damp cell, I lick my lips, picturing all the ways I'll pay her back. For first fucking my life up, and now, this inconvenience of losing my freedom, even temporarily. If she believes what she's experienced over the years has been bad, then she'll despise what's next. I was never cruel to her. Every time I fucked her, every slap, every cut, was because she begged me for it. Deserved it. But it's nothing compared to what she's earned now. What she's witnessed me do to others will be nothing compared to what she'll experience.

Maybe then, my little redhead will truly understand who and what I am to her. What a horrible idea it was to follow her old friends in their attempt to ruin me. I'm her fucking master—the one who decides if she breathes or not.

She'll soon learn. They all will. It's simply a matter of when, not if.

Because this *isn't* over. Not until *I* decide it is. And I'm far from being done with any of them, especially my doll.

Thank you for reading! Next up: Burning Notes (Captive Writings #4). Read the series' conclusion and the traumatic events that bring Willow and Hawke together.

Order your signed STORE EXCLUSIVE hardcover Captive Writings omnibus from my online store. It has a different cover and formatting from the regular paperbacks. Scan to order

More Books

Fractured Ever Afters

A 6-book (& 2 novellas) mafia romance series of interconnected standalones based on fairytales, featuring the Montreal mafia and the New York Famiglia.

The Desire in Deception (Prequel Novella)

The Hunt in Elusion

The Craving in Slumber

The Beauty in Scars

The Freedom in Captivity

The Sound in Silence

The Obscurity in Wishing

The Bonds in Christmas (Epilogue Novella)

The Bratva's Elite

A 4-book mafia series of interconnected standalones featuring the Russian Bratva.

Merciless Queen

Deadly Knight

Defensive Rook

Violent Pawn

Captive Writings

A new adult suspenseful romance series that progressively gets darker with each book

Ruthless Letters

Obsessive Messages

Vicious Texts

Burning Notes

Twisted Holidays

A series of dark romance holiday novellas

Silent Night

Egg Hunt

Fright Night

Be Mine

Midnight Kiss

Lucky Clover

Black Magick

A 5-book paranormal romance series of interconnected standalones featuring witches, vampires, shifters, mortals, and demons.

Dark Flame

Dark Mist

Dark Storm

Standalones

A Vampire for Christmas

Audiobooks

Silent Night

Acknowledgements

This book is seriously owed to two people in particular: Megan and Colleen. Who knows what this book would be without you two?! This is my hardest book to write, to date. I wish I could say it was the content, but how many character rewrites have I done??? I love you both and thank you so much for working through this book with me.

And then as a direct follow-up, thank you to Rebecca Barney from Fairest Reviews Editing Services. For making my words better and pointing out the few plot holes I still needed to fix.

Thank you to The Next Step PR. Colleen, Jill, Megan, Anna, and of course, Kiki - you're all amazing. Thank you for everything you do. You're the best team to have!

Thank you to Cat Imb of TRC Designs for giving Brent his gorgeous cover!

Thank you to all the bloggers, booktokers, and bookstagrammers who helped with the release of this book. Your help doesn't go unnoticed. Thank you for continuing on this insane trip with me.

And thank you to all the readers who took a shot on this book. My dream would not be possible without YOU. I hope you enjoyed Teagan and Brent's insane tale, but there's more to come in Burning Notes.

About

USA Today Bestselling author M.L. Philpitt writes both dark romance and paranormal romance. When she's not writing made-up realities, she's reading them. She lives in Canada with her four pets and survives life with coffee and an obsession with fictional characters, especially the morally grey kind. By day, she masks as a therapist.

TRIGGER/CONTENT WARNINGS

- Non-consensual sex (not done by main characters)
- Explicit sexual content
- Slavery
- Reference to murder
- Depictions of trauma
- Violence
- Psychological manipulation